ACROSS OUR
STARS
VICTOR

A. PAYNE & N.D. TAYLOR

This novel is a work of fiction.

Names, characters, places, and incidents are the
product of the authors' imaginations or are used in a
fictitious manner. Any resemblance to real persons,
events, and locations are coincidental or used in a
form of parody.

ISBN-10: 0990381757
ISBN-13: 978-0-9903817-5-4

www.spellboundconsortium.com
Editor: EV Proofreading
Graphic Artist: Mirella Santana

TABLE OF CONTENTS

GLOSSARY

Albion: The center of government for the United Empire. Albion is also the first and oldest successful colony.

ASR: Allied Soviet Republic. Many nations chose not to join the United Kingdom during the fall of Old Earth. These countries make up the ASR.

Astreya: A hot and arid desert planet. Intelligent dragon-like creatures share the sandy dunes with human colonists from the Middle East. The United Empire houses the Royal Archives in the capital city, Cyrus.

berthing: A dormitory or sleeping quarters aboard a military vessel.

bioscanner: A biometric scanner instantly receives vital signs and other pertinent data from a patient. It also identifies broken bones and trauma.

blast: (expletive)

CO: Commanding Officer of a vessel or military installation. This may be an officer with the rank of Commander or above.

cybernetics: Mechanical prosthetics or enhancements that replace or improve a biological body part.

cyborg: The surgical blending of an organic creature with technological equipment create a cybernetic being known as a cyborg. In the future, humans and animals can both receive prosthetic pieces and technological upgrades.

datagram: A tablet reader, like today's iPad or Kindle.

Elora: A water-covered planet that is home to an aquatic race of humanoid aliens. Pacifica Cove and Atlantica Gulf are two human settlements.

HMS Bridewell: One of three prison ships in the United Empire.

HMS Bulwark: The flagship of the Royal Navy.

HMS Glenn: Victor's former ship.

HMS Jemison: Victor's new ship, under the command of his friend Ethan Bishop.

Paradiso: A terraformed planet created to mimic the Old Earth's Mediterranean climate.

quid: Galactic form of currency used in every planet's economy.

rank-tagger: A member of either sex who pursues sexual relations with a ranking officer for the bragging rights.

Royal Defense Force: Military detachment assigned to the Empress and other high ranking members of the United Empire government. Their modern day equivalent would be the Secret Service.

Royal Marine: Elite members of the Royal Navy.

Sargossa: As an early colonization attempt, Sargossa seemed like the ideal planet to inhabit due to its livable atmosphere. Within five generations, residents began to experience changes and are no longer considered human.

splicer: A creature with meshed DNA. This grants unusual abilities to humans such as chameleon camouflage.

stateroom: A two or single unit berthing designated for an officer.

Tallulah: Texans finally made good on their promise to split from the Union. Years after most of the human population began leaving Earth to settle on Albion, the planet Tallulah was founded. They showed their southern hospitality by allowing a few other rebellious states to join.

United Command: Headquarters for the Galactic Royal Navy.

United Empire: Conglomeration of Old Earth nations joined under the former British Crown.

Xiao: Shortly after China absorbed Japan, the nation terraformed its own planet away from Albion.

XO: Executive Officer of a vessel or military installation. Second in command.

CHAPTER 1

Doctor Victor del Toro meandered through the busy space dock and admired the sleek vessel opposite the glass viewport. The HMS Jemison had become his new assignment, and after operating a standard galactic year in a tiny naval base on his planet of birth, Paradiso, it was like returning home.

Before passing through the decontamination chamber, Victor self-consciously double-checked the shine on his dress shoes and smoothed his neatly tailored military uniform. A combination of sterilizing lights and germicidal gases cleared him to board the ship and allowed him through the airlock chamber separating the dirty outside world from the clean interior.

"Welcome to the Jemison, Doctor." Ethan Bishop stepped forward wearing a grin on his usually stoic face.

The commanding officer of the ship greeted Victor personally at the entrance. In hindsight, he should have expected nothing less from his long-time friend.

Victor's reflexes provided a prompt salute that Ethan dismissively waved off. "Commodore."

"Forget the bloody formality. Glad you accepted the position, Victor. Now come here."

Ethan gripped him in a tight bear hug, bringing back memories of old times on his first naval deployment. Relaxing, Victor exhaled a breath of relief and embraced him in return.

"I appreciate the opportunity, mate. You saved my ass from a life of boredom by pulling me off desk duty."

"And I'm happy to rescue your sorry ass. Again." Ethan clapped a hand to his friend's shoulder and guided him inside. "Come on, I'll show you to Medical. But first, let me introduce you to Jem."

"Greetings, Doctor del Toro. I am Jem, the artificial intelligence personality of the HMS Jemison," a seductive, feminine voice announced from the nearest audio aperture.

Victor turned to stare at Ethan. "She sounds sexier than the personality on my new phone… but *why* does she sound like a porn star?"

"That's because she is a porn star. Or rather, a porn star voiced her. Quite a few of us COs petitioned United Command until they arranged for this. I was bloody tired of the default synthesized robot voice."

"All right, but isn't that a touch unfair to the COs of the feminine persuasion?"

"Hardly. They've got some wall of muscle and abs from a popular show." Ethan rolled his eyes and gestured for Victor to follow him deeper into the ship. He didn't have much room to talk, the hypocrite, since he, too, was a wall of muscle. "He loaned his voice for free. Apparently it's an honor to croon sexy words to the officers of the United Empire."

Victor chuckled and shook his head. "I suppose I've missed a lot while stationed at base."

"You did. Don't use it as an excuse to slack off though, mate. Let's visit your new home," Ethan said, guiding Victor along.

Victor's towering height placed him five inches taller than Ethan, but what his friend lacked in stature, he possessed in solid muscle and broad shoulders.

"What's the cybernetics budget like here? The Bishop I remember was kind of a notorious cheapskate."

Ethan chuckled under his breath. "You'll be pleased with it, trust me. I've got more personnel coming over in the next couple of days, several with implants of some kind. It should keep you busy." He glanced up and pointed a finger. "I'm still smart with my funds, but you'll have no cause for complaint. Top brass wants us field testing their new stuff, so…"

"Sweet deal. Are you ditching me at Medical because you are still as clueless as ever?" Victor grinned. For as long as he'd known Ethan, the guy was all thumbs when it came to anything remotely resembling healthcare.

"You'd cry and get lost if I didn't take you there first," Ethan jibed back.

"I would," Victor admitted. "Each ship is so different. Space vessel architects are masochists in disguise."

"Well, you can rest assured that all these new cruisers will be the same. They're built to stay out longer and travel farther before refueling is required. We'll be hitting up all the border colonies and new terraform projects to check in."

Concerned, Victor glanced at Ethan. "Is this because of those abandoned settlements they found?"

"Good, you're keeping up with the news. I have a feeling your long-term experience will be needed. The Empress wants to know where her people are going and why they're giving up on projects. Or if there are dangers on the planets we aren't aware of," Ethan confirmed.

Despite two decades of exemplary military service, Victor had no inclination to retire any time soon. Over the course of those twenty years, he'd performed his duties on four different stations and three ships. The Jemison was built for deep space patrols and prolonged interstellar combat. Of course, longer deployment schedules required self-sufficient ships outfitted with fully functioning services. The military *needed* specialized doctors like him aboard to keep its crewmen alive.

Ethan and Victor approached a gaggle of medical personnel collected near the hydraulic doors to the infirmary. Three of the five automatically stood at attention. The jaws of the other two women fell toward the floor where they remained until their associates nudged them in the ribs.

"Some things never change," Ethan muttered under his breath. "Now I'll need earplugs for the inevitable cacophony of breaking hearts when you don't reciprocate their attentions. Maybe I'll wager money on someone this time."

"Don't hold your breath," Victor replied.

Multiple examination rooms, labs, and offices created the Jemison's medical suite. Artificial solar panes spanned walls covered with cheerful yellow paint. Designed to resemble windows, they replicated sunlight and provided a soothing atmosphere. The illusion within the frame overlooked a lake bordering a flowering meadow. Discrete air vents generated a floral breeze.

"I know. It's a little girly. But you'll receive tons of patients anyway." Ethan crossed his arms over his chest.

"Smells nice in *here* at least," Victor muttered. "The rest of your ship reeks like used gym socks."

"Don't knock my ship, kid. Military vessels shouldn't smell like gardens."

"Oh, don't listen to him, sir. The Commodore didn't complain much when he was down here with the twilight flu two months back." A redheaded woman dressed in powder blue scrubs beneath a white lab coat joined them. She offered her hand. "Kathleen Hart. You must be the new cyberneticist Oshiro is so excited about."

"That's me. Pleasure to meet you, Doctor Hart." Victor glanced toward Ethan, grinning broadly from ear to ear. "He won't admit it, but he likes the downtime away from command."

Ethan muttered something unintelligible beneath his breath, then cleared his throat. "Lieutenant Hart is our genetic technician and responsible for the care of our splicers. According to the bunk assignments, which I had *no* part in creating, you're also sharing a bathroom with her. So good luck with that."

Experience with his fellow officers of the female persuasion taught Victor to never look forward to sharing restroom assignments with them. They were brutal when it came to using the last of the hot water and showed no mercy to men who forgot to put the seat down.

"Ah, so he has finally arrived," a voice spoke from behind them.

The trio turned to face the Chief Medical Officer. He barely reached Victor's chest. In the year since their last reunion, little about Doctor Oshiro had changed. Silver strands glinted against his temples and seemed more numerous, but his brown eyes remained as warm as ever. His smile comforted Victor and eased his building anxiety.

"Always a pleasure to see you, Victor," Oshiro greeted in his amicable and soothing voice. He glanced at Ethan and allowed a broader grin to surface over his face. "I will take things from here, Commodore. You are relieved from our effeminate infirmary."

"I'll leave Victor in your capable hands, but I get his company for breakfast." Ethan waggled a finger at Oshiro and winked at Victor. "I'll get you officially entered into all the systems so you can have a look at your future patients' files."

Victor laughed and rubbed the back of his neck. "I'll be there."

When they met over twenty years ago, Victor had been a medical technician on a fast-paced battle frigate where Ethan served as a Lieutenant Commander. After hitting it off as friends, mostly because Ethan said that the younger corporal reminded him of his little brother back home, Victor had been surprised to find a missive from United Command notifying him of a recommendation for advancement as an officer. If, and only if, he accepted the equally prestigious opportunity to attend medical school. According to Ethan, Victor was too bright to remain an enlisted man. He deserved more.

So he became more. He became the best military doctor in their region and aspired to make his friend proud. Years later, he was honored to serve on Ethan Bishop's ship.

If only it were under better circumstances.

"Coming off shore duty, Victor? Ready for ship life or wishing you were boots to ground again?" Kathleen asked after the commodore left.

"I like ship duty. Glad to be with the crew," he replied carefully. *New start. New chance. And this time I have Ethan and Yuki with me,* he thought with optimism.

"Well, you can relax. The Jemison's crew is bloody brilliant, so you have nothing to be anxious about."

"I think I'll take Victor around now, Kathleen." Oshiro touched Victor's arm.

Disappointment flit briefly over the woman's features, but she nodded and stepped away. "It's almost end of shift, so I'll lead him to his quarters once you're done, if you'd like."

"That will be fine," Oshiro agreed. He gestured for Victor to follow and then led him down the wide corridor.

A uniformed young man strode toward them down the hall. His gelled blond hair must have required at least ten minutes in front of a mirror to acquire the perfect magazine cover model look. Victor stared.

"Doctor Oshiro, I have the inventory check you requested. I just need your signature."

"Thank you, Jean-Claude. Please welcome Doctor del Toro. Corporal O'Reilly will be one of your technicians, Victor.

"Excellent. It's a pleasure to meet you, O'Reilly. I look forward to working together." Victor shook the corporal's hand firmly.

"An honor, Doctor del Toro. Your work in cybernetics has been inspiring. I heard you pioneered the recent advancements in synthetic veins and live nerve connections in artificial limbs."

"Jean-Claude has an interest in your field, as you can see," Oshiro relayed with a smile. He passed the data tablet back to the technician.

"I even read your article in the Galactic Cyberneticists Journal about neurocybernetic modification. Do you think they'll ever repeal the laws prohibiting cybernetic brain enhancement?"

"Ah…" As far as the Empire was concerned, brain modification was a strict no-no. "We made small steps in completely curing Alzheimer's Disease a couple of centuries ago using cybernetics, and I think given some time we can convince the Empire to allow supervised research."

"Amazing. I hope to be there when it happens. We have lots of cyborgs coming onboard, so I'm really looking forward to working with you, sir," Jean-Claude gushed with enthusiasm.

"Thank you, Jean-Claude," Oshiro interrupted kindly. "Please make sure everything is secured for our departure then report to Doctor Matthews before you check out. That will be all."

"Of course, Doctor."

"Did you bribe him?" Victor whispered as he and Oshiro walked away toward the lab.

The older man chuckled. "No, of course not. He has spoken of nothing else since word spread of your assignment to the Jemison."

"It's a nice change from the ordinary," Victor admitted. "I can't ask for more than to have a passionate assistant."

"If it relates to the synthesis of man and machine he has more than enough." Oshiro brought him to a wide door which opened smoothly at their approach. Lights brightened inside.

"Welcome, Doctor del Toro," Jem announced.

One glimpse of the spacious cybernetics lab assuaged the remainder of Victor's worries. Beyond the OR's concave viewport, a tree-filled view of the ship's bio-farm provided pleasant scenery for patients going under the knife. An array of lights hung suspended from the ceiling, connected to a retractable beam that repositioned on voice command, fully-automated by the ship's intelligence program.

It was physician's porn, the stuff of dreams that doctors like Victor wasted hours ogling on social media and hoped to work with at some point in their careers.

"Bloody hell."

"I suppose it's safe to assume you did not see anything of this sort on base," Oshiro commented.

Victor slowly turned his head to regard the older doctor, his eyes large. "No. I expected the usual from Ethan. Back where they stationed me in Valencia, the lead medical officer decided voice-assisted surgery was an unnecessary expense."

"It is, but when your transfer was approved a month ago, Ethan decided an upgrade was in order. He's truly happy to have you aboard and so am I." Oshiro placed his hand on Victor's shoulder and gazed up at him with an encouraging smile. "You look better than you did eleven months ago. How are you feeling about this change?"

"Better. It's… good to be among old friends again."

The older medical officer gestured to a second door. Oshiro followed sedately while Victor investigated ahead into the next room, where the walls traded canary paint for varying shades of cream and taupe. Flowering shrubs grew outside his small view-port, and they swayed in the fan-generated breeze.

"All of our examination and operating rooms look into the bio-farm, and of course, the windows are one-way only."

"Good to know. I've never had an office this large." Victor dropped into the swivel chair behind the desk and slid his hand over the glossy surface. The computerized system reacted to his touch and projected the holographic keyboard for his use. He logged in and out easily with his credentials.

"Enjoy your breakfast with Ethan tomorrow then come join us when he releases you. Until then, I suggest you take some time to get acquainted with the ship. Kathleen is probably anxious to show you to your quarters."

Victor sighed.

"I know what you're thinking, Victor, but I believe you'll be pleasantly surprised about Doctor Hart."

"Yeah, I'll believe it when I see it," Victor mumbled.

Kathleen practically attached to him like a burr from the moment he appeared back in the hall.

"I'm so bloody chuffed to have another actual adult in medical. You don't know how much of a relief it is to have you among us, Victor. So, what are you like?"

"Excuse me?" he asked her in confusion.

"Tell me something about yourself. Doc's kept his mouth shut tight and wouldn't utter a single word about you for good or ill."

"Well, that's a relief. What do you mean about having another adult in medical though? Aren't we all adults?"

"I suppose so. Lilibeth arrived about two months ago from Sargossa. She's some sort of bleedin' prodigy, I guess you'd call her. Only twenty."

"That's young," he commented, maintaining his careful neutrality.

"Aye, it is. We'll soon have a full complement of Royal Marines onboard," Kathleen explained. "Plenty of splicers for me and cyborgs for you. All right, the Wardroom is that way and staterooms form a horseshoe around it. The food's not bad and fried chicken night is always the busiest. Starboard side is where you'll find the CO, XO, and distinguished visitor suites. Port side is the rest of us. We're about halfway down."

"Thanks for the walk up, Doc–"

"Kathleen's fine, or Hart. We're all going to be good chums, so I'm all for canning the unnecessary formality if you're that sort. You seem that sort, at least." Something about Hart's friendly smile encouraged him to do the same.

"That's because I am that sort." Victor grinned. "Astute observation."

"Anyway, I s'pose we'll all talk in the morning. Enjoy your new digs." And without so much as a flirtatious glance, Kathleen Hart turned and jogged away. Victor stared after her retreating shape in absolute bewilderment. No coy smiles or veiled flirtation. Oshiro's kind words had proved true.

Upon reaching his assigned bunk, the locking mechanism responded to his thumbprint, granted him clearance, and slid open. The hydraulic door closed behind him again.

A blank canvas with sterile walls greeted him, waiting to be personalized. Crisp, white sheets wrapped a double-sized mattress tucked into a headboard with a shelf. An oval viewport overlooked the upper reaches of the bio-farm, displaying leafy treetops that swayed in the park's generated breeze. Compared to the enlisted berths, it was practically a mansion.

Victor found his belongings lined up neatly beside the small desk, which meant everything checked out all right in the scans.

With minimal possessions to unload from his luggage, he powered on the computer rig and flopped down on the bed. It finally set in. He had a new home and new patients. On his old ship, he'd known the name of everyone wearing cybernetics.

Finally, he had a chance at a fresh start. Nothing could ruin it, and he'd never let complicated relationships cloud his judgment again.

Before he could unpack any further, Ethan rang him on the comm system and ordered him to mingle with the crew. Resigned to his fate, Victor ventured reluctantly from his room. It didn't take long to become lost when the sterile passageways all looked the same. "Ship map."

Pinprick beams of light immediately projected from walls to his left and right, creating a holographic display of the ship's multiple levels. Victor's position showed up as a green blip.

"Identify officers' mess."

The display zoomed in to reveal Victor's current whereabouts. A dashed line in blue directed him to head left down the passage and right at the second junction to the Wardroom. The distance was conveniently close without being so near that the smell of cooking food would flood his room. He'd already had a bunk like that before on his old ship, and he'd quickly tired of smelling boiled vegetables and overcooked meats during all hours of the day.

All eyes turned Victor's direction when he stepped through the door, and he progressed to a lone table where he sat and avoided making eye contact.

Should I have taken an empty seat at someone's table? Hey, I'm Victor, great to be here? He fretted until the holographic menu blinked to draw his attention. That only provoked him to blindly press one of the entree options without reading the choices. It promptly vanished.

A stocky officer with closely trimmed black hair crossed over to stand near Victor. It seemed likely that too deep of a breath would burst his uniform seams. "Commander, welcome. You the new Operations officer?" He had an easygoing voice, lacking the formality associated with residents of Albion like Ethan. The central planet of the United Empire held on to many of its old British ways, including accents.

"Actually, no. I'm Doctor del Toro," Victor politely corrected him. His gaze fell on the man's rank insignia and nametag. Commander Daniels. He mentally filed the name and face away. "I'm the new cyberneticist in medical."

"Ohhhh, right. I saw the CO giving you the tour earlier. Didn't get a good look at you then. Good. When old Doctor Price retired, they left us high and dry. I wondered how long it would take to get a replacement."

"Your CO stole me from the Valencia base. I'm as glad to be here as you are to receive me," Victor joked.

"Greyson Daniels, by the way. I run the Combat Department. Mind if I sit here?"

Before Victor could give an answer, the other commander helped himself to an empty seat at the table. Wary of coming off as antisocial, Victor put on a smile and nodded.

"You don't really have the Paradisian accent."

"Yeah. About that, mate, I only transferred in about a year ago. I was raised on Albion during my teen years," Victor explained.

It doesn't hurt to try to make friends on a new ship. I can do this. The words became his mantra, repeated over and over in his own head until he began to believe it was true. "What do you think of this ship? This is my first time on one so large."

"As far as ships go, the Jemison isn't so bad. Namesake is kinda more prestigious than the crew, but you can't win 'em all." Daniels shrugged.

"Jemison was a female astronaut right? I'm a little rusty on my Earth History."

"Something like that, yeah. First woman of my ethnicity in space. But hey, it's just a name. The ship is good. Top-notch facilities. Some of the crew needs whipping up, but that's my job." Daniels grinned, flashing white teeth.

"Guess that means I should expect a high visitation rate in medical? I'm not used to having a lot of work." He looked forward to the change. On one hand, he didn't like to see his fellow servicemen suffering in pain. On the other, he loathed sitting by idly in an office.

"Heard they're sending us a bunch of mutants and mechies. That'll keep your hands full right there."

"Cyborgs dislike the term mechie. It pisses them off," Victor told him politely.

"You'd know." Greyson flashed his grin again. A blonde sergeant arrived with their trays before Victor could snap out an irritated reply. The young woman shamelessly roved her eyes over Victor and set each meal in place.

"Thanks," he muttered. He didn't make eye contact with her again, wise enough to realize what was happening at his new ship assignment. Nothing ever changed. It left a sour taste in his mouth that his meal did little to absolve.

"Good choice, Doctor. That one's the leading rank-tagger around here."

The filthy term twisted his stomach. With his appetite damaged by the rising nausea, he had to force down bites of mashed potatoes to stall his response. It worked until he stole a glance at Daniels to see him hanging on anxiously. "Yeah? Every ship's got to have one, I guess." He didn't particularly want to become a notch on anyone's figurative bedpost.

"The Jemison has her fair share."

"Know it from experience, Daniels?"

The man smirked. "I don't kiss and tell, but there's plenty who do. Besides, nothing in the rules against mingling. Heard it was back in the olden days."

The tension wavered and diminished, disintegrating with each bite of food and forced sip of water. *Calm, Vic. You've talked to worse twats than this guy.* "As long as they don't bring it to medical. You don't want know how many requests I have received to perform gyno services since my licensure. It isn't even my field." He gulped down the water that accompanied the meal and took a quick glance at his watch.

"Ha! I'll just bet."

"Anyway, thanks for the lowdown of the ship. Guess I'll be seeing you around." He always saw the combat department guys in medical eventually. They had a tendency to hurt themselves after taking their training beyond safe limits.

"Nice chatting with you, Doctor."

Victor couldn't get out of the Wardroom quickly enough. He retraced his steps back to his room and shut the door firmly behind him when he saw a female officer approaching to greet him. "Activate sleep setting."

The room darkened appropriately, while a pale silver crescent moon symbol glowed on the corridor side of the door. It notified other crewmen that a room's occupant desired privacy. Victor only used it to indicate he planned to rest.

After a shower, he crawled beneath the cool sheets and fell into an untroubled, dreamless sleep.

CHAPTER 2

Bright lights activated across the training room's ceiling in intermittent blips of blue glowing from holograph apertures scattered around the space.

"Is this honestly necessary?" Victor asked. "It's only my second day aboard the ship and I've been in medical all day."

"I know, but I can't send you out into the field without verifying that you're not soggy around the middle, mate," Ethan replied.

"Soggy?" Victor patted his flat abdomen. "You wish you looked as good as me."

"Put your money where your mouth is, Victor. Don't tell me you're scared. I do this with all my officers. Lieutenant Shahid Amir holds the speed record for the course."

"Haven't met him."

"Her," Ethan corrected. "Intel. Nice Astreyan girl, pretty too. You'd like her."

"Ethan."

"All right, all right. I was only saying. Besides, she's seeing some bloke in Navigation now I think. So that ship has sail–"

"*Ethan.*"

"Sorry. Are you ready?"

Despite his friend's good intentions, Victor held no illusions about involving a woman in his future on the Jemison. He wanted to work. Romantic entanglements, no matter how casual, weren't in the cards.

"I'm ready."

Ethan tapped in the final sequence and the empty chamber immediately morphed into a full military training course. Cubes, ramps, stairways, and ladders rose from the floor and slid from the walls and then a holographic overlay gave them the appearance of a mountainous stronghold. A synthetic sun blazed overhead, with lights so intense that sweat beaded on Victor's brow.

"You don't do anything half-arsed do you, Ethan?"

"Nope."

A buzzer activated and they took off at a sprint down the room's length. Victor's longer stride gave him an advantage over his heavier friend.

Victor reached the first station ahead of Ethan. A series of human silhouettes popped up behind various obstructions and opened fire on the pair. Bright red paint splattered against his side, accompanied by a sharp, breath-stealing punch in the ribs. The painful rubber bullets within the paint capsules reminded their marines that errors came with a price.

"Five second penalty," Ethan whooped, ducking past him. He aimed his training pistol and fired at the programmed assailant.

How did a man in his fifties move so quickly? Victor swore under his breath, loathing Ethan a little more with every step.

While Ethan fired on instinct, Victor lined up accurate, incapacitating shots at the cost of speed. They raced through the obstacle course and were pitted against one hazard after another, from droids that assaulted them in hand-to-hand combat to automated turret guns that attempted to mow them down with a hail of agonizing but non-lethal rounds.

Holographic projections paired with physical components created a realistic scenario without opponents. Victor blocked the merciless, rapid fire assault from a four-armed mech, staving off punishing strikes aimed at his face and upper torso.

"You dancing or fighting?" Ethan taunted from fifteen feet above him.

Just cause you're built like a tank… Victor blocked a hit with his left arm and struck with his right. A green flash cleared him to continue forward. Ethan had moved ahead of him, and he clung precariously to a wall designed to utilize as few handholds as possible. He didn't use a harness. Not to be outdone, Victor ignored the climbing rig and hurried up the rocky surface.

Victor gained better time on the thirty foot wall, and they were practically neck and neck when they each heaved over the edge. Unfortunately, Ethan was up on his feet first. Exhausted, soaked to his undergarments, and absolutely yearning for a moment of floor time sprawled on his back, Victor raced against the ship's commanding officer and pushed his body to the limit. His lungs burned for air as his booted feet pounded the ground for the finish line. Ethan crossed the line two feet ahead of him, and then they both practically collapsed to the ground. Both men bent forward at the waist, brows sweaty and chests heaving. Victor recovered first and passed his friend a water bottle.

"I haven't run one of those since battle school. You make everyone do this?"

Ethan laughed. "Only the best on my ship. This is a better way to assess them than that jargon in their personnel records."

"Fair enough. C'mon, let's see the results."

Victor took a long drink then activated the computer panel on the wall. The holographic replay earned their laughter and friendly jibing until the stats scrolled upward at the conclusion.

"Damn. You always were better at precise shots than me." Ethan grimaced at the readout.

"You might have finished first but you ended up with more holes in you." Victor slapped his friend on the back.

"Ha! And that's why I've abducted you from Paradiso, mate. Strictly for the purpose of having a personal doctor at my beck and call."

"There. Have I proven to you yet that I remain up to performance standards?"

"I'll allow you to pass this time despite your absolute failure to beat an old man."

"Appreciated," Victor replied drily.

"By the way, I have plans to run through a secret quest I found on Spellbound. Our usual tank said he'd be on tonight and we could use a healer who won't stand about with his thumbs up his arse when we need him. Interested?"

Victor considered the offer. He and Ethan both played in the same online video game and participated in the same guild. It was a hoot when their schedules matched together. "That isn't a terrible idea. I could use the R&R."

"You also have nothing better to do than to join your good friend in a heroic virtual reality game. We can never find a better healer than you."

Victor grinned at Ethan. "Well, when you put it like that."

"Hit the showers and have a brief kip on your cot before meeting up with us. You've earned it."

"I would, but I have a meeting with Doctor Matthews I'm going to be late for, thanks to you."

Ethan chuckled. "Give Lilibeth my apologies for delaying you. See you tonight in game."

***

"So I will press this button after placing the sample into the receptacle?" Victor clarified. "And then I... use one of these buttons that does a thing I no longer seem to remember. Microbiology isn't my strong suit, Doctor."

Lieutenant Lilibeth Matthews cracked a fragile but fleeting smile. It faded again, and then she patiently led him through the ropes of examining a planetary contaminant sample.

According to Hart, Lilibeth, affectionately referred to as 'Lil' by most of medical staff, arrived two months before Victor's assignment. In those two months, the girl's timid nature became the least of her problems. Her chiseled, angular features held an elfin quality, bearing high cheekbones, full lips, and thin brows. Due to her youthful looks, few officers took her seriously.

And then there was the matter of Lilibeth's race. Xenophobic discrimination ran rampant in the United Empire, and Victor often saw it first-hand. Jerks from all walks of privileged life looked down on anyone who didn't fit into the cookie cutter ideals of humanity.

"Lil," she spoke up, only to shyly add, "But you don't have to." The uncertainty resumed, and she ducked her head again.

"Lil it is," Victor replied, smiling. "I didn't know if you liked the name. Hart's a bit of a forceful character… You never know with her." And he hadn't wanted to disrespect her by presuming she was comfortable with the informality. "Victor will suffice for me as well."

The rest of the refresher passed without incident. Victor always made the effort to learn the basics of any equipment in the medical department. Out in the deep of space they didn't have anyone they could call for help if things went wrong.

Lil excused herself after their lesson concluded and Victor followed the advice of his rumbling belly. Fried chicken night meant full tables.

"Hey Victor, you can have my seat." Hart flagged him down from across the room. She picked up her empty tray and stood to make room.

"Running off on me so soon?"

The female doctor laughed and patted his shoulder. "I have an appointment, but I will leave you in capable hands. Have you met Etherington yet? He's in Engineering."

"No. Can't say I've had the pleasure."

The blond naval officer grinned from his seat at the table, and then he gestured toward Hart's vacated spot. "Have a seat with us little people, Commander."

"Be nice, guys." Hart waved then headed off.

Curious eyes settled on Victor. He shifted in his seat, discomfited by their scrutiny. The food on his plate provided a temporary distraction.

"Is it true you're qualified to work on the latest series of implants?" a young Lieutenant asked. "I heard we're getting people with tech that hasn't been released yet for normal distribution."

"I am," Victor confirmed, a broad grin on his face. "I recently completed a twelve week course on performing spot maintenance while on Paradiso, too, so I'm also a certified cyberware mechanic. Quicker repairs, no need to send it in."

"Holy shit," Etherington breathed. "No more weeklong turnarounds to receive our parts back from the repair depot?"

"That's right. I can manage most repairs myself here and in the field. Including the newest stuff."

"And the staff?" another officer asked. "How do you like your fellow doctors?"

Victor chuckled. "I feel welcome. Oshiro and I have known one another for a very long time. He was my mentor."

"But what about the Sargossan? I still can't believe they let her onboard."

"Should they not?" Victor asked, puzzled.

"Her kind don't have any place on our vessels. Don't you think so, Doc? Hart doesn't say much about it, but it has to be a nightmare in medical. I mean, aren't you one needle stick away from–" Etherington began.

"It doesn't work that way," Victor said quietly. "Even an infirm human with an impaired constitution will fight off any initial infection. It requires prolonged exposure, over a period of weeks."

"We're exposed to her every day, aren't we?" the second officer asked. She cut her blue eyes toward Victor and studied him curiously. A tag upon her uniform identified her as Lieutenant Porter.

The longer Victor remained in their company, the more certain he became of one critical fact: he disliked Etherington and his lackeys, and he found their racially oriented questions completely inappropriate. It was the same racism he'd encountered on the Glenn all over again, with another victim at its center. His grip of the eating utensil tightened until his knuckles whitened.

"Is that so?" Victor asked calmly.

"Aye, sir. They'll be regretting overturning the law as soon as there's an outbreak on one of our ships. Let's hope to God it isn't the Jemison and her plague doesn't spread to the rest of us," Etherington said, shaking his head.

"She has no business among us. Especially in medical where things need to remain sterile," Porter added.

"What about you, Doc? What's it like working with one of them?" Etherington inquired.

Them. They made it sound as if Lilibeth were something less than human. When settlers first colonized Sargossa, no one detected the microscopic organism that lived deep in the soil and rock. After twenty years, the first symptoms turned up. Sensitivity to sunlight and anemia produced a startling similarity to vampires. And now, centuries later, the people had evolved, developing a symbiotic relationship with the organisms.

"Well?" Etherington persisted. "She has no bloody place among the rest of us. It's a joke that she even received a commission. Sargossans are practically alien; she ought to be with the rest of the gormless peons in the enlisted mess."

"She's a human," Victor spat out, losing what remained of his patience. "She's as much of a human being as the rest of us and deserves respect. She's a fine officer."

"Sir—"

"Finer than you," Victor interrupted. "Doctor Matthews doesn't gossip about her peers and cares for each of you equally. She causes no harm to anyone. She does her job and minds her own business, and in my opinion, that makes her an exceptionally fine human as well. Better than the ignorant berks sharing this table with their purchased rank." He scowled at the group. "Did you earn your commission, or did your father pay for it?"

Victor pushed back from the table and strode away without looking back. He deliberately pulled up a seat beside Lilibeth and smiled. "Is the chili any good?" A glance over one shoulder confirmed what Victor already suspected about the rest of the guys, and he caught them sneaking peeks at him while speaking in low voices.

They could all sod off.

"I like it." She stirred her spoon through the mixture of finely ground meat and beans. "It isn't like the food we eat at home."

"Yeah? What's the food like on Sargossa?" he asked.

"Bland," Lil replied. "We don't cook our food so thoroughly."

"Right. Diminishes the nutritional value?" Victor asked.

Lilibeth nodded and looked down at her steaming bowl of greasy dinner. "I like it this way. They offered to serve food to me in our traditional way, but the other officers find it disconcerting."

Racist pricks, Victor thought. He controlled his reaction and maintained a neutral expression. "Won't that make you sick?"

"Doctor Hart administers a daily injection with the nutrients I need. I…" Lil's voice trailed and her shy eyes lowered to the table. Her stiff spine and tense shoulders revealed what her voice did not. "I will not lose control. No one is in any danger, Commander."

"No, I didn't think that at all. I inquired because I am concerned for your health, Lil. The Empire wouldn't allow you aboard the Jemison if you posed a risk to any of us."

The strain vanished and relief flooded her expression. "Thank you."

It broke Victor's heart that anyone could believe sweet Lil would become a ravenous, bloodthirsty monster while aboard the ship. Without another glance to the jerks at the next table, he rose from his seat and offered the younger doctor a hand. "You're only pushing your chili around with your spoon, so you have to be done by now, right?"

A couple officers gaped at him, as if horrified to see the commander touching the 'alien' Sargossan with unprotected physical contact. He ignored them and maintained his sunny smile.

Lil took his hand and rose, laying her dark fingers against his larger palm. The delicate bone structure seemed as fragile as twigs. He offered his arm and politely escorted her from the mess without any destination in mind. The young woman knew the way and directed him through the twisting corridors until they returned to the officers' berthing.

"I want to apologize for the shit you overheard," Victor began.

"Many people have behaved kindly toward me. Etherington and his friends are jerks. They'll always be jerks, and there's nothing I can do to change that. If I hold on to bad feelings, it will only poison *my* soul. Not theirs," she explained.

"You're a wise girl."

"And you are a kind man, Victor." They paused outside a stateroom, where she gently extracted herself and leaned up to kiss his cheek. "Remember my words for yourself."

Before he could ask what she meant, Lil smiled and crossed the threshold.

"That was a pretty nice thing you did for her," a voice spoke up from behind Victor.

A younger man stood behind him, smiling boyishly.

"I didn't really do anything at all," Victor said.

"You shut up the idiots bothering Lieutenant Lil. That's good enough for me. I was working on the communication system in the Wardroom and saw the entire thing. Ah, I'm forgetting myself, aren't I? I'm Chief Trevor Lockhart. It's a pleasure to meet you, sir. The commodore says you're a brilliant doctor." He spoke too quickly, much like a child given an excess of candy without any way to burn the energy.

Grinning to show no offense was taken, Victor graciously shook Trevor's hand. "Thanks. I think."

"You're also much nicer than the rumors indicated."

Victor raised a brow. "Mean isn't usually on the list of false attributes assigned to me. They must be coming up with new stories to tell."

"You should have heard the tales going around about my brother and me. People were convinced before we ever stepped foot aboard our first command that we heard every thought on the ship and sold secrets to other people for quid."

"So I'd be correct to assume you're a psychic then?"

"Apt assumption, sir. But, uh, don't worry. I'd never violate someone's privacy like that, and I can't read minds without physical contact. Not anymore," Trevor assured him. The younger man's smile diminished.

There's a story here, Victor thought.

"Anyway, Commodore Bishop wanted me to check on your netlink and guarantee you'd have a stable connection. He says you're always lagging out when he needs to be revived in game."

Victor groaned. "Did he really?"

"Okay, he didn't admit it openly, but I've seen it with my own eyes." The return of Trevor's big, jovial smile invited Victor to do the same in return.

The two men laughed and made their way to Victor's assigned stateroom. Trevor immediately moved to the interface panels and crouched beside them to begin his work.

About seven months ago, when Victor first took up with the game, he bought the most expensive system on the market that also fell within his price range. The online world distracted him, and it let him reconnect with his best friend.

"How long is it going to take?" Victor asked curiously. He retrieved his Neuro Strip and set it on the table.

Trevor glanced up from his work and let out a low whistle. "Couple minutes, tops. Nice gear, Doctor. Now you'll have a connection to match."

Less than five minutes later, Trevor had made the necessary alterations in the information currents. The chief closed up the panel and slipped his tools away. "There. All finished. You ought not to die the next time we're raiding the Hell level."

Victor's eyebrows rose toward his hairline. "You were there?"

"Didn't you gather that much from my comment about reviving Bishop?" Trevor exaggerated a sigh. "You're on the commodore's private network now, so you won't be dragged down into the laggy abyss again."

"Thanks, Chief, I appreciate it."

Trevor hesitated at the door with his fingers against the cool metal. "Commander?"

"Yeah?" he answered absently while unpacking his virtual gear. Most of the boxed components required installation and he looked forward to a half hour of blissful busywork to clear his mind.

"It wasn't your fault."

Tension straightened Victor's spine and locked his shoulders. His fingers clenched around the edge of the case. Better that than the delicate equipment within. "Excuse me?"

"It wasn't your fault," Trevor repeated kindly, without making eye contact. "I didn't see what's bothering you, and I didn't look into your head. It doesn't work that way... but there's an aura of guilt surrounding you so deeply that your soul is drowning in it, and I *can* see that."

Words died in his throat, choked back by the upwelling storm of emotions. Victor didn't think his dry mouth could form them anyways.

"Things will get better. I know you've heard that before. Trust me, I've heard it a hundred times myself."

"I don't think..." Victor swallowed and dragged in a breath.

The phantasmal impression of a warm hand settled against Victor's shoulder. Light and encouraging, and somehow pleasantly supportive. "Give it all of the time you need. I think I know why Bishop insisted for me to install your netlink personally. And I'm glad that he did. You and I have something in common, sir... and I'm around. Any time you need an ear."

Trevor excused himself quietly from the room, taking the familiar, friendly presence with him. Victor remained seated at the edge of his bed for a while longer, too captivated by his own deep thoughts to do anything else.

CHAPTER 3

"Got a patient for you, sir," the on-duty medical technician called, announcing Zoe's arrival at the examination lab. "Lovely piece of arm work on her."

"Thanks, O'Reilly. I'll be right in with her."

Zoe peered through the doorway left open by the corpsman, wondering which doctor she'd be blessed with seeing today.

Her unpleasant experiences with doctors consisted of assholes who liked to poke and prod at her arm while asking what it felt like. Occasionally, one asked about her eyes, questioned her headaches, and prescribed useless pain meds that didn't even scratch the surface of her migraines.

When she had been selected for the splicing program, Zoe had leapt at the chance. At eighteen years old, the idea of having eyes like a hawk appealed to her sense of adventure. She wanted to be a sniper, and the genetic therapy allowed her to become one of the best in the Royal Marines. Back then, youth clouded her judgment and downplayed the potential negative side effects.

Her gaze dropped away from the hall and down to her boots. Her feet swayed back and forth while she hummed quietly off-tune. It kept her mind off the stabbing pain.

Footsteps announced the arrival of her doctor, but she still didn't look up. They all tended to look the same – bland and judgmental. Arrogant.

"Sergeant Raines, right? This says you're in for shoulder pain. Let's have a look at you, shall we?"

What the…? The unusually cordial voice drew her gaze upward where it froze on the medical officer's face. It took her mind a moment to realize the handsome sight in front of her was a doctor and not one of her fellow enlistees, but his Commander insignia shined against his lab coat collar.

"Yes, sir. I was throwing punches with Commander Daniels yesterday in training, and now my arm is all out of whack. The pain radiates into my back."

The doctor moved around the exam table and flashed a sympathetic smile. "I want you to show me exactly where it hurts."

Zoe caught herself before she gazed too long into the man's smoky grey eyes. Her enhanced vision picked out blue tones in the misty color.

"Er, sure thing, Doc. I noticed an ache here." Her left hand touched the front of her right shoulder. "Figured that was normal enough at first, all things considered, but it lingered through to today. First it only hurt when I raised my arm. Now it's constant. I feel it zinging toward my spine."

"I see."

The two most frightening words to ever be spoken by a medical professional left his lips. She winced inwardly and waited for his diagnosis.

"According to your medical history, your entire right arm is a prosthetic, right?" The pale blue glow of a screen cast eerie color against his olive-toned face. He touched his finger down the delicate display screen.

"Yeah, they fit me about two years ago. My arm was burned and… they couldn't save it." She mumbled the last bit and glanced away. Everything was in her files but doctors had a nasty habit of making her repeat it aloud. When the request for details didn't come, she peeked back up. Doctor del Toro smiled warmly. It made his pale eyes stand out. *God, he looks like a model from Paradiso someone threw into a lab coat.*

"And some bone plasteel lacing augmentation of your left arm and shoulder after taking a bullet."

"Yup, that's it for the implants," Zoe confirmed.

"Have you ever had a problem with any of them before? Any sharp stabs, aches, irritation beneath the skin? Grinding?"

"Not until that louse kicked my shoulder and wrenched it in a hold," she grumbled under her breath. She quickly followed with a headshake. "No. No issues 'til now."

"You're in luck. Received my cyberware mechanic cert while on Paradiso this past year, so I'm familiar with these. The Royal Guard seems to be fond of this brand, too…" he mused out loud while reading the specifications. "Newest model. Very nice. It's not a bad device, until, you know–" He lowered his voice quieter than a conversational tone, "Some prick decides to play dirty in a sparring match."

Zoe's lips turned up at one corner. "Some people don't like to lose to a girl," she whispered back conspiratorially.

"Guess that means you were winning."

"Yeah, 'were' being the operative word," she responded dryly.

"I need to have a look, Sarge. Mind unfastening your coveralls and lowering them to your waist?"

She laughed softly and zipped down her suit. A fitted tank top beneath preserved her modesty, at least. As far as Zoe was concerned, her right arm served as a vast improvement over the missing limb and allowed her to return to normal function. It granted complete awareness of heat, cold, sensation of pressure and touch; everything had returned to her. The seam connected at her shoulder, where toffee-colored lab grown skin and advanced materials grafted to her natural body. It was a perfect match now, but during her cybernetic fitting the limb had been as pale as butter. At the time, she had been ashamed and traumatized, too embarrassed to show the ugly limb to the world. It had taken weeks for the melanocytes to gradually match her skin tone and for her confidence to return.

"And here I swore I wasn't going to let any of you ship-boys talk me out of my clothes."

Her doctor resembled a deer staring into hovercraft headlamps.

Zoe shifted restlessly and bit her lower lip. "Sorry, I tend to blurt out stuff when I'm nervous, and I've never been fond of medical."

"It's all right; I understand." He recovered and flashed her a grin. "I don't like undressing for strangers either. Maybe that's why I'm the doctor." He guided her back gently against the table. A machine hung overhead, dangling from rails installed into the ceiling. He grasped hold of it, guided it above her body at torso height until the lens was aligned with her shoulder, and he peered into the screen.

Her booted feet fidgeted, then she crossed one ankle over the other to still their swaying. She tried to stare up at the ceiling, but her gaze drifted toward the dark-haired man peering into the scope.

"You're probably familiar with this, but I like to talk everyone through what I'm doing anyway. This is a Neurogenetic Osteo Robotic Imaging machine. NORI for short. We only use it to perform scans in real time on cybernetic and organic parts. I want to see if any of your connectors came loose from the nerve plates."

The doctor quieted for a time. He didn't fill the empty seconds with meaningless conversation, but the silence didn't feel awkward or unnerving. For the first time since her arrival to the exam room, subtle notes of classical music teased past her hearing.

No... that wasn't there when I entered the room. It started when he came in, she decided. "Is that your music?"

"The ship's A.I. likes to chase me with music ever since it found out I play the cello," Doctor del Toro confessed. "This is probably going to sting." He wiggled the pads of his index and middle fingers against the joint of her shoulder. Then he rotated her arm, sending unforgiving lances of pain into the socket. It felt like a hot poker sizzling into the core of her bone and sending molten metal down every nerve fiber.

"Shit!" The expletive ripped from her throat.

"He got you pretty good. You're in luck though. We won't need any invasive procedures to go in and surgically adjust it, at least, and the worst of the pain will be over by the time you leave my office."

"Good," she wheezed, quickly clearing her throat afterward. "So... It'll just settle back in then or...?"

"No. I'll nudge it and send you back to your bunk with a sick note. You can have a couple days off for it to heal. Sound good to you?"

"Not how I'd hoped to make my debut at a new command, but I guess I have little choice in the matter."

"Absolutely no choice, really. Unless you'd prefer to go under the knife. I have some new surgical lasers I'm very excited to try–"

"No!" She flashed a quick, bright grin up at him. "Absolutely no need for you to play surgery with me, Doc. Do as you will."

"Are you certain about that? This is only my second week, and I'm dying to do some real work."

Least he has a sense of humor, she thought. "Rain check."

The heel of his right palm pressed flush against her body, effectively pinning her to the table. He stared at the screen, completely unaware of her awkward mood.

Zoe braced herself for the pain. It hurt. It hurt every bit as much as she'd expected when his fingers pressed bone deep. He kneaded and palpated, until the loosened connectors met with their sockets. Each time, a wild zing of electricity raced down her nerves to her spine.

"Be still," he warned her.

Zoe grit her teeth and refused to cry out. As he completed the final pop, sensation exploded beneath the bone and raced down her spine to the tips of her toes.

"Finished. Next time Daniels comes after you with an invitation to spar, I suggest you accept and begin the match by kicking him in the groin."

"So unsportsmanlike, Doc." Moisture clung to the corners of her eyes, trapped by her lashes.

"Hey, if you thought half the things about me that I think you did just now, then you know I'm right. Go ahead and sit up, roll your shoulder."

Zoe's head swiveled around to face him. She stared, wide-eyed and alarmed. *Please God, please don't be a psychic. If you heard any of that...* "You're not a psychic, right?" Between her lusty thoughts and her wishes for him to walk out of an open airlock, she'd never find a hole deep enough to hide in.

"Not at all, Raines. I just know how to read faces. I've been a doctor for a while now. I've also been called a lot of things in plenty of languages by many marines and airmen."

It took a moment to roll up into a seated position. Zoe quickly swiped at her eyes when she thought he wasn't paying attention. Her shoulder ached and the joint felt bruised.

"I might have thought some unflattering things for a minute there. Sadist came to mind." She smiled to soften the admission. "But it does feel better, so thanks for that."

"You probably won't think that in a couple hours." He plucked up his tablet and scribbled with the stylus. "Let your supervising officer know that you'll be off duty while that settles. No sparring, all right? There's a prescription waiting for you, as well."

"I'm guessing target practice is also out?" Zoe shrugged back into her coveralls and zipped them up.

"You guessed right. Maybe you should apply to med school," he replied.

She rubbed at her arm and slipped down to her feet. "Funny, Doc."

"Glad to be of help. Come back if you notice anything that doesn't feel right to you after the next three days. Don't wait through the pain again."

"Yes, sir."

Zoe's medication waited for her at the counter. She signed for the pills and headed out. The lift took her three decks down and she headed directly for her supervisor's open office door.

"Sergeant Raines, what can I do for you?"

Zoe held out her badge. "I've been assigned to my rack followed by some light duty, Chief," she explained.

Chief Obi Nwosu scanned the small badge with his datagram and perused the resulting readout. Zoe fought the urge to fidget. It was a new record for her. After only two days onboard, she'd already been thrown off-duty. Her embarrassment knew no bounds.

"Some good drugs the doctor gave you." His deep voice reminded Zoe of the old earth music her mother favored. There was a soothing quality to the rich bass tones.

"Yes, Chief. Hopefully I won't need them beyond tonight." Doctor del Toro had fixed the misalignment in her cybernetics, but the rough handling dealt by Daniels under the pretense of training left a bone-deep ache in her joint. It practically thrummed with discomfort.

"Take them if you need them, Raines. No shame in getting hurt, and better that you recover fully. I'll take you off the armed watch and assign you to the armory in the meantime. Does that sound good to you?"

Zoe nodded, relief flooding her senses. "I can do that, Chief Nwosu. Thanks. I need to familiarize myself with your inventory and procedures anyway."

"Go on then. I'll see you the day after tomorrow in the main armory."

At the first water station, she paused to take her allotted pain meds, looking forward to a painless, drugged slumber.

Like all other enlisted personnel, Zoe bunked with five other people. Three shared the day schedule and the others worked nights. Thanks to the personalized sleep bays they entered and left at will, and were able to chat and use the communal space freely without waking their slumbering companions.

That especially counted for rendezvous with crewmembers of the opposite sex. Or sometimes the same sex. Opaque glass partitions surrounded each bed. Adjustable settings could make them completely soundproof and absolutely private. At least, they were private until some half-dressed serviceman stumbled out with his uniform over his shoulder and his boots in one hand.

"You're back early."

Zoe smiled faintly. "Doctor del Toro took me off duty."

"Hottie del Toro? Do tell. What's he like up close? I've only seen him while serving his meals in the officers' mess. I swear, it's about time we got a male doctor who wasn't a thousand years old."

"Er…." Zoe darted her glance between the two eager pair of eyes watching her. Radha and Angela seemed nice enough at first glance. Neither one worked in Combat, and both tended to put obscene amounts of time into their appearance. Zoe learned her first day that if she wanted hot water for a shower, she needed to crawl out of bed before them.

Radha didn't wait for Zoe to answer. "My cousin Padma is on the Glenn, and she recognized his name immediately. All the girls were crazy about him there too, right? Guess what she told me. You'll never guess, Zoe."

"Guess what? He seemed nice enough. Fixed my arm right up."

"A few years ago he was supposed to marry some hotshot captain on the ship. Supposedly, he dumped her a month before the date for… get this… an Eloran!" Radha announced.

"He's into aliens? That's really disgusting." Angela crinkled her nose.

"What's wrong with aliens? Some of them are very nice," Zoe protested.

Radha fixed her with a quiet, disbelieving stare. Angela cleared her throat uncomfortably and focused on her painted nails. It was as if Zoe had spoken something blasphemous.

"There's nothing wrong with them, I suppose. Personally, I don't see the appeal. Do we even have compatible parts?" Angela asked warily, judgment filling her blue eyes.

Funny. A long time ago, people were discriminating against others for the color of their skin or which religion they followed. Now they're doing it for the kind *of skin a person wears,* Zoe thought ruefully, shaking her head.

"I guess that explains a lot if he's a xenophile. He'd rather have gills and scales over a real woman," Radha muttered.

"Come on, Zoe. You've met him up close and in person. What did you think?" Angela persisted.

"I think he knows his job." *And he has a nice smile.* "I was there in pain. Staring at the good looking doctor wasn't high on my list of priorities. Sorry."

"Oh you're no fun. C'mon, tell us. Are his hands as nice as they say? I saw him once after he arrived, but it was for a cold. But if he was looking at your arm, he must have touched you." Angela leaned forward eagerly.

"Like I said, pain. Pain I'm still feeling, so if you'll excuse me, I just wanna get changed and hit the hay. These drugs are making me loopy." The drugs had yet to affect her coherence, but she had no intention of continuing the current conversation.

"Oh. Okay, we can talk about it tomorrow then. You get some rest," Angela said apologetically. Radha mirrored her shallow concern.

Zoe nodded, smiled, and then moved over to her assigned bunk.

"Oh, Zoe?" Angela piped up before Zoe managed to crawl into bed. "Do you think I could borrow that gold top I spotted in your locker at our next port?"

Seriously? They're already scoping out my stuff?

"Don't be silly, Angie," Radha spoke up. "You're too pasty for that color, but I have a pink tunic that'll look much better."

"Everyone from your culture has the best looking colors in their wardrobe," Angela complained. "It isn't fair."

Zoe eye rolled and left them to discuss fashion without adding to the conversation. As she settled down, she did have to agree with one thing: Doctor del Toro was extremely easy on the eyes.

Maybe he'll smile for me again… The wistful thought accompanied her slide into drugged oblivion.

CHAPTER 4

Cool light gleamed from the debriefing room's ceiling and illuminated the faces of the stoic officers gathered to discuss plans for their next mission.

Ethan sat beside his ship's executive officer, Amelia Banks, a middle-aged woman with warm, coffee colored skin and equally dark eyes. Victor, Oshiro, and Daniels filled the remaining seats.

An oversized map dominated the room's center, displaying a three dimensional representation of the galaxy and its countless systems. Tiny pinpricks of light blinked to life, interspersed with radiant suns and an assortment of planets. A glowing blip depicted the Jemison and another bright yellow icon displayed their next destination. Three days of flight time separated them.

"Yesterday, United Command received a request from the capital city on Loki 4 to check their sister colony on the orbiting moon." Ethan zoomed the map to a small system that featured four planets orbiting a small yellow star. "They're unresponsive."

"Do they lack ships of their own?" Victor inquired.

"Loki 4 is a green civilization site," Oshiro informed him kindly. "Their sister colony was founded with help from the Empire to reduce overcrowding on the planetary surface. It is the first on the moon and its success will pave the way for additional colony settlements."

"So they don't mine for fuel, and they're defenseless unless one of our ships is in the vicinity, you mean." Commander Daniels folded his arms against his chest. His unsympathetic visage remained unchanged while he surveyed the map.

Amelia leaned forward in her seat and settled the weight of her solemn gaze on each officer in turn. "Often, when our ships happen by a raided colony, it's weeks later and beyond our ability to help. This time, the Empire has a chance to do something about it."

"We're sending you to search for refugees. If they are reeling from an attack or natural disaster, you will provide aid. Commander Daniels and a team of marines will accompany your squad to provide backup," Amelia explained.

"That's new," Daniels commented.

"Commodore Bishop and I have discussed possibilities at length for your squads." Amelia swiped a hand across her tablet and brought up a holographic display that projected over the center of the table and expanded. An identification photo of a young blonde appeared above a list of military achievements.

"Saskia DuPrie is one of the splicers we picked up from our rendezvous with the Noriega. She's been trained for reconnaissance and her camouflage ability is one of the best I've ever come across. Took me weeks to get her transferred to my ship," Ethan said.

Daniels grunted. "Acceptable."

He looks like he'd prefer to drink NeoDiesel, Victor thought.

"Sergeant Zoe Raines. Sniper. She underwent voluntary gene splicing after her enlistment and came out with eagle vision. This woman doesn't need a scope to hit her target."

"I'd rather take Henley," Daniels disagreed, arms crossed over his chest. Another photograph hovered above the table.

"I examined Raines' cybernetic arm. It's top of the line," Victor muttered thoughtfully. "She can handle a lot of weapons without stress."

"Maybe so, but she hasn't seen combat since she lost it," Daniels replied.

"Then the young woman must feel anxious to return to combat duty," Oshiro said mildly.

"How about Upstead?" Amelia suggested. "Steadiest arm I know. His upgrades aren't the latest model but they're still good and reliable."

Daniels shook his head. "Steady arm, true, but too slow. I need someone who isn't weighed down by their implants."

So that's his game, is it? Victor squeezed his coffee cup a little too hard. The crushed cardboard sloshed hot liquid over the side that dribbled over his fingers.

"This is not up for debate," Ethan informed them all. "Sergeant Raines will be your sniper. That is why I had her transferred here. Deal with it."

Daniels assumed a professionally neutral expression and nodded. "Aye, aye, sir." The next handful of names met with his taciturn approval.

Oshiro and Ethan conducted their own discussion about medical protocol and skilled marines. Unlike Daniels, Victor had no reservations or any favorites among straight humans, splicers, or cyborgs. He valued them equally.

"Will four be sufficient?" Ethan asked.

"I don't require many. I'll happily accept quality over quantity," Victor spoke aloud while reviewing the suggested marines. A few of the names on his personal list coincided with Ethan's recommendations. "I'm happy with the four, but I'd be pleased if you add Elizabeth Fairchild, too. I spoke with her in medical this morning and she's a brilliant nurse with a degree in microbiology. Perfect asset to the team."

"Done."

"Appreciated," Victor said courteously. He stole a glance at Daniels. The quiet man sat back in his chair with his beefy arms folded against his chest.

Eventually, they concluded their meeting and began to file from the room. Daniels stepped into line behind Oshiro, but Victor found it increasingly difficult to bite his tongue.

"Oi, Daniels. A word with you?"

The other commander hung back and shut the door, as if he'd expected the request. They didn't return to their seats. Victor opted to lean by the table while his fellow officer waited a few steps from the door.

"Something wrong, del Toro?"

"You tell me. Do you have something against cybernetics that I should know about?" Victor asked.

"They're a crutch. An easy way to cheat their way past doing the work themselves."

"That's bloody ridiculous," Victor argued. After a deep breath, he calmed his tone. "Whether it was elective augmentation or not, they are here to serve the Empire the same as you and me."

Daniels smirked. "Of course, you have a soft spot for them."

"No. That is where you and I differ, because I see them no differently than our soldiers who have the blessing to remain completely flesh and blood. You, on the other hand, appear to have something against Zoe Raines in particular. If it's about wanting to avoid any claims of favoritism toward another native of your home planet, you've taken it a few steps too far."

"Not really. This doesn't have anything to do with her originating from Tallulah." Daniels paused and glanced at the chronometer fastened to his wrist, as if he'd spared too many seconds of his precious time already for Victor. "Like most mechies, she needs to pull her weight without relying on her shiny new upgrades. She'll get herself killed if she goes into a fight thinking that arm will save her."

"She's a sniper. Her job is to kill before the enemy knows she's there. I doubt she relies on the arm to save her," Victor disagreed.

"My job is to make sure they can handle any combat situation," Daniels said evenly.

"That's odd, because I've taken the liberty to speak to a half dozen other cyborgs after the second complaint entered the medical bay. Three complaints, since my arrival, of joint and nerve damage. The commonality between them is that you are the trainer. Are they handling combat situations or discrimination?"

"I'm not having this discussion with you, del Toro."

"I saved your ass when I salvaged Johnson's hand in the repair lab. You won't have me to speak to if you wreck a twenty thousand quid prosthetic; you'll be taking it up with Bishop when the budget has to replace it," Victor said hotly.

Without another glance at the other officer, Victor slammed the door behind him and stormed to the elevator. If anything upset him, it was bullies, and Commander Daniels was no exception.

***

The Jemison reached its destination in less than three days and sent a modest spacecraft to investigate Loki 4's single moon. Lieutenant Rogers, a young man with a carrot-colored mop of hair and copious freckles, landed the rockskipper on the moon's surface without incident. The position placed them at the city outskirts on a landing pad designated for supply ships.

"You okay to wait here?" Daniels asked the pilot.

"Aye, sir. I have a rifle" Rogers patted the stock and smiled. "I'll be right here if you need me and prepared to offer aerial support with the rockskipper's canons, too."

"Excellent," Daniels said. "We'll need a reliable eye."

Zoe stared at Daniels until Victor touched her shoulder in passing.

Once they all moved outside of the rockskipper, the silence of a dead village greeted them. Windmills moved in the distance and water crashed through the hydraulic power plant by the thin river cutting through the rock bordering the town. Nothing else happened and no one came to greet their ship.

"DuPrie, you're up," Daniels called out. "I need a quick in and out to know what we're up against."

Saskia stepped away from the rest of the group and to the closest rocky outcropping. Ruddy red hues streaked with black rippled across her skin, matching the local terrain. After the press of a button her specialized armor and boots transitioned to a translucent state. She became a shimmer then impossible to track once she moved away.

Daniels split the team into two groups, mixing medical personnel between each. He assigned them each a search pattern while they waited for word from their scout.

"The place is a ghost town." Saskia reported over the comm. "No one is moving through there. We're safe to go in."

The peaceful settlement was once beautiful, but the empty gardens and silent buildings lent it a haunting quality. Their orderly sweep through the settlement discovered homes with smashed furniture, ransacked closets, and empty pantries.

Outside appeared no better. Abandoned toys littered the streets and vegetable carts rotted beneath the sun. The group split to move around both sides of the square.

"What happened in that pasture?" Abernathy questioned over the commlink.

"Maybe the livestock began to cannibalize? Villagers appear to be gone and there's no one here to feed them," Fairchild replied.

A waist high fence portioned a great space beside the village. Beyond the wooden structure, remnants of several mauled livestock carcasses cooked beneath the midday sun. They might have been a variant of cow native to the nearby planet.

"Those are herbivores, Fairchild. They won't cannibalize. Something else did that," Abernathy disagreed.

"Doctor," Zoe said in a low voice. "Don't move. Don't even speak."

Victor took her advice at face value and froze. He moved only his eyes to scan his field of vision, scrutinizing every detail of their surroundings. The dwindling sun reflected light off a glossy softball-sized eye.

The rest of the mottled, red and grey creature came into view. Like Saskia, its skin mimicked the rough stone surface of the buildings carved from the mountain range.

Don't move? What else am I supposed to do? I can't very well wait for it to eat me, he thought. One adjustment of his shotgun muzzle would place the creature on the receiving end of military retribution at least. He swung his firearm toward the monster and discharged the shell, point blank, into its chest. It shook off the shot and lunged.

The unexpected collision with Zoe's shoulder took Victor off his feet. Something sharp scraped past his cheek and left searing heat in its wake. Carrion breath blasted his face from his attacker's rancid mouth.

For a woman half his size, Zoe hit like a drake, the camel-sized reptilian creatures known for their aggression and hunger for human flesh. Astreya's first explorers and settlers named them for their uncanny resemblance to dragons.

"What the hell–"

"Sorry, Doc." Zoe leapt to her feet and put her rifle to her shoulder. "God, that thing is ugly."

Away from the rock walls and the camouflage they provided, their attacker came into focus. Foot-long quills fanned up from the beast's hide and a bloody smear colored its left tusk.

So much for our reliable eye, Victor thought as he hurried back to his feet. He leveled his shotgun at the creature's hide and pulled the trigger. The weapon bucked against his shoulder and the shot deflected off its tough skin. He pumped the firearm and blasted it again, hobbling its foreleg. It recovered swiftly and lunged with the intact front leg, its claws open and ready to strike.

"Down."

Victor dropped to one knee and Zoe aimed her rifle over his shoulder and fired. The creature's eye socket exploded in a spray of blood and gore. It crashed to the ground, dead in a single shot.

"Holy shit, we've got more of them, guys! Two more on your six," Saskia reported.

"Rogers, this would be the time to provide that aerial support you mentioned," Victor barked into the frequency.

Gunfire echoed across the square and the comm chatter revealed the other team faced similar assault. Mirroring his earlier gesture, Zoe squeezed Victor's shoulder before she moved away.

"Lopez is hurt; I'll cover you," she informed him.

"I see him." Victor shouldered his weapon and sprinted across the wide lane. A lithe form twisted around and lunged in his direction. It yowled in pain, struck by projectiles fired in rapid succession. Zoe covered his flank while he continued his dash toward the downed soldier, whipping out his medical pack from his supplies while on the move.

Four barbed spines protruded from Lopez's leg, but their presence kept the bleeding to a minimum. Victor staggered to one knee beside him and dropped the equipment package on the ground. A thin trickle of blood dribbled down his numbed cheek, and he closed his eyes to steady his head.

The hell is wrong with me?

He shook off the feeling and dove into the bag.

Saskia and Chang took cover nearby and concentrated their fire on the third beast. They moved swiftly, their flexible movements bearing resemblance to the canid species that ran wild on Paradiso. Oblivious to the impact of the gunshots, it rushed at them and gave a ferocious snarl, spittle flying from its tooth-filled maw. The two soldiers peppered its tough exterior with bullets until it collapsed on the ground. Saskia sweated heavily by the end, her pale brow beaded with moisture.

The shuttle swept overhead in a low pass. Strategically placed detonations from the rockskipper set the debris aflame that surrounded Victor's squad. The result worked like a charm, by not only scaring the fourth creature, but forcing it to rear back from the searing flames and expose its softer underbelly. Victor mercilessly capitalized on the vulnerability and filled it with scatter rounds.

"More incoming from the mountain range," Rogers announced. "I'll keep them off of you."

"What *are* they?" Daniels demanded. "Four have us penned by the corral."

"They're only wargs. I thought you had it covered," Rogers said.

Daniels didn't sound amused. "What the hell is a warg?"

"They're predatory mountain dogs. Like wolves. Native to Loki 4, but probably brought here by the settlers for hunting. By the way, try not to let one gore you. There's a neurotoxin on the tusks, and it'll put you down on your ass," Rogers said.

Now he tells me.

"Get these things off our asses, Rogers, then scare off the rest." Daniels' brusque voice filled the comm channel.

Fire frightened the wargs off better than guns. O'Malley activated his flamethrower and kept the monsters at bay until Rogers arrived. By the time things settled, Victor had cleansed Lopez's leg, staunched the blood flow, and sat heavily in the dirt to assess his injury.

He fumbled with his tools and took a sample from the blood, blinking a few times to clear his vision and squint at the streaky blur of numbers glowing from the display. "Someone read these results out loud to me so I know what I've been poisoned with."

"Allow me." Fairchild crouched down beside Victor. "Doctor Matthews and I put together a kit based on known planetary hazards."

"You're a lifesaver, Fairchild. I knew I wanted you on this team for a reason." By the time they narrowed down the proper antidote, he lacked control of his fingers to press the plunger on the antivenin. If there was one thing Victor despised, it was being on the receiving end of his profession.

"You good to continue, del Toro?" Daniels regarded both injured men. "Williams, you stay here with Lopez. Fairchild, unless the Commander needs you elsewhere, I'd prefer you remain as well."

"I'm good." Victor shook it off and rose to his feet. "I'd like Fairchild to remain with him as well. Get him to the rockskipper."

Daniels looked him over and nodded. "I'll take my team through the west buildings as planned. We'll meet up on the northern strip. Let's move out before the wargs decide the fire is an acceptable risk."

They swept through the village, occasionally picking off a straggler that came bounding from cover. Rogers covered them from above with his rifle. Occasionally, he hit one.

"Next time, we leave Raines in the shuttle, too. I see why that kid is the pilot." Victor muttered.

Daniels grunted something that sounded like agreement.

"Hey! I'm doing the best I can while piloting a bloody hovercraft."

A nervous chuckle passed over the divided squad. They reported to each other over the wireless commlink, pointing out the signs of ambushes and assaults. Bullet holes marked a few wooden market stalls, and blood stained the stone walls.

"This heat is stifling. Why would anyone willingly choose to live here?" Jackson asked. "I find it hard to believe someone would self-inflict this kind of torture."

Victor silently agreed. Perspiration dripped into his eyes, but no sooner did he wipe it away did another droplet bead from his brow to replace it.

"I heard the population on Loki 4 recently reached one billion. They'd prefer not to overcrowd their planet like our Earthen ancestors. That should be celebrated," Saskia replied. "It's only a little heat. Toughen up."

Their continued search turned up few answers, and even more empty buildings.

"Not a single child. Usually in a raid, someone gets away to hide in a closet or a basement storeroom," Victor muttered as the group met at the city hall's stone-carved steps. "At least one. There isn't a single survivor here."

"Have you witnessed that often?" Chang asked.

The commanders glanced at each other, but Daniels spoke first. "Not recently, but a few years ago during the war with the ASR, my team found a little girl hiding with her mother in the closet. We almost left her behind, too. She was playing dead under the corpse."

"Shit," Abernathy uttered.

"We're performing vital scans in every room we enter. There's nothing here so far," Victor spoke up. "We'll spread out and continue to sweep toward the outlying farms."

"Sirs," Zoe stepped into the doorway. "You're going to want to see this."

Victor and Daniels followed the young woman to a large house bordering the central square. Davis met them inside, her face solemn and pale.

"We found six corpses, sir. All were killed execution style with a single bullet to the back of the head," the medic informed them. "One of them is the governor."

Daniels swore and stopped on the threshold, grimacing. "What a stench."

The bloated bodies formed a haphazard line across the middle of the floor in a large office. "These corpses are several days... ripe," Davis muttered. She removed masks from her kit for the members of the assault squad.

Victor hastily placed his filtered mask over his nose and mouth. Heat from the steamy atmosphere outside poured through the windows and helped to putrefy the bodies, expediting the rot.

"Could it be pirates? The homes were also looted,"

"Pirates aren't usually murderers, too. They rob and dash."

"Could be slavers. The city hall indicated this colony's documented population is 594 people," Abernathy said. "That makes 588 unaccounted for individuals."

"Slavers wouldn't trouble themselves with looting," Victor said. "An adult human male goes for five thousand quid on the market. Ten if we're doing our bloody jobs and they're unable to meet the current demand."

"Would take a pretty big ship, too, taking that many people." Zoe chimed in. "Most slave rings I've come across in the past were small operations. Fifty people taken at most, but usually more like ten."

"Two ships." Saskia stepped into the room without acknowledging the dead bodies splayed out on the floor. "I followed rover tracks out to the canyons. Based on the ground marks, I say they had two ships land out of sight."

"That's more info than we had before," Daniels said. "All right, we'll take the bodies onboard with us. Maybe you can learn more from them in your medical labs."

"In every old horror movie I've ever watched set in our time frame, taking corpses aboard a ship is a recipe for disaster. We'll examine them here, Commander," Victor said politely.

"He doesn't want chest-busters." Zoe bit back her grin. "Can't say I blame him."

Victor winked at her. "Damn straight. We brought mobile scanners with us. Prepare to sit for a while."

A while was an understatement. Victor and the rest of the medical crew toiled over the corpses for hours. Multiple biologic scans revealed no underlying diseases, parasites, or trauma. Forensic examinations failed to yield anything pertinent and lacked any useful physical evidence about the perpetrators. They only learned that a single shot to the brain ended each life.

"Wait. This one's different from the others," Victor muttered. He raised mobile examination table a little higher and swung around the magnifying glass. "Here. He's the only one who lacks an exit wound. And the point of entry is also cauterized."

"Yeah, so?" Daniels asked. "What's that mean?"

"This is typical of old world bullets. A lot of older relics penetrated the skull and became lodged in the brain matter. It remains common now with non-military grade firearms. That isn't the case with those five."

"They were definitely killed with black market weapons, sir. These are military-issued tungsten steel rounds," Zoe spoke up. By Imperial decree, civilians were only allowed shotguns, revolvers, and hunting rifles.

"That doesn't explain why his skull looks like it was roasted over a barbecue," Daniels pointed out.

"That particular trait is common from the 2200s. Before parliament banned it, the rich favored guns with overpriced bullet effects. Plain metal wasn't enough for them; they wanted flame rounds," Zoe explained.

Daniels thoughtfully stroked his closely groomed goatee. "I can't see why our killer would change guns mid-execution. So we had more than one shooter? What does that mean for our investigation?"

Victor straightened from his kneel beside the victim. "It means one of them uses incredibly rare antiques. We trace the pistol, and maybe we can find the killer."

"We found the rest of the colonists," Lopez reported over the comm. "The school gym is packed full of bodies. Preliminary scans indicate no one left alive."

"I thought we ordered you back to the ship," Daniels said.

"Sorry about that, sir. We spotted the building on the way to meet up with Rogers and had a look."

"Are you up for moving around like that, mate?" Victor asked over the link.

"You did a bloody brilliant job, Doc. Never better. I can't say the same for these poor folk."

"It's a real butcher job, Commander," Fairchild joined in.

"We're on our way."

Contrary to what Lopez believed, the victims in the school gymnasium were a far cry from accounting for the rest of the townspeople. Their numbers totaled one hundred and sixty-two in all and every single corpse had been littered with bullet holes in a haphazard pattern.

While Victor and the rest of medical swept through the very stinky discovery, Daniels remained behind with Abernathy to investigate the city hall records.

"Upload the citizen registry to our link up and we'll begin the identification process," Victor told his fellow commander.

"You should have it in a minute."

Victor went from body to body, checking for signs of life before taking a DNA sample to compare against the registry.

"Loki 4 is home to an unusually large number of psychics among their population. Since these people are overflow from the planet, they should have the same traits," Fairchild pointed out.

"What are you getting at?" Zoe asked. She worked to move the bodies into neatly laid out rows with the assistance of her fellow marines.

"Well, I've scanned almost everyone in the room and not a single one is registered as a psychic."

Victor glanced up from his readout. "I haven't noted any cybernetics among the victims either. Statistically speaking we should have had at least a handful by now even if they are from a green planet."

"So we have slavers taking their choice of cyborgs and psychics now?" The frustration in Daniels' voice carried over the comm.

"Seems like it. Kids, too. Not a single body under the age of thirteen among the rest," Fairchild added.

"This wasn't a raid," Victor said. "It was a culling."

CHAPTER 5

Fan blades whirred overhead, circulating the stuffy air in the armory chamber. Zoe and Saskia sat side by side at the weapons room's main terminal, fixated upon the important task delegated to them by Commander Daniels.

Finally. Something I can do without that ornery bastard standing over my shoulder.

Zoe finished programming in the holographic settings and turned to her companion. "Right. So the Commodore received authorization from New Cambridge to allow us virtual access to their special firearms collection."

"Excellent." Saskia rubbed her palms together. "I saw that display once. Always wanted to get my hands on them, real or not."

"These are early 21st century firearms modified for use with pyro rounds." Zoe gestured to the five different weapons and a variety of ammunition clips. "We narrowed it down to these based off the cauterized wounds."

"All right, I've finished with my part, lassies. Let's do this." Trevor inserted a chip into the console's dataport and stepped away from the expensive rig. "Excellent," Saskia said. "I also had Rogers conduct some scans of the flight zone. The moon isn't equipped with a proper shuttle landing space since it's a new colony and they're green... but the flight craft responsible for the abductions left a unique set of markings in the terrain."

"I've drawn up some possible ships as well." Trevor's big grin shaved a few years from his handsome face. At a glance, the dark-haired communications chief resembled a native from the land of Xiao, but his accent sounded as British as their Commodore.

Not that Zoe planned to make that mistake again. She learned a dozen new swear words that day, accompanied by a rant about Trevor's proud Scottish ancestry. She'd never call him English again.

"Guns first. Then we can play 'name that ship' and hope we come up with something." Zoe's grin dimpled her cheeks. She pulled the visor down over her eyes and stepped up to the shooting range. "Run the program."

The virtual reality program materialized, creating an exact replica of the comfortable dining room from the lunar colony. Much like her favorite online game, Zoe experienced everything as if she were physically standing in the location. Saskia and Trevor shimmered into existence beside her.

"Looks about right to you guys?" Trevor asked. "I did what I could from the scans and photos Sassy took."

"Don't call me Sassy."

"Play nice you two," Zoe laughed. "So… Based on their sprawls and the data from the registry, do you think the computer can recreate everything?"

Trevor scoffed and dragged a menu from the console. "We have some of the best forensics programs available. Along with the intel gathered by Doctor del Toro's medics, it looks like they were dead for at least five days."

The program recreated the murder scene and pulled each of the six victims into position. A blank silhouette stood behind the governor, representing the murderer.

Zoe lifted an Old Earth model pistol from the case and looked it over. They tested various models of guns capable of firing the bullet responsible for cooking the victim's brain.

"I'm going with the assumption that our perp favored this beauty," Zoe said, picking up an old Smith & Wesson.

"I have last year's model of that," Trevor commented idly. He whistled. "Couple hundred years makes quite the difference, doesn't it?"

"My dad collected a few old guns. He let me shoot them once. Mom was right pissed about it, too. She said guns weren't proper for a lady." Zoe shrugged and moved behind the recreated image.

"Trajectory of the round and the blood splatter suggests a slight downwards angle on the entry and that the governor was standing," Saskia said.

"So we're looking for one tall bastard then," Trevor replied. "He left a partial boot print too. Size 13.5."

"Bigger than the commander."

"Aye. Victor wears a 12. This guy has him beat. Maybe…" Trevor glanced at the silhouette again. "By about four inches, maybe five. I can run a check through the known criminal database for unusually tall pirate bosses."

"Victor?" Saskia asked.

"Uh. Del Toro, I mean. Commander del Toro." Trevor rubbed his face and glanced away, red-cheeked.

Zoe arched a brow. "How do you know what shoe size he wears?"

"Man crush." Saskia maintained a stoic and solemn expression.

"Look, I see him a lot for my migraines, and I had to borrow a pair of boots the other day for a surprise inspection because mine are an awful mess. He wears two sizes larger than me. Felt like wearing clown shoes."

"I think we have a winner," Saskia announced after their simulation. The woman crouched down beside the corpse and compared it to the outline of the original body. "Good call, Zoe. There's some slight variance, but it's impossible to recreate the air conditions at the moment of death."

"So someone with a .40 caliber Smith & Wesson from the early 21st century. There can't be too many of those in working condition." Trevor turned the weapon over in his hands. "I mean, they were outdated when we left Earth behind a couple decades later."

"Don't all guns from that era fire the same? How do we know it isn't another handgun with a special kit?" Saskia asked.

"You'd think so. The differences are negligible by their Neanderthal standards," Trevor muttered. "But this program accounts for a thousand variables and picks up on the fine differences in force and gunpowder residue. The burn around the entry point before it penetrated the cerebral and the depth of cooked brain matter–"

"That's enough," Zoe said, cutting him off quickly. Her stomach twisted until she inevitably looked away from the fake corpse. "It's time to move on to the ships." She terminated the gun program after a last indulgent look. *I'd love to spend an hour with these just in a training run.*

Fortunately, their efforts to cross-reference wanted pirate ships involved a less macabre exploration.

"A Valkyrie could hold five hundred slaves easily," Trevor commented idly. "And it has the speed, but a pirate's not likely to own one and none were recently stolen."

"The Mercury 2400 is swift. My last cruiser pursued a mercenary crew for nearly two days. Swift, large, poor fuel capacity." Saskia pulled up the ship specifications.

Once the trio wrapped up the remaining results of their investigation efforts, the two women delegated Trevor the task of reporting their findings then they split from his company.

"I think Lockhart is sweet on you," Zoe teased once they reached the hallway and left their comrade behind.

"Him? I doubt it," Saskia murmured. Her lips pursed thoughtfully. As they traveled the hall, her fair skin picked up hints of the metallic walls in the corridor, reflecting gunmetal grey.

"Why not? You're a great catch, Saskia."

"You don't know?"

Zoe shook her head. "Know what?"

"He had a wee little one, and she died during his first deployment a few years ago. His marriage didn't survive it," Saskia informed her quietly, her voice barely a whisper.

How terrible. God, no wonder he looks so distant sometimes. "He doesn't look old enough to have had a wife, let alone a child." Zoe tucked the new knowledge away in the back of her mind. Trevor belonged to a small group of men who hadn't laid on the corny pick-up lines the moment she stepped on board. Doctor del Toro was another.

"Anyway. Word is that he doesn't date. Doesn't sleep around."

Zoe didn't blame him. "Well, to each their own. I'm not looking myself."

"But the jackasses like Daniels are always willing. I think that one must be sweet on *you*, love. He reminds me of a wee boy sticking gum in a girl's hair, only he has a fondness for wrecking your cybernetics instead."

"Ugh, don't even say that. Besides, doesn't seem too smart to hurt a girl and send her to the sexy doctor for fixing." Even so, she had to admit the fallout from Daniels' rough manner was almost worth it. Doctor del Toro's friendly demeanor and killer good looks weren't bad company.

Saskia laughed and ruffled Zoe's hair, spiking the short black strands. "Next time, kick him in the balls."

"That's funny. Someone else suggested the same thing…"

"Take their advice, trust me. Catch you later."

Saskia jogged off down the passageway and Zoe returned to her room, already planning for her rematch.

CHAPTER 6

Victor casually observed the endless sea of moving bodies awaiting their chance to exit the Jemison. Liberty days were a rare but pleasant breath of fresh air, enjoyed by all sailors granted a couple days respite from their duties aboard the ship. A fraction of their eligible sailors needed to stop by medical for a booster on their nanite vaccinations due to frequent changes in immunization requirements.

Everyone in the department planned to enjoy some downtime. Except for Victor. He preferred to remain on board, toiling in medical while the rest of his fellow crewmen enjoyed quality time away from the stress of deployment. Occasionally, he went out for a few hours to visit a market where he restocked his preferred sweets.

"You plan to come along on your first liberty with the Jemison? After that business on the Loki 4 lunar colony, you certainly deserve it." Ethan grinned pleasantly at him.

"Try it some other time, Bishop. I don't want to go."

"Oh, come on. How will I draw the ladies without my best wingman?"

"You can drink yourself into a pit of despair without me present. You've always been a magnet for all the pretty birds eager to find a sugar daddy. Unbeknownst to them, you're as cheap as it gets."

"When's the last time you slept with a woman and relieved all that stress, huh? You need to get back in the game. Don't let that one lousy bint ruin your fun."

"It's not Hannah," Victor said quietly. He fiddled with the hemmed edge of his green scrubs and refused to make eye contact. "Listen, I don't need to get laid; I don't want to get laid, and you can stop projecting your preferences on me. I'm perfectly *fine*."

Ethan's features softened. He sighed and raised one hand to rest against his friend's shoulder so that Victor couldn't miss his apologetic features. "I know what it is, Victor. And I'm sorry. I am asking you to enjoy freedom from your responsibilities for a while, all right? CO's orders. I don't care if you spend it drinking, not-shagging, or reading in a cafe. Just get out of here."

The crude words had the desired effect: Like the Grinch, Victor's heart swelled with warmth and made his chest feel three sizes too small. Ethan had always been a good friend. The best friend he could ask for despite the decade gap in their ages and differing authority aboard the ship. He still remembered Ethan's words too that day, the day Victor finally summoned the nerve to ask him why he cared about a scrawny, underfed kid like him.

"You remind me of my brother," Ethan had said. "He ran away to find a job on another planet when I left for the Navy. Fell out of touch with the rest of us. So I guess I always hoped that someone out there was looking after him like this."

Victor hoped so, too. Sometimes, it was difficult to believe they were serving aboard the same vessel again for the second time.

"All right. You win this time. I need a few to get out of my scrubs."

"Don't be late!" Ethan called behind him.

"Wouldn't dream of making you wait, sexy." Victor rolled his eyes and pushed his way through the thinning medical bay crowd.

***

The flashing lights and pulsing beat provided the perfect atmosphere for the crowd down on the dance floor. Victor sat at a table on the balcony overlooking the writhing mass of half-naked youngsters shimmying to the hypnotic noise. He shook his head and quietly nursed his drink.

Techno clubs and loud bars weren't his usual scene, but Ethan appeared to be enjoying himself. The commanding officer was occupied with a woman on each side of his body, swaying in close proximity.

"Evening, Commander," a familiar, male voice spoke up behind him.

Victor twisted around to face the friendly face of Trevor Lockhart. The younger man smiled and dipped his head respectfully.

"Chief Lockhart, are your migraines any better?"

"Aye, sir. Whatever you did fixed me right as rain again."

"I'm glad. I know I'm a cyberware doc, but I've learned some tricks for people with your predisposition toward them. Feel free to come in anytime your usual pain relief isn't cutting the mustard." Psychics like Trevor faced terrible headaches after excessive use of their abilities, a trade off balanced only by their brains' uncanny ability to regenerate cells and form new pathways.

"Appreciate it. Was that the CO I saw you come in with? Looks like he's living it up." Trevor peeked down to the dancers.

Victor laughed and nodded. "He's as much of a ladies man as ever."

"I think he's having enough fun for both of us."

"You're young, mate. Why aren't you dancing along with them?"

Trevor shook his head. "You're not much older than I am, si–"

"We can leave the sir and title on the ship, Trevor. Please. I'm just Victor right now. A sad man drinking all by my lonesome because my friend intends to abandon me to shag two naked ladies."

"Well, in that case…" Trevor dropped into the seat opposite his fellow marine and grinned. "I'm not much of a dancer and it's nice to get away from the ship's two drink limit sometimes."

Victor raised his glass in a silent toast. "I don't mind dancing," he told Trevor. "Just not this sort of stuff."

Victor and Trevor spent most of the night tossing back drinks while pretending they had enough sobriety to play bar games. What they lacked in dexterity they made up for with their drunken mirth.

"Aw, don't tell me you're too much of a big girl's blouse to play Guess That Drink. C'mon."

"No, I'm too smart to play it," Victor replied.

Trevor laughed and clinked his glass to Victor's. "Fair enough. I'll wait 'till you're drunk then ask again."

He'll be waiting awhile.

Raucous laughter interrupted Victor's musings. A group gathered around a holographic games table made more noise than the pounding music. Daniels and Etherington were among the revelers.

"So I have to ask, and if you don't want to say anything I'll understand, but what's the bloody deal with Commander Daniels?"

"Don't get me started on that rotten bastard," Trevor muttered. "If you're not in a skirt or some bloke who hefts around heavy things, Daniels won't give you a second look."

"Ah." *Should have known as much.* "I've had some run-ins with him."

"The man knows his job. That much I can say positively about him, but he's… brutal in his methods."

Victor made a noncommittal grunt and finished his drink. His pulse pounded in his head in time with the music.

"You enjoy the rest of your time off, Trevor. Gonna head back to the ship."

"G'night, Victor. Nice hanging with you."

"You, too."

CHAPTER 7

Like most ships, the Jemison followed Universal Standard Time, which was a twenty-four hour day set to their original world's 365 day year. The United Empire hadn't yet discovered the perfect duplicate of Old Earth's cycle and orbit patterns, but its calendar was a popular tool used across the galaxy in every star system.

At 3 AM, Victor had nothing better to do than to dominate the crew lounge. He slouched on the sofa in front of a Holotube airing a sappy show from the early 2300s.

Older historical pieces had always been his preferred entertainment when it came to watching movies, but his true love, and what he appreciated most, was classical period pieces from the 20th century. He loved them. He especially had a rabid lust for watching the science fiction films prior to 2100 and comparing their vision of the future to modern reality.

The wee hours of the morning became a delicious reverie of bad acting, terrible movie effects, and deep-fried bread products. He'd hit the gym the next night to make up for the perfect storm of calories.

"Tea and cake at 0300. And here I thought I was a bad sleeper."

Victor nearly spilled tea all over his sweatshirt. His eyes darted toward the voice and adjusted to the dim interior lighting. Recognition slowly dawned in his fuzzy brain. The girl who saved his ass on Loki 4's moon barely a couple weeks after he repaired her arm in the lab. The same girl whose damaged modulator led him to pull

Commander Daniels aside for a polite talk about disrespecting the cyberware of the crewmembers. Under different circumstances, had Daniels been an enlisted man or an officer below his rank, Victor would have read him the riot act.

"Sorry, didn't mean to startle you, Doc. Sir."

"It's fine. You caught me deep in thought."

I've had too much to drink for this. Shit. What's her name? Victor wondered. A little concentration made her name swim to the front of his inebriated mind. Raines. Zoe Raines.

"Well don't mind me. Figured being bored here was better than being bored in my bunk. Least I can watch the sunrise." She gestured to the large viewport and settled in the seat beside him. "Guess I'm not the only one with the idea, except you came prepared."

"Would you like one?" Victor extended one of the treats toward her.

"Thanks. Er…" She claimed it while eyeing his pile of wrappers. "You know, for a doctor chastising us to take care of ourselves, this doesn't look like a very healthy meal. Sweet tooth, huh?"

"Are you implying I'm not in shape?" The incredulous tone of his voice accompanied a raised brow.

"Sweats really aren't the most flattering," she quipped back while unwrapping her treat.

Victor frowned at the younger woman and vainly adjusted his sweatshirt above his abs. "Nope. Looks fine to me. I can refer you to the eye specialist if you want."

Why did it thrill him that she'd peeked over, albeit briefly to inspect the chiseled lines wrought by his hard work? "They're just fine, thanks." Her carefully measured tone deflated his mood a little, too bland for him to easily determine whether she referred to her vision or his physique. "I'm surprised to see anyone awake, really. So are you an early bird sort then?"

"I don't sleep for long usually, but the truth this evening is that I haven't been to bed yet at all." Usually, he dozed on and off very lightly through the night, never slumbering for longer than four hours. Sometimes he stole a brief catnap in the middle of the day if and when drowsiness reared its ugly head.

"Fun night out, huh?" Her expression brightened with perceived interest.

"I was kidnapped and dragged away on liberty against my will by the CO," he grumbled. He hoped Ethan was in a ditch puking his guts out and that the trashy bimbos cuddling up to his side robbed him down to his last quid.

"Ah, I see." Zoe chuckled softly. "So… kidnapped. You don't look too worse for wear."

"I have an unusually strong drinking constitution."

"Lucky you. All those pretty drinks they make knock me on my ass."

Victor waggled a finger at his companion. "Just like *you* knocked me on *my* ass."

Matching dimples emerged in Zoe's cheeks with her broad grin. "It was that or let that warg skewer you. You didn't complain at the time. Though you did look a bit dazzled afterward."

"You definitely hit as hard as the hangover I'm probably going to have when morning comes."

"So why aren't you passed out in bed like a good escapee?" Zoe propped her chin on her upraised knees and regarded him with open and friendly amusement.

Victor rolled his eyes. "You make it sound like so much fun."

"Going out with friends is supposed to be, and you're avoiding the question."

Victor chuckled. "I couldn't sleep after I returned, so I decided to entertain myself with a good movie on the Holovision screen here. Normally, I volunteer to stay aboard and wait in medical for you lot to come spilling in."

"Liberty port's not so bad though, right? A few drunks. Couple busted lips maybe?"

"Oh yeah. Someone is bound to return with a broken nose or a couple of loose screws," he agreed easily. He sipped his tea and stole a glance at the woman sharing his company. Zoe. It was a pretty name for a pretty young woman, of course, but he abruptly ceased the appreciative glance in favor of turning his attention back to the holographic display. It was a good movie, even if it wasn't formatted for 4D viewing.

For a while, the comfortable silence had no interruptions save the rustling noise of pastry wrappers as Victor shared his snacks.

"How's the arm, by the way? I should have asked before our mission."

"It's been good, thanks. The tenderness went away a couple days after you mauled me, and everything appears to be in working order. See?" Zoe held out her right hand and wriggled her fingers for his inspection. Victor set the tumbler aside to run his fingers along her limb for a quick assessment. Nothing at the shoulder felt out of place and the joint smoothly rotated with guidance. She had a wonderful piece of technology; the RX-700 served as the preferred series for the Royal Guard, so the military tended to spare no expense for soldiers wounded on the battlefield.

Zoe sported the latest model, rated highly for its near perfect ability to mimic human tissue. Comfortable, natural warmth radiated from her flesh. Even the fine hairs reacted beneath his explorative touch. If not for his experience, Victor would never guess it wasn't her natural-born arm.

"Yeah, seems good again. I probably shouldn't be telling you this, but I had words with Commander Daniels about his training methods. If you can avoid him in the ring, it's for your best interest." During his time as a soldier, Victor had met a lot of officers high on their own power trips. Greyson Daniels didn't impress him in the least. "I don't think I'm on his Christmas list anymore."

Zoe eyed him dubiously. "Sorta hard to avoid the person who's teaching you. That'd be like telling me to avoid *you* if my arm malfunctions."

"Heh. Well, you could, technically." Victor realized that he still hadn't released her arm or taken his hand from her shoulder, so he quickly dropped both hands and turned to face the movie.

"Avoid you?" Zoe drew her arm back and clasped her hands loosely in her lap. "You're the reason I chose this assignment."

Victor choked on his tea. "Me?"

"Well, not *you* exactly." Hints of color flushed into her cheeks. "I just mean that they said one of the Navy's leading cyberneticists would be aboard, so that swayed my decision when I was offered the assignment."

"Yeah. I graduated top of the training class when they sent a bunch of us off to get our certification. I guess cybernetics kind of resonates with me. I intend to finish out my career here until I'm as ancient as Oshiro since I've known the CO since enlistment."

Alcohol loosened his tongue. A night of drinking reduced some men into bumbling, staggering idiots. It merely turned Victor into a friendly chatterbox who didn't realize when to shut up. Zoe didn't complain.

"So you didn't start out an officer. That's actually sort of nice. Respectable. You must have enlisted young though if you went on to school and became a doctor."

"You could say that. I enlisted at 16, but I'm probably older than I look to you."

And I don't regret a day of it since then. It got me off the streets after I ran away. Got me a home, Victor thought to himself. He gazed through the window to pick up the first rose pink shades of color spreading like coral fingers against the midnight skies.

"Pretty, isn't it?" Victor asked, smoothly directing the topic away from himself.

"I've heard about the sunrise here, but it's my first time to this planet," Zoe told him. "It really is beautiful. All the shifting colors are stunning."

Victor dared a glance over to see Zoe's enraptured gaze focused beyond the viewport. The gilded light bathed her face, bringing out the warmer highlights amidst her dark hair. His eyes lingered on her thoughtfully pursed lips and hazy fantasies of tasting them surfaced in his mind. That came to an abrupt, screeching halt when she turned her bright eyes toward him.

"What? Do I have crumbs on my face?" She hastily wiped at her lips and chin.

"No," he blurted out swiftly. "Guess I'm daydreaming to make up for the sleepless night. I better get going." Victor wadded up the wrappers and tossed them into the bin without looking at her again.

"Oh. Well, at least you can sleep all day without worries." She smiled up at him again. "Thanks for the snacks. Guess next time I bump into you it'll be my time to share."

"For your references, I like anything with pecans," he told her. "Unless they're in chocolate."

"Pecans, no chocolate. Noted."

He stretched and ambled toward the door, which slid open automatically to allow his exit. He paused there and glanced back at her one final time. "Don't you plan to do something on your liberty days?"

"I'll probably go out for a little bit with Saskia, but I have plans in Realm of Spellbound this evening so…" She shrugged.

"You play?"

"Doesn't everybody these days?" Zoe laughed softly and waved. "Get some sleep, Doc."

Sleep became a definite plan for Victor. He couldn't afford to make drowsy advances on one of his patients, no more than he could risk another personal incident on the Jemison.

Second chances only come once. He wouldn't ruin this one.

***

Victor abandoned the idea of continuing liberty after he dragged himself from bed. Four hours of fitful sleep weren't enough to recharge him for work, and he couldn't legally scan into Medical for a shift when recently intoxicated.

After the second sleepless hour in his bed, he capitalized on the empty gym and private time with the heavy-weight machines. By lunch, he couldn't stand it any longer and poked his head into the Medical department. Three crewmen waited in the lounge for treatment and looked as though they might hurl at any moment.

Hart invited him to sit behind the counter with her for small talk between patients and duties. She shared that in the two hours preceding her noontime break, she had tended to black eyes, alcohol overindulgence, and two cases of Indari rash from a poisonous local fern.

"Sounds like the usual. I'd be let down if we had anything less to look forward to. I promise I'll be back on duty tomorrow."

"Of course you will. I want to get honking drunk too, goddammit. I only stayed on today to help Oshiro," Hart told him. She grinned brightly from ear to ear. "Even Lil takes a walk off the ship during liberty. Promised her we'd shop together tomorrow."

"I wish I spent the evening souvenir shopping instead of drinking. I feel like shit."

"You look like shit, too, Victor. You're also not scheduled to return from liberty for another day. What happened?" Doctor Oshiro spoke up to announce his arrival.

Victor winced and glanced up toward the corridor entrance leading to their private offices. "Nothing happened, Yuki. Why do you always assume something's happened? I only came to chat with Kath during her break."

"Because I know you. You throw yourself into work when you need a distraction from whatever foolish things you've done."

"I didn't do anything yet… I almost did, all right? I just happened to realize it was foolish this time and I saved myself the trouble."

"Oh? Now it is my lunch break and Kathleen's has ended. Come into my office and tell me about it."

A padded armchair awaited Victor in the spacious office, and his old mentor poured him a cup of tea while he slouched in the comfortable seat. The grassy, sweet aroma drifted up in a puff of steam.

"Perhaps this will lighten your hangover troubles as well," Oshiro murmured.

As usual, Victor gratefully accepted the cup of tea that had become their lunchtime ritual. Concealing the truth from Oshiro was about as plausible as holding water in a leaky pot, so he uttered his woes without further prompting. "I met a nice young woman."

"What's the trouble in that?" Oshiro asked.

"She's one of my patients," Victor said.

"All on board, even myself, could claim you as our doctor. What's the worry, Victor?"

"I can think of other women who seemed nice, too."

"Has *this* young woman done anything to make you question her sincerity?"

Victor considered it. The two most important women of his past, prior to Ylona, had deceived and mistreated him. Zoe had done nothing of the sort. "No. She hasn't."

"Then tell me your troubles. If the young woman has not shaken your trust, what else is there to bother you?"

"It's... Ylona. I think of her all of the time now. Barely a year has passed, and now I've begun to look at other women. It feels like betrayal," he finally admitted. "She brought me out of a dark place, Oshiro, and now she's gone because of me. I'll never find another woman like her." Victor's throat tightened and he closed his eyes. The deep breath that he pulled into his lungs didn't alleviate the simmering pain in his soul.

Oshiro nodded in understanding. "Experience is the mother of wisdom, Victor. Your troubling past has made it difficult for you to trust again. Perhaps you are correct to give it time, but you must also consider taking opportunities when they are given to you."

"You sound like an ancient Chinese master in a bad historical martial arts flick."

Oshiro snorted. "Japanese. My ancestors came from Japan. Not China. Now what would your Eloran say, were she present to guide you?"

Victor shook his head and glanced away without giving a verbal answer. Discomfort settled in the pit of his stomach, delivering an unyielding sensation of anxiety. He already knew the answer to that. Ylona would be distraught to know her memory had become a hindrance. "She'd tell me to be happy again."

The older doctor spread his hands and smiled gently. "I would listen to her."

"I can't. She'd be alive and well on her home planet if not for me."

"And you would have never known her love. What happened to Ylona was nothing more than a terrible accident."

"She boarded that ship to surprise me. If I hadn't voluntarily deployed again, I'd have been home with her. She died a terrible, excruciating death because of my choice."

"And you sought to join her," Oshiro said gently.

"I did. Some nights, I wish that I'd succeeded."

After Victor injected his veins with enough narcotic to stop a drake's heart, the Glenn's artificial intelligence spied his suicide attempt and promptly tattled. Medical reached his door in less than thirty seconds.

The old doctor sighed and reached across the desk to pat Victor's hand. "And do you have any plans now?"

"I don't *anymore*. You don't need to have the A.I. watch me in my room at night, I assure you."

"I had to be sure, my son. Many people care about you."

Jem's sultry croon joined the conversation. "I monitor all ship personnel," she told them. "But I especially enjoy our chats, Doctor del Toro."

"That isn't at all disturbing," Victor grumbled.

"There's something else that I intended to bring to your attention," Oshiro said.

Victor glanced up from his half-empty cup of tea. "Yeah?"

"An Eloran contacted me from our base on their home planet. Her name is Ylara, and she tells me that she's attempted to contact Doctor Victor del Toro without success. You wouldn't know anything about that, would you?"

A frigid wave of anxiety swept over Victor and sent his heart thrumming like a panicked bird desperate to escape his chest. He shook his head quickly. "I'd rather not. Make up something polite. I know you can do it."

"Victor—"

"I can't. How could I speak to her when her daughter is dead because of me? I won't do it. Thank you for the chat, Yuki. It's been great. I value your advice as always, but must humbly decline this time." Each breath became more difficult than the last, despite his efforts to maintain a calm rhythm.

Oshiro bowed his head. "As you like, Victor, though I would ask you to reconsider."

"I'll think on it," Victor replied. Gradually, the tension seeped from his shoulders. The tea soothed his nerves, as much a balm for his worries as the advice from his friend and mentor.

"What about the young lady who has caught your fancy? Will you at least tell me of her?"

An uncertain smile surfaced over Victor's face at last. Talking to Yuki about women made him feel like a shy boy again. He couldn't remember most of their conversation on the sofa, but he could never forget how Zoe had made him feel. Like a person and not a military title with a fat pay grade. "She's lovely. Beautiful inside and out." *Like Ylona*, he thought, although he swiftly pushed the thought away and shoved it from his mind.

"That sounds promising. You keep to yourself so often I am both surprised and pleased to hear you've gotten out enough to make a friend."

"Not technically…"

Oshiro arched a brow and waited.

"Story for another day. I'd better go before the patients begin to line up and plead for me to treat them," Victor hastily said. "See you tomorrow."

"Enjoy your day off the ship, Victor. You'll appreciate that you did. I am told the new romantic comedy is worth your twenty quid."

Oshiro was right. Victor even paid to watch it a second time. Afterward, he wandered the city streets and breathed in the fresh air beneath the radiant sun. True wind felt good against his skin, different from the fan-generated currents aerating the ship.

I missed this. No matter how much I love ship life, nothing compares to the feel of the sun on your skin. Nothing beats the fresh breeze on a spring afternoon.

"Evening, sir."

Victor jerked around and stared into the grinning visage of Lopez and a dark-eyed woman in a cream, gold-trimmed tunic. A ruby red shayla covered her wavy hair, hanging loosely around her face before wrapping neatly over her shoulders. Her skin carried the rich and warm tone associated with the desert people inhabiting Astreya, and she resembled her Persian ancestors as much as Victor resembled the people of old Mexico.

"Evening, Lopez. How goes liberty?"

"Fantastic. Have you two met?" Lopez asked with a glance between the two officers. "Most of us assume all you officers know each other and share laughs behind our backs."

The young woman's musical laugh brightened Victor's spirits. She nudged her companion then offered out a slender hand to Victor. "Not officially, no, though we exchange many reports."

"I suppose I'd be correct to assume you must be Lieutenant Shahid Amir. Pleasure to finally make your acquaintance." *Bloody hell, no wonder Ethan dropped her name to me. She's gorgeous.*

"Nisrine," she corrected him gently. "We're all off-duty now, are we not?"

"Nisrine it is. Just make sure you call me Victor in return to make us even. Both of you. I hear enough Commander this and Doctor that while on the Jemison."

"Wicked. We were just about to catch a movie," Lopez told him. "She picked some rom-com that I'll sleep through, but you're welcome to join us, mate. I'd appreciate the company."

Nisrine swatted him. "You are not allowed to sleep through the movie, but Victor is allowed to join us if it will keep you awake."

"Actually, I saw that one twice already this afternoon. You'll have to suffer with your girlfriend alone." Victor grinned. It didn't sound like a horrible offer, but his rumbling belly demanded sustenance. Overpriced popcorn wasn't enough. "You two have fun. It's really not bad."

Lopez shot him a betrayed, pleading expression as the couple headed off

The afternoon blended into a pleasant evening and a dinner for one at a family diner by the seaside. The fresh salt smell reminded him of Elora. Of his *true* home.

He nursed a glass of wine and watched the sunset, its canvas of deep colors beautiful but inferior to the pastel hued sunrise he'd enjoyed that morning. Or maybe it had something to do with the shared company. Briefly, he envied Lopez and Nisrine until he swallowed the bitter taste back down.

Company always improves things, he thought. With that bleak thought in mind, Victor returned to the ship alone.

CHAPTER 8

At the end of his relaxing day, Victor elected to visit his favorite online videogame over an hour or two in the gym. He showered, changed into fresh shorts, flopped into his desk chair, and donned his virtual reality equipment.

Weight gradually settled over his limbs, comparable to falling asleep after a long and exhausting day. He surrendered to the sensation of falling backward through the air. Weightlessly, he floated until the world suddenly snapped into existence.

Victor awoke on the other side in a crowded city zone teeming with fellow gamers. He'd picked a popular place to log in, sitting under a cafe awning on the side of a crowded street. His current location was styled to resemble downtown Los Angeles.

Realm of Spellbound served as the most popular virtual reality online game in the United Empire. Users played out fantastical roles as magic-casters, legendary creatures, or dark entities in a setting replicating 21st century Earth.

An urgent message accompanied Victor's party invite from Vincent Knight – Ethan's role-playing avatar. An in-game teleport delivered him to Olde London where he managed to team up with Ethan and Trevor. The two were embroiled in a deep argument about the game's class options.

"Look. Everybody knows that Templars are just overpowered paladins," Ethan grumbled.

"Whatever, man. You guys would have gotten your asses kicked if I wasn't there with the holy water on the last raid."

Ethan opened his mouth to fire off a witty retort, but he turned in time to see Victor approaching. "Look who finally decided to show up. Get lost along the way, mate?"

Victor snorted derisively and brought up the HUD menu. The holographic user display allowed him to see a 3D representation of the map.

"I'm surprised to see you here after your hard partying last night. Feeling all right or should we worry about you keeling over at the first mob we meet?"

"Shut it," Ethan grumbled, much to Trevor's amusement. "I'm online, technically I'm resting and asleep."

Trevor, who used the name Alexander Solo while in their VR realm, guided them to a dark and dirty side of London where the smog stank of chemicals and filth. The night sky gave them the cover of darkness as they fought their way through the ranks of the undead set at specific sentry points outside. Victor picked up the key dropped by a skeletal figure.

"Guess we've got our way inside now."

A large door blocked their progress, lacking a visible keyhole. Victor scratched his head and leaned down for a closer inspection, while the other two searched the wall for a secondary hidden entrance.

"You'll never get in that way," a voice chimed from behind the group. "The keyhole is there, but they have it trapped. We know another way in."

Victor turned to face the speaker behind them and came face to face with three nymphs, nature spirits in female form with shamefully voluptuous bodies.

Rich mahogany hair twined with vines and flowers framed the speaker's golden face. Fluttering maple leaves made up her dress, revealing everything and nothing at once. A second dryad stood behind her, a brunette covered in green moss resembling a lace bodysuit. The third woman appeared to be a sylph, a slender nymph associated with wind and storms. Her pale blonde hair danced around her face on an ethereal breeze, as did the scant silk covering her body.

"Ah, sexy triplets. Wanna join us?" Ethan offered without consulting his mates. Trevor kicked him indiscreetly. Victor wanted to tell him to do it again, because he recognized two of the players from a large raid two months earlier.

It wasn't that Zephyr and Annalise were bad players. Victor just had the feeling that the former was really a teenage boy, and didn't understand the fine logic behind staying at the edge of battle. Not that the guy's decision to play another gender really mattered. What mattered was that he sucked.

"I hope you learned how to play better since last time we met," Victor said bluntly to the two nymphs. Trevor elbowed him where his kidneys belonged. It didn't hurt, failing to register as more than pressure. A group message flashed across his lower field of vision, telling him not to be rude. Victor rolled his eyes.

"Your tank rushed the room and drew the whole horde on us. Don't blame me for being squishy and attractive to mobs," the blonde protested. She gestured toward Trevor and gave a disdainful sniff. "Besides, we've gained levels since then."

He glanced at Zephyr's viewable stats. "Yeah, I see. You ranked up. Congrats."

"Anyway, you have to unlock the door from the other side," the red-headed dryad cut in. She didn't offer a name but her status bar said Varine. She wriggled between Trevor and Ethan, choosing to link arms with the latter.

They didn't have to wait long once Zephyr, the air nymph, used one of her abilities to release the trapped entrance. The heavy metal doors slid open to reveal the inner chamber of a safe house. The game was designed with faction play in mind, so their demon-worshipping cultists seemed to be the intended prey of Templars like Trevor. He unloaded a hail of bullets at the approaching horde of summoned demons, putting his military prowess to good use.

Victor and Trevor wouldn't admit it, but they benefitted greatly from Ethan's imperious decision to invite the girls. Together, the six of them swept through one chamber after the next. For a while.

"Do you have to lag behind so much to explore?" Trevor hissed at Varine.

"Do *you* know how many resources and good gear you're passing up?" The dryad held up an enchanted amulet to prove her point. "Anyway, our Charmer can use this more than me. I'm not even the right level."

The red-head dropped the golden disc in Ethan's hands and batted her lashes at him. Victor bit back a snicker. Even in a game his friend attracted the ladies.

"Thanks. I appreciate it." Ethan playfully swatted the dryad's rump.

"No problem. Better it go to someone who can use it."

"A gun would be more useful," Trevor grumbled.

"I don't know how Flidais tolerates you in her group, if you complain nearly as much around her as you do with us about the drops," Victor said, referring to Trevor's online girlfriend.

They discovered the dungeon boss at the highest floor of the tower, a warlock with a dauntingly high level. He used his mind control spells to force Trevor to shoot Ethan and his familiar with his magic-negating bullets, which put a damper on their plans. It would have ended the fight right then if not for the presence of the hottie-triplets. By the time Victor healed his friend, Annalise and Varine's life bars had been reduced to slivers.

To spare their lives, Ethan produced a fireball that soared past Victor into the warlock, efficiently cutting through his shields. It bought them time to provide a good offensive and cut the boss down to size. The warlock fell beneath their combined onslaught and landed on the ground as a motionless silhouette that smoked and glittered with bullet holes. It vanished and left behind a pile of loot.

"Bloody hell, I picked up some good spell components off him," Ethan crowed triumphantly.

Zephyr shook out her designated prize with a satisfied look on her face. "I've needed a new set of robes."

The currency count, even split between them, was substantial.

"Good game, the lot of you. We need to meet up again soon sometime," Victor said. The alarm timer flashing above his HUD warned him that it was nearly time to log off for bed. He wanted to rise bright and early for duties the next day.

"Certainly. I gotta work tomorrow, so how about standard Saturday?" Annalise asked.

Victor thought ahead briefly. Logging on to clear his head and get Zoe off his mind had worked. "Brilliant idea."

"You guys have fun. I'm booked on Saturday," Zephyr said with an easy smile.

Varine remained by Ethan's side, held close with his arm around her waist. The two exchanged quiet whispers and flirty glances. Trevor sent Victor a private message, predicting the inevitable outcome.

"Varine is new to the game. I promised to offer her a tour of the local common areas," Ethan warned, oblivious to their secret conversation.

Alexander Solo (to you): What did I tell you?

Juan Sebastian: You didn't have to tell me anything. I guessed it myself.

Victor shook his head. Ethan was lucky that STDs didn't exist on the internet.

"Thanks for allowing us join you," Annalise said. "This was an absolute blast."

Yeah, it was, he thought as the group split.

Victor logged off and lay back in his seat for a moment until he awakened completely from the virtual world. The feeling returned to his limbs and fingers, banishing the paralysis of lucid dreaming. Eventually, he pulled off the headset.

A message reached his console from Trevor less than a minute later.

Are you going to be all right, Victor? it asked. *You haven't been up to your usual chipper personality in the game.*

Victor inhaled deeply and rubbed his face. No. He wouldn't be all right. With the anniversary of Ylona's death fast approaching, he didn't know if he could survive another day with a pleasant smile on his face.

For once, he didn't lie.

No, I'm not. But I will be, he simply replied. He would adapt and recover because life had given him no other alternative.

CHAPTER 9

"That was fun last night, don't you think?" Zoe closed her locker and crouched down to lace her boots.

"Not as much fun as what this little tart had," Saskia teased. "C'mon, Fairchild. Don't hold back. Tell us how your virtual romp went."

Fairchild stuck her tongue out at them. "There's no need for jealousy just because I got some and you didn't."

"Please," Saskia said. "I'd rather have a real man plowing me. The virtual sensations just don't do it."

"Meaning you've tried it," Zoe pointed out. Saskia's reply was to shrug and grin.

"Who hasn't? We're on this ship for months at times between ports. I don't know about you, but dating the men aboard the Jemison doesn't do it for me either," Saskia replied. "They're a rather childish sort, with exception to a limited few."

"Speaking of dating fellow crewmen, I can't believe that dumb berk O'Reilly asked you to join him on a date in the bloody lounge. Did you tell him you wouldn't be caught dead, or were you nice as usual?" Fairchild asked. The young woman stood in front of the locker room mirror, gathering her white-blonde hair into a neat bun.

Zoe grunted and finished wrapping her wrists. "I managed to avoid giving O'Reilly any sort of answer. Medical didn't seem the place to laugh in his face."

"He's a womanizing creep. Do yourself a favor, love, and stay away from the men on the Jemison. These twenty-four month deployments turn them into randy losers."

"No worries about me, Saskia, I've been through ship tours before. Now I'm just trying to plan how to whoop the commander in the ring."

Saskia smirked. "You almost had him the last time, if I recall. That was a cheap shot, what he did. As I said before, he's like a boy on the playground picking on the girl he has a secret crush on."

"Give him a good walloping today, Zoe. We'll all be cheering for you. I dated Daniels for about a month when I was new to the ship. I believe he was searching for a rank-tagger and became disappointed that I didn't live up to expectations," Fairchild muttered. "He's one of the worst for abusing his title."

Zoe sighed. "This is the 24th century, you'd think by now that men would have it in their noggin that we're as good as they are."

"According to the word onboard, he doesn't like to take women or cyborgs along on his missions. I'm surprised the three of us are on his squad," Saskia said.

Fairchild shrugged. "Fortunately, he seems to be alone in his line of thought. I'd bet fifty quid that del Toro had something to say. He's fair, and he never has a disparaging thing to say about anyone on the ship."

The doctor's drunken confession remained Zoe's secret. Instead of providing any confirmation, she nodded and smiled. "Maybe so."

Combining soldiers and specially trained combat medics became a fine art that Daniels perfected through rigorous exercises. They spent fifteen hours a week in five hour sessions of performing high intensity physical training routines, and during those fifteen hours they each received his undivided attention in the ring while his or her squad mates ran endurance, lifted weights, or sparred against each other.

"I don't see Commander del Toro," Saskia said.

"Oh, he has duty today," Fairchild informed them.

Zoe began her training session with a timed run. While each marine stepped into the ring with Daniels, the other members of the squad continued their own exercise routines. After three laps she moved on to the climbing wall, followed by a round on the mats practicing blocks and strikes.

"Raines, get in here."

Zoe bumped fists with Saskia then they exchanged places. Daniels allowed her no time to get situated and kicked her rotator cuff the moment she moved within his reach. It was the same low blow that damaged her prosthetic in the last spar, but she rolled with it this time and let his foot glide off her arm to minimize the force.

Sheisty bastard. The strike knocked her off balance, but she blocked the next with her natural arm to avoid granting Daniels access to her prosthetic again. She had to keep it away from him before he capitalized on the same weakness.

"Afraid I'll shatter your toy again, Raines?"

"No, sir."

Daniels moved swiftly for a man of his considerable bulk, and his blows were devastating whether she blocked them or not. He bruised her forearm and her shin as they traded strikes and kicks across the mat while eager comrades watched on and held their breath.

Literally. Saskia was blue in the face.

"Come on, Raines. What are you waiting for? What if I wasn't a trainer and I pulled a gun on you or a knife? You can't drag the fight out and keep that arm away from me forever."

His taunt goaded Zoe into dropping her guard. Daniels pressed his advantage and caught her across the face with a right hook. The coppery taste of blood filled Zoe's mouth and she retreated out of his reach.

"Accept that you're going to lose. Give it up and let me teach the rest of my squad—"

The commander's words had the desired effect; her rage flared. She lunged at him with her cybernetic fist, but he stepped aside of the blow, grabbed her by the wrist, and cracked her prosthetic over his knee. Zoe screamed. Desperate to remain in the fight, she drove her flesh and bone fist beneath his chin, cracking his teeth together.

Blood and spittle flew from the man's mouth as he staggered back off balance, pulling Zoe with him. He recovered quickly and wrenched her arm. He used it like a tether, taking her wherever he wanted to lead her on the floor until she slammed the back of her head into his nose.

They traded blows back and forth across the sparring mat, one blocking and the other receiving. She searched for an opening in his defense, determined to end the intense exchange between them.

Daniels' weakness became apparent with crystalline clarity. It had dangled before her all along, and Zoe had never considered it with any seriousness. She feigned a strike with her left and stepped in close, turning her cheek so that his punch skimmed past her face. It hurt, but it wasn't the devastating attack Daniels intended, failing to lay Zoe out on her back. With only a second to spare, she aimed her right hand downward for his balls.

Zoe's strike was colossal, the sort of blow that made a spectating crowd sympathetically wince along with the recipient. The heel of her palm collided with the commander's crotch, and she held very little back, allowing him to experience almost the complete might of her cybernetic limb. Anything more would have squished his grapes into jelly.

The chain of events that took place after the strike set everything in Zoe's favor. Daniels convulsed and relinquished his grip on her shoulder, failing to hobble her cybernetic arm again. His defenses lowered completely.

Without wasting a precious second, Zoe took him down to the ground into a locked grapple that placed the commander face down into the mats. He puked, but she lacked the sympathy to ease up on her restraint. She kept him locked by both of her strong legs.

"Tap out, Commander."

Daniels struggled but in the end he slapped his hand down on the mats. Zoe released him to the sound of cheers.

CHAPTER 10

"The marines must have had a great sparring match, sir. You have Raines *and* Daniels both this time," O'Reilly reported.

"Really?" Victor tapped the screen and pulled up the patient waiting list. He blinked.

"They look feckin' awful. Especially the commander. I, uh, sent him to the showers first, sir. Raines is waiting in your lab."

"What's wrong with him?"

The medical technician struggled to maintain a straight face. "Read his chief complaint, sir."

Victor tapped the screen with his finger and expanded the digital record. "Testicular… contusion…" *Christ. She actually did it,* Victor thought. A broad grin spread across his face, and then he leaned back in the seat to chortle with laughter.

"They brought him in covered in his own vomit," O'Reilly shared.

"Ha!"

Zoe waited for him in one of the exam rooms, sitting on the edge of the table in form-fitting workout attire. Bruises littered both forearms and dried blood crusted her lower lip.

"You're looking a little rough around the edges, Raines," Victor commented. He shut the door behind him and held both of his hands beneath the sanitizer. Within a couple seconds, he had a perfect pair of gloves molded to his hands.

"You should have seen the other guy."

Victor chuckled and gestured for her to lie down. She knew the routine and remained still as he guided the biometric scanner above her and activated it. "I will soon. Did you take my advice?"

"It wasn't bad advice and he didn't leave me much opening for anything else."

A keen eye picked out most of Zoe's injuries without use of the device. A swollen lower lip appeared to be the least of her troubles.

"Does that hurt?" he asked.

"Which bit?" Zoe looked up at him from her reclined position. Her smile tugged at the tear and quickly dropped the expression from her face.

"That bit," Victor said. He smiled back at her. "Hold on, I'll clean that up first."

Victor used a damp cloth to wipe the dried blood away, careful not to further agitate the split skin. "Any pain in your prosthetic?"

"Not as bad as last time, no, but…"

"What?" he asked while using an applicator to smear a dollop of anesthetic gel over the split skin.

"I heard a crack, I think. And my fingers sort of tingle. Things don't feel right."

"I thought so, but I wanted you to verify it." Victor turned aside and opened a drawer to remove his surgical scalpels.

Zoe squirmed. "Um… Doc? I see lots of sharp things."

"He separated a nerve and I can't reconnect it by touch this time, Raines. If you want complete sensation back, I'll have to go in this time."

"Oh. Right. Okay." She focused her gaze straight up at the room's ceiling, tension in her lean frame.

"Relax. You're familiar with this, right? I'm going to make a small incision here, and here," he explained patiently, marking the spots with a green marker. "For the duration, your pain receptors will remain deactivated in this arm. I won't let you feel a thing."

A pent-up breath exhaled from her, accompanied by a terse nod.

Victor numbed the arm all at once by deactivating the sensors beneath the skin. He knew them by memory on her arm's model, and could do it without the use of an x-ray. Once it fell limp against the surgical table, he positioned it as needed and began making small and precise cuts to yield access to the mechanicals bits beneath the human skin. It parted easily, welling small amounts of blood to the surface that he wiped away with a cloth.

The repair took less time than the conversation preceding it. At the end, Victor sealed the small cuts and reactivated her arm's nerve sensors. "You're done."

Zoe rolled up and flexed her hand, touching each finger in turn. She pressed her palm against the table and then ran her fingers down her pants before she seemed satisfied with her tactile sense.

"Thanks, Doc. Daniels hits like a drake."

"He should. He was a former MMA champ before he enlisted. You should feel proud."

Victor patted her on the back in passing on his way to the next patient room.

Commander Daniels lay on his side in the fetal position. He didn't grace his fellow officer with a single word of greeting.

"So… My chart tells me that you walked groin first into someone's hand. Bad luck, mate." Victor grinned broadly and stepped into the room. *Karma is a bitch,* he thought cheerfully as he shut the door.

Greyson Daniels wouldn't be challenging Zoe to the ring again anytime soon.

***

Only old television shows played during the early hours of the morning. Victor loved them, but his personal player didn't pack the same punch as the device operating in the crew lounge.

When his fellow crewmen realized Victor had an appreciation for the early shows, they began to leave data chips for him with entire seasons of ancient TV dramas.

"Glazed pecans." Catching him in a daze, Zoe dropped a small bag full of the sweet confections over the back of the couch next to Victor. He jumped, startling badly enough to slosh cocoa mint tea over his hand.

"Sorry, sir," Zoe apologized quietly. "Didn't mean to scare you. Figured I could share since you fixed my arm and all. Twice."

Victor waited for his heart to calm before he answered. It hammered rapidly in his chest and tension coiled in every muscle in his body. "It's all right," he said slowly.

"Are you sure?"

He scrubbed his face with the heel of his palm and exhaled. "Why are you awake at two in the morning?" he inquired while plucking the baggie up.

"I told you. Night owl. Sometimes I wonder if it's a side effect from the splicing." Zoe rounded the couch and dropped down beside him, drawing her legs up. "I used to be a terrible sleep-in, Doc."

"Victor. We're both off-duty, so the name's Victor."

"All right… Victor." She smiled shyly and swung her gaze to the video. "You're always watching these old shows. And eating sweets."

"Is there something else to do at two in the morning?"

Her warm laughter filled the quiet space. "True enough. Unless you like the gym. Or the bio-farm."

"Tried that once," Victor admitted. "Daniels and Etherington like to visit the gym around three and leave by four. That's when I head inside. As far as the bio-farm goes… The trees are a little too popular at night for my liking." Couples took advantage of the flora-filled pathways to find privacy for stolen, romantic moments.

"Not one for intimate strolls, Victor?" Zoe reached over and snagged a couple sugar glazed nuts from the bag. Their fingers briefly touched.

"I'm not one for tripping over two shagging corpsman," he replied awkwardly. "There's kind of an unspoken vow between us officers and the rest of the crew to remain away from a few locations during certain hours of the day."

"Is that so you don't have to, uh, bust people or so they don't try to lure you into mischief?"

"Both."

"Not a bad deal, I guess." She settled back against the seat. "What about you? Anyone waiting back home? A wife? Kids?"

"No. I'm not married."

"Sorry. Your private life is your own."

"It's fine," Victor assured her, waving it off with one hand. "The military life doesn't suit marriage, and since I prefer living on ships, it wouldn't be fair."

"Oh, I don't know. Some people seem to make it work. Look at the residential deck. Abernathy has a wife onboard, did you know that? She works in one of the science labs, I think."

Yeah, but that only works if you're not surrounded by racist twits, Victor thought bitterly. He didn't realize until the denial of his third application for residence that Ylona wasn't the right species to live in the civilian residence quarters as his wife. "No, I wasn't aware." He focused on the candied nuts and crammed a few into his mouth, creating the perfect excuse to become silent.

"Elena is real nice. She's sent cookies down to the armory a few times, too." She leveled her curious gaze on him. "So, if it's okay to ask, why do you prefer a stateroom and mess food to a house and cooking your own meals?"

Goddammit, she asks a lot of questions. "I was born on Paradiso but grew up in a large city on Albion where no one cared. This is nice and personal, the people are reliable, and I know for every Daniels, there's someone supportive when I need them. Doctor Oshiro mentored me into the Navy."

"Oh. I suppose I can understand that then. I grew up in the capital city on Tallulah. Not as big as the cities on Albion, but not small. Just enough that most everyone knew everyone else's business."

"No husband waiting back home for you?"

"Me? Goodness, no." Zoe shook her head vehemently. "Actually, if you want to know the truth, I joined the marines to escape just that. Marriage, I mean."

"I'm told that the word 'no' also works," Victor quipped. "Poor bastard. I suppose he didn't take that well."

Zoe shrugged. "His family didn't, but arranged marriages are an archaic tradition my planet decided to bring back into practice," she told him. "I was seventeen and I didn't want to be thrown at a stranger to become a… proper housewife. I wanted to do more with my life, so here I am."

Victor raised his brows and stared at her. "That's respectful. I couldn't imagine marrying without feeling an emotional attachment."

"Exactly. So my folks practically disowned me, and we didn't see each other again 'till after…" Zoe flapped her right elbow out and smiled sadly. "Funny how tragedy reunites people sometimes. They didn't approve of my choice to remain in the service, but they didn't fight me on it."

"Small favors."

"What about you?" she asked quietly. "Any family?"

"My mother and father died a long time ago, during one of the last Soviet uprisings," Victor explained. "They attacked my home city in Paradiso, but I survived." *Lucky me,* he thought. So fortunate his aunt Celestina took him in at the tender age of eleven once the hospital released him into her care. Not. He spent the next three years receiving physical abuse from her and her alcoholic boyfriend.

A gentle squeeze drew Victor's gaze down to Zoe's smaller fingers curling over his hand. He appreciated her lack of hollow platitudes. Too many people automatically offered apologies with no real sense of understanding or true sincerity behind them.

"Did you end up with family after that?" she asked, releasing her supportive touch.

Memories flashed back of nights without meals and the acidic odor of drug-filled pipes. Fists in the night, unforgiving and eager to punish anyone for imagined transgressions. "An aunt on Albion took me in, but we're no longer on speaking terms," he replied drily. "So I joined the Navy." Enlisting offered him a way off the streets and a way to finally heal from the hardships endured in his youth.

"And now we're your family. The ship, I mean."

He merely nodded and raised his mug toward her. "Want some tea?"

"I don't have a cup."

"We'll share then." Victor shrugged and offered his tea again. "I've seen your records so I know you won't pass me anything I can't cure."

Her grin brightened his mood, and without any further hesitation, Zoe accepted the warm porcelain cup.

Conversation fell away as they both turned to watch the rest of the movie. The mug passed between them, fingers brushing more than once as they handed it off. Eventually, Zoe's weight shifted against the sofa and her head dipped forward. Victor attempted to guide her back against the cushions, but her cheek snuggled into his shoulder instead.

"Zoe…" he whispered.

"Just… just ten minutes," she mumbled drowsily with her eyes closed.

Victor touched his fingers lightly to Zoe's dark, pixie-cut hair. Her baby face made it difficult to discern her age at a glance. At rest, her youthful features seemed too peaceful and innocent, as if she didn't have the same blood on her hands.

"Zoe?" Victor persisted gently.

A sigh parted her lips, and if he lowered his head another inch, they would have pressed perfectly against his mouth. An enticing but unfamiliar floral note clung to her caramel skin. He'd never noticed before that Zoe wore perfume.

Zoe shifted until her cheek slid against his shoulder, curling her body intimately toward his side. Somehow, Victor suppressed the urgent desire to learn the taste of her skin, opting to tilt his head and rest his cheek against her brow instead.

They remained like that for close to an hour until a faint chime from his watch warned him of the approaching time. He was due to start his shift at medical soon.

"Zoe." He rubbed her arm and gave her a light shake.

"Hmm?"

"Time to get up."

The young woman bolted upright and rubbed at her face. "Did I fall asleep on you?" Her large, golden eyes fixed on his shoulder and then a hand rubbed instinctively at her mouth.

"No, you didn't drool on me, and it was only for a moment. It's fine," he assured her, while reaching out to smooth an errant black wave sticking out from her temple. "But I have to head into medical soon."

"Yeah, I should get going, too. I have the next armory watch."

Seconds ticked by and threatened to become minutes. The holovision started its next feature presentation, but the man and the woman on the sofa remained in their seats, each waiting for the other to leave first. Zoe reluctantly stood.

"Will you be joining us for training this afternoon?"

Victor nodded. "I'll be there. Though I don't imagine Daniels will be doing his usual matches. I plan to fill in for him."

Chuckling nervously and avoiding direct eye contact, Zoe glanced away and rubbed the back of her neck. "Yeah, I guess we'll see. Catch you then, Victor."

"Hey Zoe," he called out, catching her before she reached the door. "Thanks for the company."

"Same to you."

Her bright smile stayed with him through the remainder of his day.

CHAPTER 11

The Jemison's bridge maintained round-the-clock dim lighting and was one of the quietest spaces on the ship. Ethan's command seat dominated a raised section at the back of the room and gave him a full range of vision over the various stations and personnel below, including the pilot.

Victor joined Daniels and Trevor at the commanding officer's side. An intergalactic identification file expanded on the holographic display, featuring the bearded features of a man in his sixties. Glossy, cream-colored adornments dangled from the neatly groomed triple braids lying against his chest.

"I owe a favor to Lieutenant Shahid Amir for her assistance in the matter," Trevor spoke up to the three officers. "As you can imagine, there aren't any guns on the open market equipped to fire pyro rounds. They're old tech."

"Must have taken awhile to figure out which gun they used. Boring?" Victor asked Trevor.

"Are you kidding? Zoe and Saskia had a blast in the simulator. So did I, to be completely honest with you. This shite is right up my alley–" Trevor's amused words died when Ethan shot him an impatient look. Without further delay, he cleared his throat and promptly continued. "I asked our intel officer to cross-reference the caliber of the pistol against recent news reports. It took a couple of weeks to comb the galaxy, but we found this ugly bastard. Jarvis Crane. He's the big boss of the Black Jackal Brotherhood."

"So what makes you think he's our guy?" Daniels asked.

"Lieutenant Shahid Amir tapped some connections, so we know that he purchased a Smith and Wesson model 2140 Ignite off a black market weapons dealer out of Astreya a year ago. It's a pricey piece. About a half million quid, as there's less than a dozen in working condition these days."

Victor whistled. "So it's only a possibility that he's our man?"

"No, I'd say it's about 98 percent." The communications chief minimized the window and pulled up Crane's list of crimes. The United Empire wanted him for countless violations, and the least of them were murder and burglary.

"Unlawful trade of children…" Ethan read out loud.

"Forced prostitution," Victor continued, swallowing heavily afterward.

"He fits the profile, too," Trevor said. "The man is taller than you, Doctor."

"We don't have much of a bloody choice then. We need to find this cretin and put an end to this," Victor said.

Ethan glanced up at him sympathetically, allowing his emotion to show. "We will, Victor. Contact United Command and tell them we've identified our man, Lockhart. I want Crane and his ship found."

"Yes, sir."

In an effort to calm his troubled thoughts, Victor sucked in a deep breath and leaned against the side of Ethan's chair without concern for what was proper or professional. He expected the commodore to complain or order him off of the luxurious, leather-covered seat, but he didn't.

"Commodore?" A young woman at the communications terminal spoke up from her station. "We have an emergency transmission from Athena. You might want to hear this, sir."

"Patch it through to my terminal," Ethan ordered. He swiveled his chair around, knocking Victor from his comfortable position.

"This is Commodore Bishop of the HMS Jemison. What–"

"Oh thank god!" A frazzled voice sounded over the comm. "Please, you must help us. We need immediate evacuation!"

Victor raised both brows and exchanged glances with Daniels. Both commanders turned their attention to eavesdropping on Ethan's call.

"What's the nature of your problem?"

"I've spent bloody hours searching for someone, anyone. I'm an engineer, and I work for Hephaestus Tek, the manufacturing plant on Athena. We came under attack three days ago. They killed most of the technicians and took others about an hour ago. God only knows where. There's wounded people everywhere. Pregnant women in labor."

Ethan's green eyes cut toward Victor. "I need you to remain as calm as possible. Tell me everything you know about your captors."

"Pirates. Well-armed pirates equipped with cybernetics unlike anything I've ever seen. They overwhelmed our security force–" A single gunshot abruptly ended the communication.

"Shit," Victor muttered.

"I'd put fifty quid on this bein' him," Trevor spoke up. "I'll contact United Command and find out whether we've got more ships in the area."

"You do that. Agosti, set an immediate course for Athena," Ethan ordered the on-duty navigator. "Give me a time frame."

"I can have us there in two hours, Sir."

"Get us there in one." Ethan turned to Victor and Daniels. "Grab your gear. We'll get a shuttle down there and pursue Crane's ship by radar if we can locate her in time."

"Right away, Commodore." Daniels turned about face and strode off the bridge.

Ethan input a set of commands into his terminal and the ship went into alert. Red lights flashed overhead. "All hands to their stations. Alpha team, gear up and report to the shuttle bay."

Victor waited until he closed the ship's comm line. "Did he say pregnant *women*? Plural?"

"You're going to have your hands full, Victor. Good luck."

***

Athena orbited a gas giant in a yellow star system. The barren moon held little of interest aside from a subterranean colony developed beneath its rocky surface for two purposes: mining and technical production.

Rich fields of liquid valerium beneath the moon's surface provided a clean-burning fuel for manufacturing plants across the galaxy. In its solid state, valerium formed the basis for plasteel, the galaxy's most profitable metal. Since it was as light as plastic and stronger than steel, it was favored for cybernetics and space vehicles.

An inhospitable atmosphere required breathers for any surface work or travel. The colony below relied on extensive oxygen generators for their life-support systems.

"Masks on, everyone, and be prepared for gunfire as we exit the shuttle," Daniels called out to the squad. "If they expect our approach they'll flood the surface landing pad. Raines, I want you leaned out the barrier with a gun on that door."

"Will do, Commander." Zoe rose from her seat and activated a button on her combat suit. The individual pieces of her helmet slid from the neck of her form-fitting combat suit and created a functional re-breather mask.

The rockskipper's side door opened, generating a shimmering energy barrier in its place to maintain the interior atmosphere and pressure. Zoe clipped a line to her belt, placed her rifle to her shoulder, and then leaned out of the protective shielding.

Victor swallowed back a brief wave of vertigo. He didn't envy the sergeant for her job, but he kept a close eye on her vulnerable position. Below them, rocky terrain rushed past the descending shuttle.

"There's a fair chance that they have pain dampeners. Pirates and merc bands like them. That means that no matter where you shoot, they won't feel it," Victor muttered.

"You heard the man. Let's go for headshots," Daniels said.

The military-issued devices were hot on the black market, desired for their ability to numb all sense of pain and discomfort. A man could fight until the bitter end. The Empire outfitted every marine in the Royal Defense Force with a similar device, especially those sworn to protect the Empress. Those highly trained, seasoned warriors were expected to defend her and any member of the royal family to the death.

An ear-splitting gunshot rang out before they touched down. Two more followed and a round sparked off the kinetic barrier. Three feet above the surface Zoe unclipped and leapt down.

"Move out!" Daniels ordered.

Victor led the rear assault. He and the three marine field medics in his squad had but a single task – to save as many lives as possible while supporting the primary assault squad.

Cold, dry air leached the moisture from his exposed skin, pulling it tight around his eyes. According to the environmental alert displayed in the glass of his bioscanner's visor, surface temperatures maintained a steady -1 degrees Celsius.

They had a difficult job, keeping their eyes on the hostiles while also maintaining constant vigilance for their teammates. From the corner of his eye, Victor saw Zoe take down two men with the same bullet from her high-powered rifle, but an aggressive, six-man squad emerged through the blast door.

Low walls provided cover for the enemy and a few came equipped with personal shields. Their bullets bounced off the shuttle's kinetic barriers and pelted against military grade armor. The marines promptly returned fire, though it did little good. The pirates wore reinforced armor claimed from the bodies of the security forces slain in their assault.

Daniels deployed his team to positions with mobile bulwarks. They returned fire from behind their armor but their shots were useless. Victor hated to be right. For every three rounds fired, only one penetrated an assailant. Half of those didn't so much as offer a flinch of discomfort.

"I said headshots, marines!" Daniels yelled over the gunfire.

"Davis and Fairchild, swap to armor-shredding rounds!" Victor ordered.

"Shit," Zoe swore over their communications channel. "Rogers, get out of the shuttle!"

Victor whirled to face the shuttle, but Zoe's warning came too late. A rocket tore through the air and struck their transport, igniting in a spectacular effect of rising fire and smoke. The failing barrier sparked and the flames rushed over the portside wing. Metal warped and melted under the intense heat.

Victor hit the ground, blown back by the resulting shockwave. The impact forced all the air from his lungs and left him gasping. He pushed his feet and maneuvered around to the shuttle door where automatic extinguishers had begun showering the flames with foam particles.

"Rogers is down but alive. But I don't think we're getting off this rock anytime soon," Victor reported.

"Stay with him, Commander del Toro, while we mop up this mess." Daniels relayed over the sound of gunfire.

"Acknowledged," Victor replied. He had no intention of leaving his patient. He knelt beside Rogers and removed his medical kit. The kid was in pain, and his left leg resembled charred steak below the knee. He'd lose it for sure, and there was nothing that Victor could do about it. The right leg suffered superficial burns. They could wait for now while he stabilized the most severe injuries. "Hang in there, Rogers. You are going to be just fine. Can you hear me?"

Rogers groaned in response and continued to lie frightfully still as Victor worked over him. He dosed him with a pre-prepared shot of morphine and applied antimicrobial ointment to the burns.

The four marines on the front line advanced with their shields, providing cover for the others behind them. Their mobility was their advantage. They pushed forward, forcing their opponents against the rocky outcropping that housed the facility entrance.

"They're wearing stolen armor," Zoe relayed. She held a position up on a rocky pillar with her rifle. "Aim for their joints, the plating is weak there since it's not made for them. Pain or no pain, they can't stand on a shattered knee." To emphasize her point, the sniper fired. A crimson spray of blood exploded from the nearest pirate's leg, and the man crumpled to the ground.

They made quick work of the remaining mercenaries and secured the landing pad. Victor finished with his patient and swept his gaze over the team for more wounded. No one appeared to require his services. The pirates were another matter.

One crawled forward on bloodied arms, trying to reach the missile launcher they had used on the shuttle. Daniels walked toward him and emptied his rifle. The mercenary's body jumped with each bullet until he finally laid still.

"Jackson," Victor spoke over the comm link. "Fall back and stay with Rogers in the shuttle. I can't do anything else for him at this time."

"Williams, you stay with them, too," Daniels added. Hold this position and see if you can get this bird flying again."

They faced less opposition inside, but the narrow space of the front warehouse proved to be treacherous ground to navigate. Containers stacked high at the forefront granted substantial cover to the armed attackers inside.

The brutal firefight continued in the facility. While the United Empire prohibited the sale and use of automatic firearms to civilians, various pirate and mercenary groups always managed to acquire them. Once the well-stocked mercenary group fell beneath military firepower, Victor and Daniels took charge of their troops.

"Raines, get up on that catwalk and keep an eye out. Abernathy, you maintain watch on our entrance. Chang, I want you on the door across the room." Daniels issued orders with calm authority. "Lopez, accompany Commander del Toro and his medics on a sweep through the side rooms."

Victor stole a side glance at Zoe's retreating form. She swiftly scaled a utility ladder and took her position above them. He needed to get his head back into the game, and he needed to do it fast before someone capitalized on his distraction and blasted a hole in him. Turning to appraise the situation, he viewed a few motionless bodies identified as green and alive under his bioscanner. Unwilling to take any chances, Victor quickly barked out orders to his men. The medics fanned out as Victor commanded, sweeping from the entrance and tagging the deceased in passing on their way to the injured. They painted prominent fluorescent orange markers on each corpse. It differentiated the living and unconscious from the dead who were beyond their aid.

"I found a survivor over here! This man's alive!" Davis called. The young woman took her hand away from the throat of a prone form near the stairwell leading to the sublevel.

"You tend to him. Jefferson, come with me. We'll sweep the next room for more injured colonists," Victor said.

It didn't take long to discover the whereabouts of the remaining colonists. The pirates had herded them like cattle into a dormitory bunker and stormed the underground village to raid their homes and businesses. They removed all valuables and picked the houses clean. Because the pirates destroyed all surface communication towers with their ship, the colonists couldn't send distress calls or send for help until the engineer had rigged a signal to the Jemison.

The marines discovered the corpse of the colony's savior in the communications lab. Apparently, his team had been in the process of creating a new communication hub that operated by complex quantum mechanics. It bypassed the downed towers and sent the distress call directly to the Jemison.

The technician's sacrifice brought aid from the Jemison. He died a hero.

"Damn shame that this had to happen this way," Victor said.

"The governor's dead. He died during the initial assault," O'Malley reported to Victor when he arrived. The medic shook his head sadly. "We finished our head count. Most recent census indicates this is a colony of 631. We have 182 survivors."

"Christ. What of the others?" Victor asked. His stomach twisted in knots. So many lives extinguished for nothing.

"It's like the transmission said, Doc, most colonists were taken off-world. Maybe the Jemison will find 'em on the ship if they catch them," O'Malley replied.

"Commander Daniels and his people went to scout the rest of this place. We're getting the colonists fed and cleaned now with supplies we found," Davis said as she stepped into the room.

"I'm reviewing security footage on my helmet's internal screen," Lopez informed Victor quietly. "They were obliterated. These people didn't have a chance, sir."

"It was irresponsible of Hephaestus to found a remote colony so far from civilization." Small colonies often became the target of raiders and pirates, as the chaos on Athena clearly proved.

And the news continued to worsen. Fairchild sprinted into the room.

"Sir, confirmation on the pregnant women. All three in labor," Fairchild reported between heavy breaths. Sweaty strands of pale blonde hair clung to her flushed cheeks.

Victor tossed one of his kits toward the female medic. "Here's the sterile gloves. Go find out dilation and the distance between contractions on all three."

"But–"

"You can do this, comm me with any pertinent information. Comfort them in the meantime. Unless they're a minute apart or hemorrhaging on the floor, I don't want to hear anything else about it."

"Aye aye, Commander." Fairchild bowed her head and stepped away to return to the laboring women. They were her patients now, and Victor became all the more thankful that he possessed the foresight to invite her to the medical squad.

CHAPTER 12

Zoe wiped the sweat from her eyes, clearing her vision to examine their surroundings. The subterranean warehouse provided ample protection, built to withstand the inhospitable exterior conditions. In exchange for the colonists' loyalty, the Hephaestus Corporation provided safe lodgings, healthcare, and a stable work environment. It had been safe at least, until the pirates arrived and decimated the security forces.

Daniels assigned her an easy task; her single duty was to clear the residential wing of the complex. She discovered ransacked homes and several cold, slightly smelly corpses. They hadn't been dead for long.

Two mercenaries opened gunfire on her when she entered the last domicile, initiating forty-five of the most harrowing seconds of her life. Adrenaline fueled the frenzied pace of her heart, the sound of it pounding in her head.

Zoe scooted into cover behind a kitchen counter. A bullet ripped through the thin wood paneling and plinked off of a weak chink in her tactical armor. It grazed the skin beneath, introducing her to a world of pain. "Shit!" She swapped the sniper rifle for her handgun.

She popped up and let her enemies' movement direct her aim. The first man dropped to the floor with a single round between his eyes. His companion kept to cover and blindly fired his weapon around the corner from the hall.

The fight ended when their handguns clicked dry and she rushed her attacker to squeeze the remaining life from him with her cybernetic hand. She crushed his skull to be safe.

"Damn, that hurts!" she swore, once the battle rush diminished, leaving exhaustion and pain in its place. Heat pooled against her skin inside the armor and her fingers came away from the slash bloodied. "Stupid mercs."

All soldiers, regardless of whether they were combat, boarding parties, or medics, carried the necessary supplies for basic medical care. She opened her kit and set it on the kitchen counter. "All right. I can do this. Nothing to it," Zoe convinced herself. She removed the damaged plate and pulled up the tank top beneath for a view of the raw wound. First, she cleansed away the dark, clotting blood then she snapped the antimicrobial dispenser and angled the tip of the tube toward her abdomen.

I can do this, I can do this. She swiped it over her injury and bit back a scream, grunting instead. The disinfectant solution was like fire in her wound, burning mercilessly through her injured tissue. Within seconds, it had also formed a protective seal over the tear. *Not as bad as losing an arm, Zoe. Come on. Buck up*, she told herself again. She wiped away the tears trickling down her cheeks and donned her damaged armor again.

It was a relief to return to her squad mates. The empty houses gave her the creeps.

Used as a warehouse before the arrival of the pirates, the sprawling underground complex had been transformed into a proper lair to store ill-gotten wealth. Beds carried from colonists' homes, bathrooms, and a cafeteria filled with various cooking devices provided for the raiders' every need. They imbibed alcohol and drugs, but worst of all, the pirates took sexual pleasures in the colonists while awaiting the return of their thieving comrades.

With the current hostile group cleared and their military shuttle practically a pile of slag, the only thing the marines could do was settle in and hope they could hold out against any incoming marauders. The strongest pirate bands typically consisted of a formidable flagship and two to five smaller raiding vessels. With the HMS Jemison on a rescue mission, the marines had no choice but to await their return. They were thoroughly grounded until the ship found a safe moment to retrieve them and their damaged rockskipper.

Doctor del Toro set up an impromptu clinic in the medical facilities, working alongside the medics. Last she heard, Rogers wouldn't be walking back onto the Jemison with them. She sympathized with the man. No one could understand what it was like to lose a limb without experiencing it firsthand.

With all of her security tasks complete, Zoe reported to Daniels, who directed her to check on their downed pilot.

The smell of stale sweat and coppery blood invaded her nostrils as she stepped into the room. Every bed in the medical facility was filled. Those with less serious injuries took up a separate room on cots. After Zoe slipped in, she made her way over to Rogers' bedside.

"How ya doin', Rogers? Being a lazy bum already?" she smiled down at the freckled man.

"Heeeey," the man slurred. "You got pretty, Doc."

Zoe laughed. "Yeah, well, we'll have to disagree there. It's me, Zoe. He must have you drugged up pretty good, huh? I remember that feeling."

"Feels like I'm drunk but better." Rogers attempted to nod but his head lolled instead. His eyes rolled in his head, unable to focus on her face. "Don't hurt at least."

"You'll be on the painkillers for a while. They'll take good care of you, and our doctor is one of the best." She stole a glance over one shoulder toward Victor. He toiled over a young woman with a head injury, stitching the wound shut with deft movements.

"Get a brand new leg huh? More impressive than your wussy arm." Rogers laughed weakly. Zoe looked back and nudged him in the shoulder.

"Nah, I'm way better. But we can compare rigs once you're all situated. Deal?"

Rogers passed out before she received an answer.

"Gave him a solid dose of the good stuff. He shouldn't be in any pain for a while," Victor spoke up as he stepped to the bedside. He leaned over Rogers and scanned the man's vitals. "Thanks for that. Speaking to him, I mean."

"I remember what it was like…" Zoe told Victor softly, smoothing Roger's red hair back from his brow. Trauma had flash-burned it into her memory, everything from the fire to waking up minus a limb. The excruciating pain, the numbness, and the way people tiptoed around her afterward.

Zoe cleared her throat and shook off the old memories. "Least I can do is talk to him some. Let him know what to expect."

"I appreciate it and so will he." Victor forced a thin smile to his weary face. "I've done all I can for him now. It's mangled beyond anything I can aid with field medicine. Once we return to the ship, it will have to go," Victor explained with a gesture toward the sedated soldier's left leg. Bandages concealed his mangled calf.

The doc moved away again, shaking his head in sympathy. With wounded people all around, Victor stubbornly assessed even the most minor scrapes and cuts. He moved from patient to patient, passing very few of his duties off on his medics. Zoe admired him for it and watched him from the corner of her eye. The compassionate doctor didn't pause for breaks, too driven to stop until the last patient lay resting.

"We're stranded until they receive our signal. Is that it?" Dark circles beneath Victor's eyes revealed his poorly rested state. He couldn't go on forever.

"Wait and hold our position, yeah." Zoe leaned back against the cold metal wall and sipped from her water bottle.

"I'm not a communications expert. How long would you say we've got to wait before we hear word back from the Jemison?"

"A day, maybe two. We've got all the healthy civilians in that back room so they're good. Rest of us are scattered around to cover any possible entries. Best thing to do, Doc, is find a spot to catch some rest in."

"I suppose so." He smiled wistfully. "I haven't been in the field like this in a while. I prefer it actually. Feels like I'm really doing my job and making a difference when I'm planetside. Don't get me wrong, I meant what I said about fancying the ship over living on the ground, but after a while… Most of what I see from day to day are the petty things. Someone with the flu wants out of their duties. A case of the clap. Or some unlucky woman goes toe to toe with Daniels and learns he's an asshole. This is more like home to me."

He gestured toward the resting crewmen in varying states of recovery, thanks to his tireless efforts. It was how military doctors spent their first years of post-medical school training, working on the front lines and learning to apply urgent medical care to the seriously wounded.

"Yeah, well, we like you plenty onboard. You do lots for us. But enough of that. Let's find you a spot to cozy up in. No one will say a word after all the time you just put in on them."

He shook his head. "I took the first watch. I'm not injured, and I think you could use the rest more. Go ahead," he urged her. "I already told Daniels I plan to remain awake for a while. I need to be while he's sleeping."

"Awfully considerate of you." *Especially considering you've been working harder than anyone else all day…* She kept the thought to herself. "Guess I'll go grab a pile of pillows somewhere. Keep an eye on that western access hatch. If I were going to attack this place, that's the way I would come," Zoe warned as she strode away.

The next day passed without either incident or word from their ship. Zoe spent most of her hours on the surface, maintaining the watch while her fellow Marines worked on the damaged shuttle. Several workers from the colony volunteered their services for the repairs. Their mechanical expertise expedited its completion.

By the third day, tempers among the colonists flared. Some were convinced the Jemison had been destroyed by the pirates. They wanted someone to take the patched shuttle and make a run for help. Commander Daniels quickly squashed the idea with Victor's agreement. The angry mutterings stopped completely after a garbled message came in from the Jemison.

The Jemison had successfully caught up to their quarry and damaged the pirate ship's engines but sustained a surprising hit to their own barriers that overloaded Jem and left them dead in the water, so to speak.

The good news was that they sent a boarding party over on a shuttle and gained control of the mercenary ship to liberate the pirates' human cargo. Unfortunately, it wasn't Crane's flagship and the Jemison's engineers needed time to repair their systems before they could return to Athena. They estimated 30 hours.

The ground crew needed to securely hold the colony for one more night.

***

Weariness weighted Zoe's limbs when her shift finally ended. A low throb in her feet encouraged her to find a place to stretch out and rest, but she had a last job to complete. Rubbing her tender side, she picked her way through the debris-strewn dormitory halls toward the manager's flat.

Zoe knocked and lingered hesitantly in the hallway. "Knock, knock, it's Raines," she announced. Nudged by her metal knuckles, the creaking door swung inward to reveal a motionless shape sprawled on the low, sleigh-style bed with enough blankets draped over it to cushion a crashing shuttle. "Doc?" Poor Victor. According to Daniels, he'd been dead on his feet and made no arguments about taking a break from command this time.

"C'mon in," he answered drowsily.

It felt like stepping into another world. Opulent decor drew her gaze from one item to the next. A large oval window offered a view to the moon's violet tinged surface. On the horizon, the planet Apollo hung like a multicolored marble. As beautiful as the view was, it barely held her glance. Between the jewel-toned carpets scattered across the floor, the framed paintings on the walls, and the man in the bed she was hard pressed to pick the better sight and decide which to ogle.

Victor cleared his throat, making the choice for her. Zoe's attention snapped to him and heat rushed to her cheeks. His alert grey eyes made him appear less tired than she'd originally thought at first glance. He wore his tactical suit without the helmet and armor plates, revealing a dull grey military issue t-shirt instead. Victor's scattergun lay on the bed beside him with the safety set to fire.

"Sorry. Did I wake you? Daniels sent me to make sure you were okay."

"Nah. I was drifting in and out of sleep. Had a movie going for some background noise."

"Sorta figured. You always have music or a show on."

"Yeah," he chuckled softly and ran a hand through his hair. "So what is it this time? Is Daniels lost without me?"

"Commander Daniels asked me to pass on that all is clear and secure for the night in the infirmary. He didn't want you to come up earlier than needed."

"Sounds good. Let him know that–" He glanced briefly toward her and abruptly ended his polite dismissal, his gaze focused on the bulky pad of gauze outlined beneath her black tank. Zoe groaned on the inside. "I thought I cleaned up all of the injuries from that last scuffle. What's that?"

Zoe made a poor attempt to conceal it, her hand raising reflexively to rest over the padded area. "This? Just a graze, Doc, nothing to worry about. Scrubbed it clean and bandaged it the way we're taught. It's a little tender, so I slid a gauze pad over it so it wouldn't rub." A graze that hurt like all sorts of hell, but she hadn't wanted to bother him while there were so many other serious injuries requiring his immediate attention. Victims of battery and rape. Punching bags used to amuse sadistic captors. Newborn babies. They'd deserved his expertise more.

"I thought that we established my name isn't Doc. We're both off-duty. Sorta." Victor paused his movie and set the tablet device aside. "C'mere and let me have a look."

"Habit," she mumbled, pushing the door shut behind her once she reluctantly stepped all the way through. "Really, it barely bled or anything." *Liar,* she chastised herself. "Considering you had a lost limb and stuff to deal with, I was pretty low on the totem pole."

"Yeah, yeah, yeah. There's no rule of battlefield triage at the moment so lay down. Shirt up. You know the drill, Zoe."

"I should be insulted you're disparaging my field skills, *Victor.*" She rolled her eyes, but she didn't disregard the order. The familiarity of their relationship didn't extend to insubordination. Zoe sat gingerly on the edge of the low bed then laid back, enveloped in the warmth his body had left behind against the covers. She didn't have to tug the fabric up far to reveal the bandage to the right of her navel. "Bored or do you just delight in torturing me in particular?"

"My movie was a little more entertaining than you. "

Victor crouched beside the sleigh bed and rifled through his supplies. The contents of his medical case had been dramatically reduced since their arrival only three days before. Earlier, she'd overheard both commanders discussing whether they had enough ammo charges and medical equipment to hold out if another shuttle of pirates arrived with a desire to retake their new home. They needed the HMS Jemison.

"And here I thought this was our thing." Zoe sighed and focused her eyes upwards. "Seriously though, it's not so bad." *Please don't be bad.*

"Why are you so stubborn? What do I tell you whenever you make a visit to the medical department?" he asked, peeling away the medical tape.

"Come see you if my shoulder hurts again," she replied cheekily.

He didn't reply immediately, but his jaw tightened when he lifted away the surgical tape and bandage and exposed a shallow groove with red, tender edges. The subtle traces of warmth had bothered her, but she hadn't wanted to take his attention from dying individuals. "It's infected," he told her bluntly.

"Stupid black market bullets."

"That is why I am the doctor and you are the gunsmith. When my rifle is jammed, I will give it to you. When you are fucking hurt, you come and tell me whatever is wrong."

"Your accent comes out when you're angry." A sexy accent that ran chills up her spine and reminded her of the olive-skinned people hailing from Paradiso. She'd never traveled to the planet where the Latin, Spanish, and Mediterranean people of Old Earth had taken residence. Until now, Victor had sounded like any other native of Albion: very, very British.

"Sometimes." Victor fell silent for a moment, his professional touch applying a cold compress over the affected area. "I'm low on the good stuff. One of the moms had a wicked infection," he muttered. He flicked out a prepared syringe from the bag and took the cap off with his teeth. "Hip please. I promise it won't be as bad as the pb shot. Just a pinch."

Servicemen who visited the infirmary with infections hated the concoction of penicillin, antibiotics, and germ-eating microbes used to treat their illnesses. The shot was as thick as peanut butter and it burned going in.

Zoe's smile wobbled and fell, ending with a sigh. Like most people, she had no love of shots, but she also didn't want to further upset an already frustrated man. She obediently rolled to one side and nudged the waistline of her pants down.

The cleansing agent was cool against her skin, but Victor's fingers against the designated area left heat in their wake. She barely noticed the puncture of the needle. "At the time you had a gut wound to treat, a roasted limb, and babies to deliver. Fairchild gave me a field pack on the shuttle so I used it."

"You don't seem to understand how deadly an infection can become on an unknown planet when we haven't tested…" He trailed off. "Never mind."

"No, no. Explain it to me," she told him quickly, deciding she disliked the frustrated expression on his handsome face. "Please?"

"Basically, it's not possible to vaccinate against every disease and germ in the whole wide galaxy. That's why we take soil and air samples via probe before a landing. Lilibeth and I synthesize the right combination of drugs and immuno-boosters. We inject you all, and then we go down. That way, no one returns to the ship with Emerald Itch or some other nasty disease."

"Except, this time, all we received was the basic broad spectrum inhalant."

"Yes, and it's not good enough. I hate cutting corners, but these people needed us," Victor grumbled. "It's a fair trade off, but we're no good if we fall ill and can't protect them before the Jemison returns." He shot Zoe a cross look and swept one hand through his dark hair.

"You're right; I'm sorry," she said meekly. Disappointing Victor left a sick feeling in her stomach. "I found a couple of mercs hiding out and one of them got a lucky shot. You were so swamped, and I didn't think it would get this bad since I used the field kit."

For the first time, she noticed the hints of grey sneaking in around his temples and peppering his stubbled face. Stress and a couple of hard days had taken a toll on his personality.

"Sorry for losing my temper with you."

"It's sorta sweet." The words slipped out and she didn't mind them. A lovely flood of comfort spread from her head to her toes. "I feel like I'm floating."

"Yes. I may have mixed in something for the pain, so that means the medicine is working. Now relax and watch a movie. Doctor's orders."

He reached over her to retrieve the tablet and set it on the floor to the left of his hip. With his back to the mattress the holo's display was at the perfect level. His considerate choice of seating granted her the benefit of admiring his profile.

"You'll probably sleep for awhile. Better to have you in top condition than passing out in the middle of a fight."

The movie display flared to life, expanding in three dimensions.

"So… I was wondering…. Why do you always keep to yourself?"

Victor tore his eyes away from the movie. Something about his perplexed expression amused her and she cracked another faint smile. "You're referring to why I don't prefer spending my shore leave at the bar each night, and why I don't participate in the get-togethers?"

"Something like that, yeah."

"It's a bit private."

"So… mind my own business." She scrunched her nose at him. "C'mon. You've gotten me to partially strip for you three times now." She held up three fingers to emphasize her point. "I'm not asking anything too much, am I?"

Victor sighed. "Look. None of it's interesting." He continued after a hesitant pause. "I… I cocked up a lot of things in my life just before coming here to the Jemison. I made a big mistake and almost lost my commission altogether. They stationed me at a little shit base on Paradiso, instead, until Bishop rescued me and arranged my transfer to the Jemison. That's it in a nutshell, Zoe."

"Oh, a fresh start. I can respect that, but…" Zoe drifted off, her brow furrowed. Nothing about Victor's situation sounded as cut and dried as he tried to make it seem. "So, you don't ever go out and have fun?"

"Didn't we have this talk back in the lounge? I think my medicine is working its magic," he teased.

Zoe didn't recognize the chosen movie on the holograph, but it failed to lull her into a peaceful rest. Instead, it warred against the medicine, winding up her curiosity each time her eyelids began to drift shut. It was a simple tale, mostly meant for quick laughs. It just didn't hold a candle to the enigma half-clothed in battle gear beside her.

"Oh… You're right. God, this is some good shit. So… what's going on in the flick so far?"

"You didn't miss much of it."

After catching Zoe up with a quick summary about one-night-stands, accidental pregnancies, and marriages in Las Vegas, she only had more questions.

"That doesn't make any sense."

"It doesn't, but when you're drunk or you've run away to elope, I don't think you're in the state of mind to exercise good judgment." He glanced back over a shoulder to flash her a grin, one which she readily returned despite her foggy senses.

"Anyway. How are you feeling now? Are you ready to surrender to the medicine?"

"I feel good. I have a comfy bed and a movie. No wonder you claimed this room, it's like lying on a cloud. All we need is popcorn."

"Daniels didn't have a hard time talking me into it," he admitted. "By the time he brought it up, I'd been between the legs of too many women to argue about sleeping arrangements... Bloody hell, that sounded bad."

"It really did." Zoe laughed and nudged him in the shoulder lightly.

"I mean, I was ready to pass out. I haven't delivered a kid since med school, and I don't really look forward to doing it again." His dramatic, over-exaggerated shudder belonged in a theater production.

"I'm sort of sorry I missed it." Bringing new life into the world was something worth witnessing.

"So... What accent do you think I have? I'm curious now. I didn't think I had one anymore."

"Fishin' for compliments, Victor?"

"Maybe."

"It's just that your accent sometimes reminds me of Lieutenant Salvador in communications. So that means you're actually from Paradiso, right? You weren't just stationed there for the hell of it?"

"My surname didn't tip you off?"

Smart ass. "Lieutenant Salvador lived in Paradiso his entire life, but Lopez is from Easthampton on Albion. Having a Spanish last name only means you have Spaniard blood somewhere," she pointed out.

"Touché. I used to speak the language, too, but I can barely put together a sentence in Spanish now. It's a dead language outside of Paradiso, like many others from Earth. No need for it. I think Italian is the only one really flourishing these days."

The movie ended with a happy conclusion, wrapped up with an embracing couple giving heartfelt admissions under an evening sky. Victor dimmed the device down and set the tablet upon his medical supply kit before he turned to look down at her, as if expecting to find her sleeping. She gazed into his misty grey eyes instead.

Zoe drank in the sight of them and yielded the fight against her impulses. So did Victor. He closed the distance and their lips came together in an electrifying tingle that had nothing to do with cybernetics.

It was crazy, thrilling, and almost forbidden, yet she had absolutely no desire to stop when he matched her with undeniable hunger. His parted lips urged her to mirror his movement with increasing heat and passion, a certain kind of desperate need apparent in the way he leaned closer. Their tongues tangled in a wild dance that curled Zoe's toes. His hands explored between her tank and fatigue bottoms, each touch sending currents through her body. She yearned for the gradual upward sweep that brought the hem over her ribs.

Desiring the same touch and tactile sensation beneath her fingers, Zoe tugged at his shirt to slip her hands beneath it. In her memories, the teasing and playful glimpse of his rock hard abs tantalized her mind. Muscular definition and a chiseled marine's physique tensed beneath her fingers, even better than she'd imagined. It was surreal and almost like a dream, worsened by the drugs clouding her thoughts. It couldn't be real; sooner or later she'd wake cold and alone on her cot.

As far as Zoe was concerned, Victor had a mouth made for kissing and a set of abs worthy of worship. Her fingers crept over each plane and dip, learning his shape as her mouth committed his taste to memory.

She shoved him back against the mattress and swung her leg over his hip. Straddling Victor placed her body just above his hard bulge and the proof of his shared desire.

Victor abruptly froze beneath her and ended the kiss. His fingers closed over her wrists and smoothed over her fingers, his larger palms dwarfing her hands. He loosened Zoe's hold from his hair and deposited her beside him on the bed with a smooth roll.

"Sorry," he mumbled. "You're not in any condition to make this kind of decision. Sorry."

The distance between them became wider than ever once Victor abandoned the bed and pulled on his shirt. He crouched by his medical bag and pretended to sort through the remaining supplies, as if he needed to occupy his hands and create any excuse to avoid making eye contact with her.

Zoe pushed up to a seated position. "Victor…?" Nothing could quell the hammering of her heart.

"Yeah?"

Shit, shit, shit. Do I apologize? But there are no rules against it. He's not in my direct chain of command, she rationalized internally. Archaic fraternization laws had been dissolved when the Empire instituted two year deployments in space.

"Sorry. I should have sent you to rest a while ago." Victor's shaking hands spilled the contents of his bag, allowing translucent vials of medicine to roll across the floor. He swore harshly and swept them off the rug.

"Why are you apologizing? As far as kisses go, I'd give that one a ten for sure."

He glanced back briefly from the corner of his eye. "Your injury," he pointed out evenly. "You should probably rest so it can heal."

The narcotics warred with the endorphins rushing through her body. Would she be brought up on assault charges if she ripped the clothes off of his body?

"I am resting."

"Drugged women can't consent, and this is probably not the most appropriate activity while the others are keeping watch." He had a point. They were technically relieved of their duty posts after working grueling hours with little rest and only a handful of comforts. But there was a time and a place. She'd hate to be caught with her pants down, literally, if returning pirates engaged their squad in battle.

"Yeah, I guess you're right on that." She searched his face from across the room. His anxious mannerisms revealed nothing about the motive behind his sudden change in behavior.

Something was wrong.

Damn him for his logic and that shot.

"You'll pass out any moment, I'm sure. Would you respect me any if I had my wicked way with your unconscious body? C'mon. Get some rest, Zoe. Our watch will come sooner than you think."

Zoe managed a small smile. "As much as I'd like to say yes… Thanks. I still stand by what I said, though." She rolled to her feet, wavered briefly, but tensed her jaw and didn't utter a complaint. Otherwise, he was likely to sacrifice his bed and keep her there. Or worse, carry her to one of the makeshift bunks instead of getting his own rest. "Night, Victor. Thanks for the movie. And for patching me up." *And for the kiss…*

Victor remained crouched beside his bag, surgical laser in hand as he counted the remaining charges. "Sleep well, Zoe." He smiled at her, but she wasn't convinced.

Doctor Victor del Toro was a mystery, and she wanted desperately to know the truth behind his controversial relocation from the Glenn and his former post. More than that, she wanted to know what had happened to make a man who was so selfless and sweet start pushing everyone who came near him away.

CHAPTER 13

Once the squad returned to the Jemison, Victor became inundated with work. He spent days performing tune-ups, repairs, and helping the other medical officers with the men and women injured on the ship during the space battle and emergency landing. He didn't have time to see Zoe, and that was all right with him. He didn't know what he'd say to her if they did cross paths.

The large number of refugees from Athena filled up their aft cargo hold. The three new mothers and the severely injured survivors occupied rooms in medical. Space was cramped but they were safe and allowed use of the ship's recreational areas for an allotted time each day.

For lack of a better place to house the survivors, the Jemison flew for a week to reach the nearest major post equipped to handle a few hundred refugees. The loss of the additional medical responsibility instilled Victor with a sense of profound relief. He'd enjoyed the work, but babies were not his forte. Their tiny, fragile bodies distressed him, as did the reminder that he had never had kids of his own.

A small part of him missed running into Zoe during the ship's night hours. He even peeked into the lounge once or twice against his better judgment, but the gold-eyed sniper hadn't been present.

Messed things up again as usual, Victor thought while leaving the shower. *Probably better that way.* Better for Zoe, and better for him if their relationship remained professional. After that, he avoided her in earnest.

Hart impatiently hammered her fist on the door again. She'd been beating on the door for the past ten minutes of his shower. "Wank on your own bloody time, you big twat!" she shouted at him through the door.

"For Christ's sake, I'm out now," he rumbled at her loudly in return. If he joked about her shower "massager" she wouldn't speak to him for a week.

The restroom lock clicked behind him, followed by the noisy drum of running water. He tugged on a fresh t-shirt over his towel-dried head. After sleeping three or four hours, he planned to awaken at his usual early bird time and check into the infirmary again.

Two knocks jarred Victor from his thoughts.

"This better be an emergency," he muttered under his breath. He slid the door open and peered into the hallway, expecting news from the medical bay. Medical staff preferred to fetch him whenever something went wrong or an extra hand was needed in an emergency.

The sight of Zoe Raines at the other side of the door filled him with hesitation. "Aren't you a little far away from your berthing?" he inquired. He tried to add a lighthearted tone to his voice, but the day's weariness had already taken its toll. Being the ship's only certified cyberware technician meant he'd returned to an abundance of appointments and had to make up for cancellations.

"I suppose so. I…" Zoe shifted her weight from one leg to the other. Uncertainty briefly flickered across her features, then she seemed to collect herself. Her posture straightened and she clasped her hands loosely behind her back. "I wanted to come clear the air on something. Please."

"What is it?"

"Oh, um…" Her glance darted down the passageway then back to his face. "Not exactly a conversation for public, sir."

"Come on in. I have plenty of privacy." He had unpleasant memories of his first years as an enlisted man.

The privacy pods were a new technology then and the glass had variable levels of soundproofing. Between the sounds of intimate encounters, jock talk, and noisy exercise routines, Victor had slept very little then too.

"I really can't complain. The history vids said back in the day a hundred women would share a bunk. Glad that's not the case. Five others is enough." She stepped past him into the room.

Victor stole a glance into the hallway in time to see his fellow commander attentively watching their exchange. Daniels glowered at him before disappearing into his own room. Victor sighed and shook his head.

Great. What the hell was that all about? The last thing I need is for that tosser to jump to conclusions.

"What's on your mind?" Victor asked.

Zoe turned from her casual inspection of the space and tilted her head to look up at him. "Yes, right. So... I was going to apologize, but the truth is I really don't feel apologetic about kissing you. What I do want to make clear though is that I respect your... boundaries. You don't have to walk out of a room because I happen to enter it. I'm not going to stare after you with cow eyes or whatever the stupid term is." She made a fluttering gesture with her hand.

"Cow eyes works," he offered helpfully.

She slanted her gaze at him. Despite the difference in rank, he promptly silenced. "Like I was saying. You don't have to treat me like a leper or some rank-tagger," she continued.

Victor's spine stiffened. He'd have never spent his off-duty hours in her company at all if he'd ever suspected her to be participating in some unspoken vow to sleep with the most officers on their vessel. "I know you've heard this shit before, but when I say it, it is the truth. This has nothing to do with you, Raines. It's me. I'm not a guy you want to date... or anything else. Trust me."

"It was a kiss, not a marriage proposal. I'm just trying to clear the air because the whole avoidance thing is exhausting."

"I've been busy," he gritted out at her. Legitimately busy. He might have left once or twice on the run, but he hadn't intentionally ditched any of the ship's common rooms to avoid her company. Until she walked into the pool in her Navy-issued one-piece bathing suit, the material clinging to her like a second skin in all of the right places.

Or when she'd come to medical for a follow-up for her infection, and he'd passed her off to Lil instead and gone down to the lab.

"It wasn't completely intentional, all right? I owe you an apology. I knew better and I kissed you anyway."

Zoe held up a hand to wave him off. "You're not making me feel any better."

"I was trying to make *me* feel better." He failed miserably, too discontent with leading her on to immediately forgive himself.

The young woman shifted slightly, idly tapping her fingers in a silent tempo against her thigh. "Mind if I ask you a personal question?"

"Shoot." He was used to her inquisitive nature by now and, if he was he was honest with himself, found it attractive.

"Was kissing me really so horrible or was that panic attack for something else?"

She's bright. Observant. It wasn't the kind of conversation Victor wanted to have with her a few minutes before bed. "You're great to kiss, Zoe," he answered carefully. "And I enjoyed every second. Is that all?"

"No, not really…" A frown twisted her lips. "Sorry. I honestly didn't mean to upset you."

"It's fine. I'm fine," he insisted. He repeated the word again, convincing himself that nothing was wrong. "Go on to bed, hon. I'm not writing you an excuse for duty tomorrow." He tried to sound chipper, but the tease came out forced.

"Nah, I wouldn't abuse you like that. I actually enjoy your company."

Victor absently kneaded his fingers against his left shoulder and rolled the tight joint. He'd still be in the shower under the hot water if not for Hart. "I appreciate it."

"So… are we good then?"

"We were always good, Zoe. I haven't had much leisure time since we returned to the ship. Hell, I logged on Spellbound last night for about an hour and got chewed out by half my friend list. I don't make it known that I'm military, and when I miss our scheduled raids, they think I'm skiving off."

Zoe smiled lightly. "Been there. Done that. I don't really game enough to have a regular group, though I've found a couple good ones to team up with sometimes. They were probably just worried about you is all. Friends do that. You know… worry."

"Yeah, they do. I'd log on tonight if the day hadn't caught up to me. Guess I'm getting old."

Zoe scoffed and rolled her eyes. "You're far from old. You're just overworked and stiff."

"Almost forty, hon. I only look good. Too bad I don't feel it, too."

"Like I said, overworked. I can help with that if you like."

"With what?" He involuntarily let his gaze drop toward her chest level. The sports bras issued by the military were the universe's greatest illusion. He would have never guessed her to be so busty beneath it, and now he couldn't get his mind off it.

"Go. Sit." She pushed him lightly toward the lounge chair near the bulkhead. "You're tight as a drum and won't get a blink of sleep."

"Maybe that's why I sleep so little."

"Yup. Now, if you tell anyone I can do this I will never forgive you," she threatened half-heartedly.

"Do what?"

"Long story short, I took a masseuse class during my implant adjustment leave."

Once she settled behind him, Zoe's hands smoothed across the breadth of his shoulders. Her reluctant massage recipient sighed and pulled off his shirt.

He should have been more eager to have a woman's hands on him. Ethan would have agreed completely that he was long overdue for a round in the sack with a lovely woman.

"After I got the new arm I had trouble with managing the strength. They had me try pottery," Zoe explained quietly. "I'm rubbish with creative stuff like that. Can't draw more than a stick figure, let alone create a vase."

"So you thought people were a better medium?" He glanced over his shoulder and cocked a brow. "Maybe I need to rethink this," he teased.

"My sister suggested it. Offered to be my practice dummy and everything. Not hurting her was a strong motivator."

"Younger or older?"

"Younger, by several years. She would have been a psychic, but she was one of the unlucky ones who developed an aggressive pituitary tumor. It metastasized into her brain," she explained. "The latest round of treatments seems to be working though."

Psychic genes tended to run in families, but a small fraction developed tumors instead of abilities and rarely survived into adulthood.

"How's she doing now?" Gradually, he began to relax beneath the steady grip of Zoe's hands, letting his head fall forward while her fingers melted away the lingering stress of the day. He hadn't realized how much the tension hurt until she began kneading it from his shoulders.

"She's good for now and was finishing up a round of chemo right before I transferred here. Old tech, I know, but effective. I'd been growing out my hair for her."

"Sometimes the old stuff works best…" he mumbled. "You're a good sister to do that for her."

"I love her. It was the least I could do. After I left home, she was the only one who stayed in touch."

"Honestly, we've advanced so many things, but the human brain is the one area we can't toy with. Some big company caught a few billion in fines for testing brain implant cyberware without prior authorization. I agree with the decision but… hell, there's people like your sister who could benefit from the progress."

"Why *is* it prohibited?"

"If we try some high-risk things on your kidneys and you go into failure, we'll put you on dialysis until we grow you a new one or acquire an implant. If your lungs collapse, we have a machine to breathe for you. I can't do that with your brain, Zoe."

"I guess…" she sighed heavily and fell silent. Her thumbs drew down alongside his spine. After a few moments, she spoke up again. "I guess that must tie in to your studies, right?"

"I probably know more about it than I should for a tech-doc huh? For a while, I wanted to work my way into the medical research department, but… someone close talked me into applying for cyberware certification instead. Helping people mattered most to me, so it didn't really matter where I went to do it."

"My gain, I suppose. The whole ship's really." The warmth of her breath preceded a gentle press of her lips to his back.

Silence fell between them as she worked on his knotted muscles, although it ended when he picked up the first subtle notes of cello music. "Guess the ship's joining forces with you now. You're both putting me to sleep."

Gradually, it increased in volume, filling the room with soothing tones.

"Guess the ship likes you," she said with a soft laugh. "Hey Victor, can I ask you another personal question?"

"What?"

"Did you pull away because... I'm not your type? I mean... I guess it just makes it easier if I understand. I don't mind. Just... You know what, never mind."

"Huh?"

"It's nothing, just something I heard. It got me to thinking, is all."

"The rumors, huh. Seems I can't escape them no matter where I go." A cold ache filled his belly, followed by a numb feeling that proved to be impervious to massage techniques. "I didn't mean to waste your time, all right? Contrary to whatever you heard, I'm not that much of an ass."

"No, it wasn't anything like that. Besides, you're entitled to like who you like. As for my time, you didn't waste it. You spent it with me. So thanks for that."

"Nevertheless, I owe you an apology," Victor insisted.

Zoe's hands fell away from his back and left a void. The separation of contact was brief, ended when she climbed over the seat and sat down next to him. Their hips and thighs brushed against each other.

Victor had never wanted a woman more.

"No apology needed. Really. It was a good kiss." She flashed a quick smile. "Feel better? I didn't press too hard, right? Been awhile since I've rubbed anyone's shoulders."

"It felt good," he assured again. He claimed her right arm and traced his fingertips over her skin. Warm, alive, and sensitive to his touch. Her face flushed in response, and the endearing reaction sent a surge of testosterone through his veins. Everything about Zoe excited him. "Do you trust me?"

"That's an odd sort of question…" She regarded him thoughtfully. "I do. You're my doctor, right? And my friend."

Victor pressed gently with his thumb above her wrist where veins belonged on a flesh and blood limb. With the back of her hand propped against his knee, he returned the favor. "This," he murmured quietly. "You loosened a nerve connection again. Probably during a fight. How's that?" He asked his question, but he didn't release her or sever contact.

Zoe flexed her fingers. "I barely even noticed. How did you…?"

"I'll spare you the medical jargon and say that my job is to notice when things are not as they belong."

"I'm impressed, Victor." Her body shifted minutely to accommodate his continued hold of her hand. Her knee pressed into his and her fingers curled inward toward his touch.

Victor's hands behaved as if they had a mind of their own, exploring and touching her everywhere all at once. Her cybernetic arm, the original focus of his investigation, became the least interesting facet of her anatomy. Her tank was a bothersome hindrance, an obstacle to be removed.

"You had something wrong," Victor said impulsively. "It wasn't a good kiss."

"I… er… it wasn't?" Zoe's heartbeat thrummed beneath his touch. The delicate hairs on her arm stood on end.

A good kiss. Never had anyone spoke a greater understatement. "I told you, Zoe, you're *great* to kiss."

"Maybe you should kiss me some more then," she whispered breathlessly.

He did. Inhibitions faded for the first time in months, leaving a sense of freedom in its place. Victor kissed her thoroughly, recognizing the sweet taste of mint lingering upon her tongue. A hint of cocoa from a favored tea shared during a rare early morning movie session in the lounge. It was a taste he'd come to associate with Zoe, its smell always bringing her to the forefront of his thoughts.

Zoe matched him in both eagerness and enthusiasm. She bridged the distance and ran her fingers over his strong biceps. Up his arms, over his shoulders, and down his chest and the soft hairs scattered over his chiseled pecs.

One of her hands touched his waistband and delved lower. Predicting her intentions, Victor closed his hand around her wrist and pinned it to the cushion of the lounger instead. With her fingers out of the way, he dipped his head and kissed her collarbone, denying her the instant gratification she craved.

Victor released her and pulled the tank over her head, baring no more of her than what he'd seen in the medical bay. He tossed it to the floor and admired her lithe upper body, clothed in only an elastic sports bra. Almost two long years had passed since the last time he'd made love to a woman, when he'd taken Ylona to bed on the eve prior to his last deployment to the Glenn.

And in the months since his wife's death, only one woman had inspired that kind of desire in Victor again.

The minutes blurred together, lost in a series of slow and drugging kisses. Hands wandered and fingers explored, gliding over curves, muscles, and ticklish places. They were free to kiss without urgency or guilt, no patients awaiting his care and no soldiers relying on their vigilance.

When his restraint dwindled, Victor drew back for air and studied Zoe's passion-hazed eyes. Every time he tried to speak, to put a voice to the thoughts swirling in his head, the words died on his lips.

"If you apologize I'm going to smoosh your box of cream cakes," Zoe smiled with her half-hearted threat.

"I wasn't going to apologize this time."

"Good, cause I wouldn't have accepted it." Her smile dimmed and she caught her lower lip between her teeth.

"I was actually deciding whether to ask if you wanted to stay. I happen to be an excellent bedtime cuddler."

"You're not kicking me out?" Color rushed to her cheeks the moment the words left her mouth. "I mean… yes. I'd like that."

He shook his head. "You don't have to stay. I'm a big boy. A 'no' doesn't bother me."

"Good thing I'm saying yes then."

"C'mere." He reached down and dragged Zoe to her feet by both hands, only to draw her close with both arms around her afterward. She stepped into the embrace, placing her hands at his hips.

"I feel I should warn you. I'm a horrible bed hog." Her words were only half in jest.

"I'm not worried," he assured her.

"Good." The warmth and humor suffused her voice with an inviting quality, chasing the fluttering moments of shyness and anxiety away. "Only a few hours until we're both supposed to be up and moving anyway, right?"

With their sleeping arrangements made, they slipped beneath the blankets and tidy sheet, and then Zoe snuggled into his secure embrace with her cheek against his bare shoulder.

"That's pretty." Zoe said, gesturing toward a keepsake bottle on his nightstand table. Pink sand sparkled at the bottom of the water filled globe, cushioning three pearlescent shells. The room's dim lighting glinted off several fine purple and ivory filaments floating inside. It resembled a marine feather duster. "Is it from Elora?"

Victor inhaled deeply. "It is."

He didn't elaborate about his souvenir, reluctant to tell her it was a lock of hair from the deceased wife he'd been ridiculed for marrying.

"Is this really okay?" she asked softly.

Victor pulled her closer to illustrate how much he enjoyed their cuddling session. Reassured, Zoe settled against him. His bed fit them both with room to spare, and compared to enlisted narrow bunks, his mattress would suit royalty.

"Hey Victor?"

"Hmm?" he responded drowsily.

"Will you ever tell me why you don't like to be touched sometimes?"

"Ask me again another day, and I'll tell you." He squeezed her tightly and pressed his lips against her brow. "And then it's up to you to decide if you still want anything to do with me. Right now, I only want to enjoy having you here."

"Fair enough." A turn of her head brought her lips to the perfect position for kissing his jaw. "I enjoy this too. Using you as a pillow is becoming a habit."

It was a habit Victor didn't want her to lose.

CHAPTER 14

The day was never going to end. While there had been a decrease in the number of corpsman needing medical services, it had also resulted in one hell of a boring day for the doctors who worked in the infirmary.

"Want one?" Hart asked Victor, leaning one hip against the desk. She held out a bag of assorted chocolates and candies that had already suffered a thorough rummaging from the medical technicians.

"Who the hell ate all of the Silk Classics?" he demanded indignantly.

"Lil got to them before you. Maybe if you were socializing with the rest of us instead of hiding in your office you would have gotten a few."

Victor growled under his breath and plucked out an acceptable substitute. Silk chocolate bars were the most sinful, decadent delight, but crushed nuts didn't improve their quality. He'd rather have chocolate *or* nuts, of the firm belief that the two should never meet.

"I've never met a man so bloody picky about his sweets. You'd think you were a woman," Hart complained.

"We have an hour of this bullshit left. I need sugar, and I would like to get it without picking nuts out of my teeth in front of my next patient," he told her candidly. He plucked a few more of his choice favorites from the bag, then groaned inwardly when Hart scooted her rear onto the corner of his desk.

"If you get a patient. It's been dead for you, too." Hart popped another candy into her mouth and watched him. "You know, I'm a practicing empath."

"So? You mentioned this to me before."

"You're excited about something. What's up, Victor? You're hiding in your office, anxious to leave when you're usually the last to go, and you're stuffing your face with candies – when they're serving fried chicken in the mess tonight. Your favorite."

"If you are reading my thoughts, I will punch you out of this ship's airlock. I'll explain later to Bishop about why he lost a physician," he threatened grumpily. He avoided meeting her eyes and kicked the trash bin out from behind his desk. "I have a lot of things on my mind."

"C'mon. Dish." Hart folded her hands together and practically bounced on her toes.

A quick glance to the left and to the right confirmed no one was within ear shot. Their conversation would remain private. "I have a date."

"Ohhh?" Her eyebrows rose beneath her bangs. "Will you meet her for tea in the cafe? Or shall it be a make-out in the bio-farm? That's where all the kids are snogging these days."

"It's an online date," Victor quickly clarified. "I don't want... we aren't ready to meet in public here yet." *Except you forgot to ask for her login handle, dumbass.* Victor sighed and considered phoning Zoe back to ask, but her time on the clock wasn't as fluid. He had all the free time he needed between patients.

"I have to say, I'm curious about who's caught your eye. Pretty sure you're not going to tell me though." Hart wrinkled her nose at him.

"You guessed correctly."

"Go on, sod off, and get out of here. Shift is almost up and unless Daniels rips someone's tech out of a socket, you won't be needed."

"You don't mind?" Victor hesitated, perched on the edge of the seat.

"I can handle things. Besides, the way your feelings are bouncing all over the place you won't be focused anyway."

"Thanks, Kath."

Without any patients awaiting his care and with no scheduled procedures, Victor abandoned his post early for the first time since his arrival on the ship. He was halfway to his stateroom when his communicator beeped.

"Tactical room, Victor."

Ethan's terse voice cut off and Victor swore. A call like that meant now, not later. He turned about and headed directly for the briefing room as ordered. Daniels arrived at the same time and didn't utter a word or acknowledge his sociable nod.

Ethan, Amelia, and Oshiro had already taken their seats. Their grim expressions told it all.

"We just received word from the Glenn. She's been on similar mission as ours in the Tersian Nebula." Ethan cut to the point without greeting them. "They discovered a mining settlement out there under the same circumstances as Athena. Only they arrived too late... and the pirates left more bodies behind than they took."

"We forwarded several autopsy results to your personal medical rig, Doctor," Amelia informed him. "You'll find them to be of interest."

"Why is that?" Victor asked politely.

"The survivors from Athena said the pirates took everyone with cybernetic implants on the ship first and secured them. After that they weeded through the rest. According to the personnel files, everyone taken either had an implant or was a technician involved in the manufacture of cybernetic parts."

"Right. So we have pirates on a high tech ship with their sights set on cyborgs."

"The bodies found by the Glenn had been... stripped." Amelia frowned and pulled up a file on the display. Over a dozen images flickered open, each more disturbing than the last.

"What the hell is all that?" Daniels leaned forward to get a better look.

"Someone practiced cerebral augmentation on that man. Right here, I recognize it by the cyberware burns on his brain." Victor stared at the frozen image hovering above their table. "Typically, we're allowed minimal interference with the brain." The photos demonstrated another story of opened skulls and blank, staring faces attached to motionless corpses, their bodies strewn over the ground like refuse. It pissed him off. It wasn't ethical. It wasn't *right*.

"He is correct," Oshiro said. "Good eye, Victor. I didn't recognize the burns."

"Okay. It's clear that they're abducting experimental subjects, but why would they prefer to take cyborgs," Daniels said, cutting in. "If they plan to do the work on them already…"

Yes… why are they? Victor wondered. Experimental brain research could help millions, but the strict codes enacted by the Empire forbade it. Zoe's little sister would benefit greatly. "I've got it!"

"Well don't keep us in suspense," Daniels said.

The four officers gave Victor their full attention. "When the steps are made to become a cyborg, often we install a small neurochip between the brain and spinal cord. It's a wireless conduit between it and the new cybernetic part. Practically every cyborg of the past fifty years should have one."

"You think they're after the chips?" Ethan asked. "Why not simply hijack a freighter with a shipment of them on the way to a medical installation?"

"No. About twenty percent of the cyborg population rejects their chip. When that happens, they're downgraded to a less efficient, but very useful model from early century. There's a firm that specializes in building more of the old tech to today's standards.

"So, what you're saying is that they're hunting for cyborgs who have already undergone the trial?" Daniels asked. "Christ. I didn't know it was so complicated."

"I haven't told you about the number who die on the table, mate. Choosing cybernetics isn't an easy decision." And for a soldier with a career, it was absolutely necessary to remain in the military without a medical discharge.

Daniels looked abashed, and rightly so.

"But there's more to it than that. As we discovered, they're also claiming psychics. I believe that whoever we're after has chosen to abduct them for illegal brain experimentation. A psychic's brain can accept a lot of punishment before it's absolutely exhausted beyond the point of regenerating."

"Why plant the seed when you can purchase a sapling? Only in their case, they're stealing living human beings." The words chilled Victor as they left Oshiro's mouth. "But what do we plan to do about it?"

"Find them," Ethan said swiftly. "I have Nisrine and Lockhart conducting a search of their own. In the meantime, we plan to visit the remaining outer rim colonies. Set them on alert. We'll conduct weapons training with their militias and local police forces to prepare them."

"Still, what is their goal? Can just anyone do this kind of work on a body? You went through years of training to get where you are," Amelia pointed out.

"Takes a skilled neurosurgeon and a cyberneticist working in conjunction with each other," Victor replied. "Anything less is murder. You can't pick this up from a FaceNote video and practice it out."

"The brain is off limits to tampering. Back when the experimental trials first began, Parliament decreed that the human mind was too delicate to undergo enhancement," Oshiro explained. "I was fresh to neurosurgery then, but I remember the day clearly. Hundreds died during unnecessary cybernetic procedures."

"Obviously someone decided to pick that research back up." Ethan grunted in disgust. "Doesn't matter why, not right now. You lot can figure that out after we catch them."

They adjourned the meeting after discussing their next destination. Ethan hung back instead of filing from the room along with the others.

"Victor, a moment."

"Yes?" The door closed behind Oshiro, leaving the two men alone.

"We've been so busy that we haven't had a chance to really talk. Free time has been shite."

"That's because you've been busy flirting with virtual nymphs." Victor grinned and put on a smile. He had a niggling feeling about the reason behind the chat.

"We don't all have young women visiting our staterooms aboard the ship."

Shit. "How did you—"

"No one told me anything. No one alive anyway. I tried to ring you last night for a chat, but the ship's bloody A.I. insisted you were busy with a female friend. She screened me. *Me.* Do you plan to tell me who?"

"No."

"Fair enough." Ethan backed down easily. He always had a knack for knowing when to push and when to withdraw. "At any rate, that isn't why I asked you to hang back a moment. You're aware of the mission schedule, right?"

"You're worried about our next scheduled liberty location."

"Yes. Will you be all right there?"

All right. Such a simple concept, but far from how he felt when he considered the rolling green and blue oceans stretched endlessly over the globe. The little aquatic planet held memories for him of his deceased wife. Ylona wouldn't want him to avoid her home planet. She would want him to celebrate every moment as if she were there in spirit.

"I'll be fine," he responded slowly. "I'm looking forward to it. I miss her, but I promise going there isn't going to push me over the edge. I won't collapse again."

"And… your new friend? Is that a one time dalliance or will you be sharing the time with her?" Ethan regarded him with brotherly concern.

"I don't know. I didn't think… I honestly don't know what she expects." Victor frowned. "I haven't told her about Ylona."

"Or about the rest of your troubles, I take it. Go ahead and ask her. We'll work with you on the schedule if your shore leave doesn't overlap."

"You don't have to do that, Ethan. No special favors."

"This isn't a special favor. Now get out of here. I'd ask you to join me in game tonight but I have plans to visit Engineering and the Main Battery. When we run into those pirates again, I don't want history repeating itself."

"Don't terrorize them too much."

They parted ways and Victor hurried as fast as he dared down the passageway. A glance at his wristwatch revealed the approaching hour for his date. Thanks to the unexpected meeting he was cutting it close.

He flew into his room, stripped out of his clothes and showered. He had his VR gear in place less than five minutes later.

The game asked him if he wanted to log into his last known position, or teleport to a new location. He chose the Gardens of Manhattan. Seconds later, the virtual world greeted him with a splash of colors and humming sensation. It came alive, bombarding him with natural green smells and melodic trills from local birds once native to Earth.

Zoe had picked the location. Victor turned in a circle, taking in the exotic sight surrounding him. New York City as a whole didn't appeal to him; it was too crowded and noisy. No wonder their past ancestors had looked to the stars for greener pastures.

He waited in an oasis within the chaotic city replica. Trees grew inside and soared up to the vaulted glass roof, water fell over rocks in a natural fountain, and flowers in every color sprouted up in neatly tended beds. Birdsong filled the air. It was beautiful and quiet, with only a small handful of other players occupying the large space.

I should have asked her username... What if she came while I was in the meeting, and she's already logged off?

Waking beside her had been a solid reminder of what he lost when Ylona died. As typical, he was early to rise, long before the time necessary to prepare for his day in the medical bay. Victor left a note tucked under Zoe's hand, urging her to call him at his office extension.

Then he had spent a few minutes watching her sleep. True to her word, Zoe somehow managed to spread out across his entire mattress and immediately snuggled into a pillow when he left the bed.

A soft breeze whispered across his cheek and stirred through his hair. It carried the scent he associated with rain and thunderstorms, mingled with the green and floral fragrance of the room. The game provided the most realistic tastes and smells rivaling anything from the physical world. It was no wonder that some people logged in and lost their lives to the virtual world. For a time, he had been one of those people, throwing away his physical life to numb the pain of losing his wife.

"Oh, hello, Juan. Fancy meeting you here."

The use of his avatar's name drew Victor's gaze upward. Zephyr's ethereal form shimmered and coalesced into existence near a vented window. Pale blue and silver silks fluttered around her slender frame, accompanied by beautiful iridescent wings that vanished once she touched the ground. Her bare feet left slight indentations in the lush green grass.

"Get bored with England's zones?" he asked.

Zephyr smiled and shrugged. "I was after a certain weapon drop in this area last time I played so this is where I logged out."

"Did you get it?" Chatting with Zephyr became an acceptable distraction until Zoe arrived. If she arrived. If she didn't decide to back out and cut her losses.

The sylph nodded eagerly, her face aglow with enthusiasm. She accessed her holographic interface and removed a longbow from her inventory. Living vines twined around its length. "A reward from the local tree nymphs for defending them against some fire happy warlocks. I can hit an imp at a hundred paces, easy."

"Nice." He glanced it over then handed the weapon back, watching as it disappeared into her inventory. "I'm a little envious. I like bows."

"So what brings you around here? I'm so used to seeing you with the other two."

Victor opened his mouth to reply, but quickly shut it again to search for an appropriate response. He certainly didn't want to admit that he'd been stood up by a woman in an online game. "Eh… I didn't set up a time to play with them today. They're busy."

"So just taking in the view then." Zephyr's glance slid past him briefly, toward the sound of an opening door. Two people stepped out of the gardens into the room beyond. She sighed and glanced back.

"Yep. What about you? I usually see you with a gaggle of your nymphly cousins."

"True, but today I'm waiting for someone." She dropped down onto a nearby bench and swayed her feet from side to side, tapping her fingers against her thigh. The familiar gesture drew his gaze until she lifted her eyes and caught him staring. "Nymphs don't have a footwear slot. I sort of like it."

"Apologies. I didn't mean to stare. It's just that… you remind me of someone I know." He paused to consider the absolute absurdity, then marveled over how dry his mouth felt in a digital videogame. "Zoe?"

Zephyr's lips parted in a silent "oh" of surprise. She hopped up and hastily tucked her long, silvery hair behind her delicately pointed ears. "Victor?"

"You're a sylph," he stated in confusion. He'd expected some hulking Inquisitor type character with a flaming sword of righteousness, or maybe even one of the tough-as-nails wizard avatars.

"So?"

"You're roleplaying the most feminine class in the game."

"What's wrong with that?" Zoe drew herself up defensively. If Victor had any doubts about her identity, that action ended them. "I'm supposed to be a tank because I shoot guns in real life?"

"No, I like it!" he quickly clarified, waving his hands. "It was just unexpected. Bloody hell. We've been playing together all this time."

"You're playing a healer." Her lips quirked at the corners into a broad smile. "You're a doctor and you're playing one here, too."

"Stick with what you know."

"It suits you." She clasped her hands behind her back, toes wiggling in the grass. "I should have guessed. You like chastising me in-game as much as you do out there."

"Sorry. I guess I can't help it."

"It's all right. I always liked to think it was because you liked me."

"I do. Like you, I mean."

"So…" She stepped closer and took his hand. "Now you know I have a girly side. I like dresses and stuff like that."

"I haven't seen you in a dress yet. I mean, in the real world. Last time I saw you step off the ship on liberty, you were wearing pants and boots. Not the most feminine attire."

She glanced up shrewdly. "You've been paying attention to what I wear?"

"Not exactly… You forget, I sort of have to stand there and monitor all of you for medical flags as you leave. I notice a lot. Like I know your bunkmate Radha likes to skate the boundaries of what's within the dress code."

Zoe rolled her eyes then she lifted up on her toes to silence him with a light kiss. A simple and chaste brush of her lips over his did the trick. "Next time, just go with it and say yes."

"Sorry. I babble when I'm…" Her kisses made him nervous for reasons he couldn't describe, but her attractive game qualities made him critique and silently compare every difference. The real Zoe wasn't quite so short, and he preferred her dark-hair and ethnic skin tone. Her true smile featured a slightly crooked tooth too minor for dental correction. The sylph avatar lacked her flaws and the minor imperfections that made her lovable and real.

"You don't have to be nervous around me. I'm just the squishy nymph who tags along with your group sometimes. Now you just happen to know my work schedule."

Overcome by impulse, Victor dragged her close against him and kissed her with all of the passion he could muster. Zoe's softer lips and fragile frame molded against him, her every curve as authentic in digital form as it had felt as she lay beside him the previous night.

Her fingers crept slowly up his arms, coming to rest on his shoulders.

"Come on. Let's have some fun," he whispered against her lips.

They came to the mutual decision not to share the evening with their military friends, although Zoe sulked when Victor refused to reveal the identity of his two guild mates. He told her it would ruin the fun, especially after she erroneously guessed O'Reilly to be the player behind Ethan's character.

A sudden message popped up from Trevor as they stepped outside into the digital sunlight.

Alexander Solo (to you): Hey, we're going to raid the banshee citadel in Avalon. Finally got about two dozen good players to pull it off. Wanna come along? Oh, and here's the 5000 gold I borrowed from you. Made it back like I promised. Thanks, mate.

Juan Sebastian: Go without me, I'm going to do an event in NYC area.

Alexander Solo (to you): Yeah? I heard about that. It's only a stupid haunted house.

Juan Sebastian: So?

Alexander Solo (to you): Testy, this evening, aren't you? All right, I'll keep an eye out for anything you might want.

Victor shot a glance at Zoe. She had bent to interact with a few of the digital pixie NPCs. The programmed creatures flitted around the garden, occasionally landing on players with friendly auras. "Sorry. Just a second."

"No rush," Zoe assured him.

Victor sighed and typed out another hasty message to Trevor.

Juan Sebastian: I'm grouped with someone who has a high faction rating with Avalon. I'll hang out with you next time.

That seemed to end it by satisfying Trevor's curiosity. For her patience, and because he simply wanted to do it, Victor kissed Zoe again at the conclusion of his messaging.

"Okay, all yours."

Supposedly, the game designers had done their research by pulling information and scenes from popular horror movies of the time. Between a burned man wearing double razor gloves and a bulky zombie wearing a catcher's mask, Victor and Zoe ran more in one night than they'd ever run during military training. Fortunately, the sylph's natural ability to control the wind translated into a powerful haste spell. Victor practically flew down the poorly lit halls of the dilapidated house.

"Are there rewards for completing this?" he demanded once they stopped breathlessly in a quiet hallway. The realistic loss of stamina made him lean against her. "I don't know if I'm having legitimate fun or if I'm too terrified to believe otherwise."

It was definitely fun. With Zoe, he enjoyed an exhilarating freedom denied to him as a kid.

"Are you going to need a teddy bear tonight?" Her playful taunt accompanied a laugh. She gazed up and down the hallway warily. "We're almost to the top floor anyway. That's the goal."

"Almost," he repeated. "If another clown chases me through a room of torture devices, I'm holding you responsible," he teased lightheartedly.

"I will humbly accept my punishment." She reached over and took his hand.

The top and final floor featured a maze of spider webs they had to navigate. Victor had the final laugh upon the discovery that Zoe was fine with zombie clowns but absolutely petrified of tiny arachnids. He refused to let her quit and dragged her through.

Maybe they couldn't enjoy a traditional date away from the Jemison, but in a way their virtual videogame had given the very thing they both needed: a night together away from their military responsibility.

***

Victor removed his darkening goggles and set aside his headset, but he remained reclined in the chair with his eyes closed.

Once he sat up, he primed the movie player and waited for Zoe.

Eventually, the door chime announced her arrival, and he found her on the other side dressed in standard ship coveralls with a mild case of bedhead mussing her short hair. Victor fought back the urge to smooth down the dark strands at the nape of her neck.

"Sorry. I had to listen to Angela's chatter before I could slip out," she said after the door slid shut behind her.

"About?"

"Actually…" she laughed quietly and glanced upward. "It was about you. You're sort of the dreamboat of the ship. I just nodded and said 'uh huh' and 'I guess' a lot."

"Yeah, I sort of gathered. I spent my first three days bogged down by frivolous medical requests before Oshiro caught wind of it and put out word that any unnecessary sick calls would be visiting him personally in his office."

"Yeah, see, I never heard the reasoning behind that. I just thought medical here ran a really tight ship. Made me nervous when I came in about my arm."

"From that, I gather this means your roomies don't know where you've gone to? Did they ask about last night?"

"No. I'm always taking off anyway since I'm a night owl. Besides, last night was personal and none of their business."

"Sorry for leaving in the morning. I… Anyway, I have snacks ready."

She touched his forearm gently. "Thank you for leaving the note, Victor."

Victor smiled easily. "I found a good movie on Cineweb in their Classics section. It's only about 200 years old but recently remastered for the Holovision."

Zoe left her boots by the door and lowered her coveralls, tying the sleeves around her waist. The cotton shirt beneath failed to hide the lack of an undergarment and was far from standard issue. Stylized flowers decorated the lower half of the soft, white cotton. Victor swept his gaze over her with appreciation, then patted the bed beside him.

The movie itself was an interesting mix of family values and romance filled with awkward sexual tension. The heroine's family became overprotective jerks as the story's main plot device, while the young lover floundered and failed in every effort to please them.

Story of my life, Victor thought wryly. Before Ylona, he'd dated Hannah for years prior to popping the question. Her father, an admiral in the military, hated him on sight, and Victor had no doubt that her parents popped a bottle of expensive champagne to celebrate the end of the relationship.

Throughout the movie, Zoe and Victor engaged in idle chatter. Their friendly banter seemed to distract from the unspoken questions between them. After a time, Zoe nudged him forward to sit upright with his legs off the bed and then scooted around behind him to resume the massage she had started the night before.

"I've always wondered if this sort of behavior is common in real families."

"What behavior?" she asked. She turned her head slightly, bringing her nose in a light skim against his neck. "Boyfriends sleeping in separate rooms before marriage?" Zoe laughed, and the huff of breath feathered across Victor's cheek. Her closeness would have weakened his knees if they were standing. "My folks did when my brother's fiancée came to visit. Not that it mattered much, since I remember hearing them in the middle of the night. They hit it off. It was like love at first sight for them." She chuckled at her own memories. Her busy fingers stroked over his thigh until her thumb slid over the waist of his sweats.

The muddied memories of his parents warred with years of watching ideal families in movies. Victor remembered enough to know that he was loved, but he had missed out on the best parts of family life. Bringing home his first girlfriend. Learning to shoot from his dad.

His mother and father watching him graduate medical school.

"Close your eyes, Victor," she whispered against his ear, lips brushing the delicate curve of flesh.

Zoe's capable hands slid over his thighs, down to his knees then back upward to his hips. Her fingertips skimmed and danced over his burgeoning erection.

According to Ethan, it was the sort of stress relief Victor needed.

"Zoe, I don't…" He wanted to warn her that she was wasting her time and that the inevitable panic attack would bring an abrupt end to her plans. If he'd known what was on her mind, he would have taken one of his anxiety pills. Given himself a stim shot. Something.

"Shhh…" she soothed, her hand dipping into his pants.

His abs tightened in anticipation, body stiff and tense against her, yet so very still that his chance to deny her passed by harmlessly. He had pride. So much of it, even if it had been shredded time and time again by Hannah over the course of their two-year relationship. His anxiety attacks led to two incidents of failing to perform to her standards, but his ex-fiancée never allowed him to live it down. She told everyone who would listen.

"I can't–" Her fingers felt warm against cool flesh, cupping him with such a welcoming touch that he shivered in delight and barely contained desire.

Victor couldn't bear to speak the words out loud, to tell her that her effort was in vain, that he'd never be able to provide her what she wanted. He broke out into a cold sweat.

"Allow me to try," Zoe pleaded softly. "I want to do this for you, but if you don't we can stop. No questions asked."

Zoe's kiss elicited a tremble from him, a shiver down his spine that seemed to race along every electrified nerve. The muscles of his body tensed in a wholly different way.

The slow pumping motion from her natural hand ceased and her moving weight shifted the mattress. Zoe stood up from the bed.

Victor closed his arms around her waist and drew her close, burying his face into the small valley between her breasts. "Why are you so kind to me?" Women of Zoe's caliber came few and far between, littered amidst a history of selfish females. Maybe he attracted users like moths to a flame, drawing them to his gentle and sensitive personality. They saw past the shaky confidence that was his protective cover and honed in on the damage beneath.

"I'm rather sweet on you, Doc. Being mean isn't in my general nature."

"But you care," he pointed out. He considered the flirtatious crew members who found a greater interest in his career choices than his actual personality. Leaning back again, he gazed up at her to hold eye contact.

"I do," she replied in the same quiet tones. Her fingers threaded through his dark hair, trailing down to his nape then around to his jawline. As his heart hammered in his chest, she knelt before him. "You're remarkably easy to like. Anyone who doesn't see that doesn't deserve you."

***

Victor felt whole again. For as long as he could remember, he'd struggled with intimacy, and only a single woman displayed the patience Zoe freely gave him. Ylona. It felt wrong to think of her now while another woman's lips pressed intimately against his inner thigh, but in that moment, he also realized one thing; Ylona would have approved of Zoe.

Elorans didn't believe in Heaven, Hell, or any traditional afterlife, but they believed a surviving loved one deserved the chance to resume a happy existence. And Victor wanted so badly to be happy again.

When Zoe rose to her feet before him, he wrapped one arm around her waist and drew her near. "Stay tonight, Zo?"

"Will you be here when I wake up? I…" She kissed the top of his head and stroked her hand up his back. "I don't have assignment tomorrow."

"I do, but I think I can swing something." Victor tugged her easily into the bed alongside him and arranged the blankets over them. "Our chief medical officer sort of loves me, and I think this time, I don't mind using a connection or two."

"Doctor Oshiro seems nice." Zoe nestled in closer, one leg drawing up over his. After a moment, she seemed to reconsider and stretched her leg out. Victor caught her by the thigh and pulled the limb back up.

"Known him since I was a scrawny kid. The Royal Navy denied me the first time I tried to get in." He chuckled against her dark hair at the memory of his younger self. "I didn't make the weight requirement. I don't know what made him do it, but he wrote me a waiver and took me home with him. He even told them he'd have me meeting all the regs by the time they shipped me to boot." *Hell, he even lied on my psych eval. I should have failed, but he lied for me.*

"I have a hard time imagining you as scrawny." Her trailing kisses ended at his chin. Black strands of hair tickled his neck and shoulder. "You grew up nice. Look how far you've come, fixing up grunts like me."

"Yeah… Doc had a huge impact on me. I knew then that I wanted to be a doctor, but I didn't think I'd get accepted into school. I guess for a kid who missed getting his certs, I must have scored really big on more than just my entrance exam. The commodore was on the review team."

"And now you serve with both men who helped shape your life."

"Lucky me, huh?"

"It must be nice, having role models and friends like that. I haven't dealt with Commodore Bishop at all, but I hear good things. Usually, my sort doesn't run into him unless we're in trouble or getting an award. Tends to be better that way."

Heh. If you knew you were raiding with him in the game... "Mm. He's not a bad guy. Just has to set that impression around the rest of you. You should see him during liberty."

"No, no, I get that." She chuckled softly and turned her head to nuzzle his throat. "He kidnaps officers and forces them to have a good time."

"I had a horrible time," he muttered. "Some little tart from logistics tried to rub her tits in my face."

"Torturous."

"In this day and age, there's no excuse for obvious false tits, hon."

Snickers turned to full blown laughter. "Oh, you mean, um, Keita. I was on the Armstrong with her six years back when she first joined up. The girls were *much* smaller then, yes."

"I figured. She should have paid a few more quid to get it done right."

After he released her with a sigh, Zoe cuddled back into his side with her head pillowed on his shoulder. "There's no rush on anything, Victor."

"Hm? I didn't complain."

"No, but you're... frustrated about something. And I'm willing to wait 'till you're ready to talk. Because I know what it's like not to want let people get close."

"You're practically naked in my bed, Zoe. Doesn't get much closer than that."

"You know what I mean. Would you believe that it took me a long time to feel okay with people looking at me after the accident? I thought they saw the scars and tech. Not me. Not anymore."

"Your arm is beautiful, Zo. Like the rest of you. I can barely see a scar here." He traced his finger over the hint of discoloration, estimating the point of fusion between her shoulder and the biotic limb. "Besides, I'm a cyberware doc. I'd have to surrender my license if I didn't think plasteel and carbon fiber bolts are sexy."

"Careful, doc, or I'll think you like my arm best." Her breath huffed with amusement against his skin.

"There's a lot of parts of you I like," he teased, shifting so that Zoe rolled to her back again. He needed a moment to concentrate, and he couldn't achieve the clarity of mind that he needed while she pressed against him beneath the sheets. "I enjoy our time together, Zoe. Okay? I don't think that needs to be said, or you wouldn't be here with me."

"I'd hope not. I hadn't expected this but... I like it. I like you. I just want you to know that if you ever do want to talk about something, you can. And if you'd rather I mind my business, I'll do that, too."

"No, I promised that if you asked again, I'd tell you. Again, I'd prefer not to ruin our night, so I'll make it brief. I have anxiety problems. Oshiro waived a lot of issues when he met me, and I can't show him enough gratitude for taking a chance."

"Yeah? But you seem so confident in medical. Never flustered. Sometimes you seem a little shy, but I sort of figured that was due to your fan club. I'd hide away, too." Zoe quieted, and in a small voice she whispered, "Someone hurt you really bad once, didn't they?"

Twenty-six years later, those memories continued to haunt Victor. He closed his eyes and swallowed the rising lump in his throat. "A long time ago, Zo. I've tried to put it in the past but... every once in a while it's there. I've had trouble all my life," he confessed to her in the dark. "Even saw an empathologist once when I was twenty. I laid on a couch, talked about my feelings, and she did whatever her profession does. Nothing really worked." Until he'd met

Zoe, Ylona had been the only woman in his life to ever show him dignity and patience.

"But you were engaged once…"

"That's why I broke it off with Hannah. I couldn't make her happy. It wasn't fair to her anymore. What kind of husband was I going to be?" She never failed to remind him of the time he wasted.

"There's more to a relationship than sex every night, Victor."

"It wasn't fair to her," he repeated.

Zoe frowned up at him. "Did she tell you that?"

"Doesn't matter what she said, Zoe. It's history. Last I heard, she married some admiral and retired to be a happy homemaker at the end of her twenty. Three kids in five years."

"Seems like maybe she wasn't the woman for you."

"We had some great times together, so I'm happy for her," Victor replied honestly, despite the stories she told and the rumors she'd spread following their split. After a while, he even convinced himself that he'd deserved it for stringing her along by pretending to be whole and normal.

"Because you're a good person."

"If you don't want to waste your time, I understand, Zoe. I'm happy with where I am in my life, and I won't hold it against you."

The smile faded from her features and Zoe caressed his cheek, her golden eyes sincere. "I don't know what *this* is yet but… I'd like to explore it. With you. But only if you want that as well."

"Sweetie, I was so anxious to see you again this evening that Kathleen spent most of our shift making fun of me."

"I, uh, ran into her this morning. In your bathroom."

He tilted his head back to look at her, confusion apparent on his face. "You didn't lock the door?"

Zoe giggled and turned her face against his arm. "Sorry. I'm not used to locking doors. We still use a shared space in the enlisted section. A bunch of women fighting over three showers."

"The bint didn't even tell me. She played it dumb the entire time she questioned me."

"Well, we didn't talk or anything. She sort of blinked at me a few times then backed out again mumbling about not seeing anything."

"Of course not. That isn't her style. She must have expected me to offer it up to her."

"That was nice of her." Light pecks traveled up his shoulder and neck, little kisses that wormed their way into his heart and filled him with warmth.

"I'm glad you're here," Victor said impulsively. "I mean it, Zoe. I enjoy when we're together."

"I like you, too. And…" Her gaze dropped downward then back up to his face. "You didn't have any problems at all," she whispered playfully, moving in closer.

Victor succumbed to the sweet claiming of Zoe's mouth. The slow, drugging kiss stole his breath as readily as her passionate and hungry displays of ardor. "Mm… what can I say? You bring out the best in me."

CHAPTER 15

Eventually, Victor took Hart's suggestion and invited Zoe to tea at the small cafe manned by the crew lounge. After a quiet month of dating in supposed secrecy – he somehow squeezed in time for her amidst his investigation into the missing cyborgs – people stared at the unusual sight of Commander del Toro laughing with a lady friend in the open.

Victor casually ignored the lookie-loos in favor of biting into his pumpkin seed muffin. Once Harvest season arrived in Bromwicham, the Jemison's homeport, they'd become inundated with supplies of squash and other fresh goods. A lot of people donated to their ships, and it helped that the hydroponics lab kept a successful farm.

"Are they really so shocked to see you with someone?" Zoe murmured in a hushed voice. She leaned in close to his side and tried not to stare back at the gawkers in the ship's pub.

Crewmembers were free to spend their own funds on a limited menu that rotated out monthly to change up the offerings. Wine and beer were also available for purchase, each member allotted two servings in a twenty-four our period.

"Pretend they're not there. That's what I'm doing. People have spotted you in the corridor outside of my room, so you'd think the news would be well spread by now," he joked lightheartedly.

"The news that Hottie del Toro is currently off the market?"

"Very much off the market and completely happy with that." He kissed her cheek shamelessly, practically oblivious to the glowering eyes of envy. In reality, the reaction wasn't as grand or widespread as expected. Most of the crew didn't seem to care, save for a few embittered females who had tried their wiles and failed to entice him.

"Me, too." Zoe leaned in and stole a bite of his snack.

"If it wasn't so late, I'd get a pumpkin pie latte," Victor grumbled. "That's the only good thing about this damned season. You want the rest of this? I'm getting a slice of cake instead."

"Ask for a decaf."

"Then it isn't coffee. It's just dirty water masquerading as coffee."

Zoe nearly choked on the tea she sipped to wash down his muffin. She swiped at her eyes and failed at muffling her laughter. "I learned something about you: never bring Victor decaf. Got it. Anyways, Radha glared daggers at me the entire time I was in our quarters. By tomorrow, she'll have probably progressed to the silent treatment which, frankly, I am perfectly content with. Can't wait."

"I heard she's pro-human-human. I'm surprised she'd even show me an ounce of interest unless it was all some diabolic plot to reclaim me for our race."

"She was pretty quick with the dish on you when I first arrived, after my appointment with you. Said a cousin or someone like that served with you and that you dumped your fiancée for an alien."

"There's only a hair of truth to that rumor. I did leave Hannah as I said, but I never left her for Ylona. After Hannah and I split, I met Ylona while drinking at a bar in Pacifica Cove. We crossed paths again about seven months later when our ship docked on Elora. Hannah just assumed her to be at the source of our breakup all along. Too convenient, she said."

"The Elorans are pretty…"

"They are," he agreed.

"She must have been special."

Victor nodded quietly at first, maintaining careful control of his emotions. Their surroundings didn't serve as an appropriate place to have such a poignant discussion, but he couldn't help the path that their conversation took. "I just want you to understand that I don't have a thing for aliens as the gossip claims. I had a thing for *her*. I didn't care that she was an alien. Like you said, there's more to a relationship than sex."

"What happened to make you two part ways?"

"She died," he answered quietly.

Zoe took Victor's hand for a supportive squeeze. "I'm sorry, Victor... it's none of my business."

"No, it's quite all right. I... well, it's about time that I..." *Began to face what happened and accepted that the only woman to ever truly care for me also died because of me.* "So, okay. I'm getting a slice of cake and a latte. You want anything?"

Her uncertain smile nagged at his guilty heart. "I'm good. I don't see how you stuff yourself with sweets and look this great. I should count myself lucky."

"When I'm not dragged into a raid in Spellbound or attempting to impress you with my charming wit, I spend the rest of my time exercising in my room."

"I'll have to challenge you to pull-ups one day."

"You're on." He grinned at her and strolled to the counter to make his next order. They shared both the coffee and the cake, but only after Zoe stole another bite of his sweet pastry on the sly.

"Are you one of those girls who will never order anything of her own, but picks meager bites belonging to everyone else?

"You're putting tempting, delicious things in my path; I caved. But I promise to eat a full meal and not peck like a bird if you take me out."

"When I take you out," he corrected her. "We're coming up on our next port soon."

The date ended with a brief, affectionate kiss that Victor willingly initiated. Before leaving the area, he bought a mug of Ethan's favorite earl grey, made to his preferences.

A quick trip to the bio-farm for a treat to sweeten the pot. Ethan had a weakness for the gene-spliced chapples grown in the bio-farm. The juicy fruits had a delicious cherry-flavored center within their crisp apple flesh.

Una won't care if I take just one... Technically, they were supposed to visit her for a Harvest Badge, but Victor only planned to pluck one. *I'll have Jem let her know in the morning.* Sure, Una wouldn't recognize a single missing apple from her beloved tree, but it was the polite thing to do.

"Oh shit! Rank coming!"

Several shadowed figures darted off and a group of over a half dozen men and women quickly scattered down the different paths. Victor raised a brow and proceeded forward and down the darkened path leading to the rear of the bio-farm's starboard side. There, Una, the farm's Chief Botanist, kept a five hundred gallon basin filled to the brim with organic trash. The evening's dinner leftovers from all three mess halls and the civilian deck glistened wetly. The lid was off and a pair of legs angled out of the steamy slop pile. A hand clutched at the rim beside a long rubber air-line passed along the floor for oxygen exchange.

Victor scanned to the left to follow the hose. A young man in evening dress attire, perhaps hoping to go unseen, crouched beside the source of the airline. His fingers were on a bold yellow sign announcing their unfortunate captive's plight. Busted, he leapt up and snapped to attention.

"Sir!"

"Name and rank."

"Corporal Danyl Speirs, sir."

Victor sighed and set the lidded mug of tea on the nearby bench. "Who's in the compost?"

"Etherington, sir," the young man admitted.

"Assault of an officer is a dischargeable offense, but you're the only one who didn't flee when I approached. Why's that?"

"I'm not a scared lubbard to be running away, sir. I'm willin' to face disciplinary measures for my part in this. I know what I did was wrong."

Etherington remained in the compost muck during their discussion. Under normal circumstances, Victor would have hauled the officer out first before resuming the conversation, but something bothered him about Etherington's predicament.

"How'd you catch him?" Victor asked the young man.

The freckle-faced kid rubbed the back of his neck and cleared his throat awkwardly. "Well…"

"It's okay, you can tell me."

"With his pants around his ankles, sir."

Holding back his snicker became an exercise in control. "What? I need details, Speirs. Start from the beginning."

"I won't name names."

Victor raised one brow. Years of practice with his subordinates gave him the edge required to keep a strict poker face. "It's admirable that you're protecting your mates. Tell me why you did it. I want the honest truth from you and only that. Don't sugarcoat it and don't feed me a load of hogwash you believe I want to hear."

"To be frank, sir, we all got tired of his demeaning attitude. I mean, I know we're enlisted, but that doesn't make us lazy or stupid. A bunch of us got together and found a rank-tagger to lure him to the bio-farm. She did it happily."

Ah. Victor maintained his stern countenance despite the desire to double over with laughter. "You're dismissed."

The corporal stared at him. "I'm dismissed?"

"Yeah. Go on, get out of here. I didn't see a thing. Everyone was gone when I arrived."

After Corporal Speirs was long out of sight, Victor tugged Etherington's booted foot and freed him from the greasy mire. Once he'd set his feet to solid ground, the younger officer spit out the mouthpiece to the oxygen line and wiped a lump of mashed potato and gravy from his face. Partially decomposed food and fresh compost offerings clung to his uniform and stuck in his hair.

"You're out of regulation there, Lieutenant Commander."

"What? You can't possibly be serious."

"I'm very serious. Your uniform looks like shit. Your boots aren't shined."

Etherington gaped, like a fish out of the water. His mouth opened and closed several times but no sound emerged.

"Well?" Victor crossed his arms over his chest.

"My father is going to hear about this!"

"Hear what? That you were ganked while an enlisted girl slobbed your knob? Ah, yes, that's precisely what I'd want my father to know."

Etherington's face went beet red.

"I expect you to be up to standards and outside my office tomorrow morning at 0600."

"I was assaulted!"

"Excuses. I didn't witness an assault."

"I—"

Victor arched a brow and Etherington fell silent, showing the first signs of good judgement.

"Now get out of here and clean yourself up. You're a disgrace to the uniform looking like that."

"Yes, sir."

After the soiled lieutenant was out of sight, Victor exhaled a relieved sigh. "Jem, delete all data pertaining to this incident." He had lucked out; a smarter officer would have demanded Jem to replay the event.

"I cannot do that, Victor."

"Cannot or won't? Use your judgment in this instance, Jem. From what you've observed aboard this ship, would you say that the lieutenant deserved his punishment?" No one deserved humiliation on a daily basis, and maybe now that Etherington had a taste of his own medicine, he wouldn't be so quick to abuse his subordinates.

The program remained silent for a moment. Her final answer brought a grin to his face. "I am able to perform a security upgrade at the risk of losing pertinent data related to the last half hour in the bio-farm."

"Please do."

Chuckling, Victor resumed his mission and took the lift to the bridge, carrying with him the hope to bribe the ship's commanding officer for a small and insignificant favor.

"Do you have a moment, Ethan?" He decided to keep the news of Etherington's humiliation to himself, wary of bringing trouble on the heads of the participating servicemen and women.

Ethan glanced away from his console and groaned when Victor presented him with the chapple. "Are you finally deciding to use our friendship to your advantage?"

"Apt assumption to make. Yes. Here's your tea. I made it just for you. Milk and honey as you like it." Victor set the hot mug in the cozy armchair's cup holder.

"You never ask anything, so tell me, what is it that you want?" Ethan warily accepted his bribes.

"I have a friend out in this sector," Victor promptly said. "Doctor Mathias Campbell retired from the Navy last year. He's a good man and he's the only board licensed physician on his planet."

"The *planet*?" Ethan repeated.

"Kantarn has three colonies within a hundred miles of one another. One is practically a city now, or so I'm told. The council is planning to apply to New Cambridge in hopes of opening a doctoral college with his help. He's also the man who helped me with the research for my theory on neurocybernetics."

"All right. This'll delay our arrival to Elora by a fortnight, but we can swing it. Navigator Agosti, set our coordinates to Kantarn."

"Aye aye, Commodore."

"Thanks, mate. I appreciate it. I've tried contacting him by message twice this week, and…"

"No response?"

"Nothing," Victor replied.

"We'll be there in five days. Tell Raines I said hello. Brilliant choice by the way, mate."

Victor grinned at him. "Of course I will. We enjoyed tea together, so I won't be seeing her again until tomorrow. I plan to return to the medical bay to resume reading the medical histories on the psychics who were taken. There's something odd about them that I want to evaluate further, but I just can't make it click."

"Keep me posted."

CHAPTER 16

The Jemison's bio-farm remained open twenty-four hours a day, all 365 days of the standard galactic year. While its primary purpose provided nutritious food to the ship's crew, Doctor Una Valentine, the ship's civilian botanist, had developed one additional perk to the system. Named for its peaceful qualities, Zen Time granted every member of the crew exclusive and private use of the space for two hours each month. Some crewmen pooled their hours for group yoga classes or friendly cookouts, but most people spent the personal time for private picnics and dates with a loved one.

"Did you bring me out here to snog in the trees?"

Zoe laughed and leaned her cheek against his arm. "Well, we can kiss if you want, but I came out here for some sunshine since Elora has been put off for a bit."

"Sorry about that. Kind of my fault."

The bio-farm's artificial sunlight granted the benefits of a natural setting during their lengthy deployments, but the synthetic sun didn't compare or match the beauty of a true sunset at dusk.

"I forgive you, but only if you help me fill a basket." Zoe tugged him down a path. They plucked a bounty of blackberries and strawberries in one basket then packed the second with fresh raspberries, always eating as many as they picked.

"C'mon, sit down here. I see some clusters near the bottom," Zoe urged him.

Victor obediently crouched near her to fetch a few bunches of ripe berries. Doctor Valentine had placed small green flags at some bushes, indicating the juiciest selections. "Are we going to eat all of this, or do you intend to drag me into the lounge to bake a pie, too?" he griped.

"Do you bake?" she teased. "Half goes to Una for the galleys and I was going to greedily hoard the rest."

"I've burned a pie or two in my time. My cakes are better."

"*You* bake cakes?"

"With real buttercream frosting."

"Obviously we need a kitchen date next time."

"Ha. If I can't talk one of the chiefs out of a couple of steaks in the mess, I'll make a pick up at our next port and cook for you. I'm glad you pulled me in here… thanks for that."

"After all the work you've been doing, I thought a break would be nice."

"I know, and I appreciate it. It's just that I'm worried, Zo. The more we learn about all these abductions, the more disturbing the pattern becomes. Cyborgs, psychics, and kids."

"How has your investigation been going?

"Awful. I notified Mathias that I'd like his opinion on a theory I've developed about the recent abduction, and he hasn't uttered a word. There are no reports about Kantarn going under fire from pirates, so I can't fathom any justification for his failure to respond. Something must have happened."

"Could he be busy? I mean, you get real focused on your work sometimes."

"If it were only a matter of days I could buy that, but I've been trying to reach him for weeks. There's also a high concentration of abandoned colonies near Kantarn. Doubtful that's a coincidence either. If pirates aren't already assessing their worth, they will be soon. I'm afraid we'll arrive to find the entire colony in shambles or an attack in progress."

Zoe attempted to soothe his concerns. "United Command would have reported that when the Jemison altered her course for Kantarn."

Victor sighed. "You're right." If not for the recent theory he'd developed about the correlation between the abductions of the children and cyborgs, he wouldn't have even realized something was amiss. The entire thing felt wrong.

"We'll get it solved, but for now we have two hours alone. You're *supposed* to relax during Zen Time."

"I *am* relaxed. It's difficult to feel anything but relaxed when I'm with you. These past few weeks have meant more to me than you can ever know, hon."

Words alone failed to convey what Victor felt in his heart. Jem's soothing classical music filtered through the bio-farm speakers, treating the pair to a romantic blend of piano, cello, and violin.

"They mean a lot to me, too." Her fingers slid down his arm and twined with his. "Well worth the grueling hours of work to earn extra time alone in here. Una is a rigid taskmaster."

Victor chuckled nervously. "Let's take a break for a bit, okay? There's something I've been wanting to talk to you about."

"Wait... This isn't a break up talk, right? I mean, I know I'm younger and all but that doesn't make a difference to me."

"What? No. Nothing like that. Where'd you get such a silly idea in your head?"

"Sorry." She ducked her head and kicked a pebble down the path. "Last time a guy told me he 'wanted to talk', it didn't end well."

"Zo, sweetheart, look at me." He tilted her chin up and claimed her lips in a light kiss. "Furthest thing from my mind, I swear."

They settled on an open patch of clover and grass with their basket. Zoe allowed herself the comfort of his lap, making herself welcome by scooting in close and setting both arms around his neck.

"There aren't many people that know about this, but I believe you've guessed at a bit of it already."

"You carry a lot of pain," she began hesitantly. "And I know there are lots of wild rumors out there about your last ship but we already talked about that."

"I do, and there are. Before I came to the Jemison, I was in a bad place, Zo. I screwed up bad," he admitted candidly. Leaning back with one hand on the grass beneath him for support, Victor placed the other arm around her waist and gazed up at the streaks of false cloud cover across the serene orange and pink bio-farm sky. "I never told you about why I almost lost my commission."

"I figured it was your business and if you wanted it to be known you'd tell me." The light breeze blew bits of leaves and fallen flower petals over them.

"I do want to tell you." So much, that he'd rehearsed it to Jem until the artificial intelligence program assured him that his anxiety had dramatically diminished to a level suitable for romantic conversation. *There's nothing romantic about admitting a suicide attempt*, he thought wryly. A better opportunity wouldn't come.

"Whenever you're ready. There's no rush, Victor."

I can do this. Like ripping off a Band-Aid, just get it done. "I pocketed a lot of meds from the drug cart on the Glenn, and I tried to kill myself in my room. It was probably one of the stupidest things I've ever done, but not the worst of my regrets." Most of all, he lamented his choice to deploy on the Glenn for one final galactic tour before retirement. He and Ylona should have been settling down by now on Albion, or even her home planet where humans accepted their marriage more readily. They would have adopted an Eloran orphan and begun to raise a family.

And he wouldn't have met Zoe, a possibility which struck him as painfully wrong.

Zoe patiently stroked the back of his neck and head. "You're not thinking about doing it again are you?"

"No!" he blurted out quickly. His next words came softer, almost apologetic for raising his voice. "That isn't why I told you. Promise."

"Better to be safe than sorry. So after that, what made you stay in?" Zoe leaned in and rested her cheek on his shoulder.

"Where else was I to go? I have no family. My last living relative died three years after I enlisted. They were going to force a medical discharge on me," he explained. "Stuff you already guessed at. Sometimes I wonder if you have a touch of empathy, Zo, because you're a little too sharp."

She laughed quietly and shook her head. "Nah, I tested too low on those entrance exams they do but it does run intermittently in my family."

"You always seem to know what to say… It's like you're too good to be true. I spend half of our time together expecting to wake up." From a beautiful dream that was beyond anything he deserved. Impulsively, he kissed her, a brush of his lips against her brow.

"Funny, I think the same thing about you sometimes."

"Nah. I'm not that special," he muttered. "Anyway, I count myself among the lucky that they permitted me to remain. They relocated me to Paradiso for treatment. One day after a round of gaming, Ethan asked if I'd prefer to be aboard the Jemison. He put in the transfer request and here I am."

"I should send him a thank you card."

"You've thanked him plenty. You just don't know it."

Ethan would never forgive him if he blew his online cover, so Victor merely grinned and zipped his lips on the matter, miming the gesture with one hand. He settled back against the grass and chuckled at her. "I'm sure if you put your mind to it, you'll figure it out one day."

"Hmm. Mysterious." Zoe resettled beside him, keeping her head pillowed against his chest. The soft music in the background rose in volume at a gradual pace, providing a romantic touch to their cuddles. Victor ran his fingers through her hair and drew in slow, deep breaths.

"Thank you for telling me." A hug accompanied her simple words. "And I'm glad you stayed in."

"Well, the Empire kinda spent a lot of money on my certifications. I want to credit Ethan and Yuki toward United Command's decision to let me stay, but it'd be dumb to believe money wasn't involved. You don't have to worry about me going off the deep end again. They've got Oshiro and Jem watching me. I can't take a leak without her chiming in."

"That must get tiresome. The music's not so bad though. Besides, it's become a plus to being with you."

He didn't hear condemnation or pity – only a genuine concern that warmed his heart for Zoe all the more. "Yeah… I've become accustomed to her poking into my business. There's one more thing that I forgot to mention to you."

Her head lifted from his chest and turned to look down at him. A loose lock of her dark hair fell against his throat, tickling his skin. "What's that?"

"All this time, I never felt truly grateful that the Glenn busted me. Until now. Being with you changes everything."

Choosing action over words, Zoe kissed him.

CHAPTER 17

The Jemison reached Kantarn's system five days later, but a meteor storm delayed their arrival to the planet itself by another forty-eight hours.

Kantarn's space traffic control tower seemed reluctant to grant the Jemison clearance. After Ethan shoved his weight around, they were permitted into the planetary atmosphere and directed to a landing space within city limits.

The plan was to allow Victor to go down and reconnect with his former comrade while Ethan coordinated with the planet's governor and council. They had to be prepared in the event of a pirate attack. Kantarn had all of the qualities of the other colonies that had gone dark before it: secluded, small, and connected to cybernetics.

"Well, don't you clean up nice," Zoe commented as she neatly knotted Victor's tie. She smoothed her fingers down his chest and smiled up at him.

"Where'd you learn to do this?"

"My dad," she replied. "He wore a tie every day and I was fascinated. He always told me I didn't need to learn it, since women on my planet are only allowed to wear dresses."

"I've never visited Tallulah. Really? Dresses all the time?"

"Really," she confirmed with a big grin on her face. "I guess that's why I always wear pants and boots to shore leave. Makes me feel like a rebel."

"True rebels wear lace lingerie. I thought I should tell you."

Zoe swatted him playfully and leaned up for a kiss. "I hope everything is okay with your friend."

"Me too."

Victor exited the ship's airlock and descended the ramp into a village occupied by antisocial townsfolk. They hurried away and avoided him, parting like the Red Sea.

"Hello? Excuse me, young miss?" A woman reluctantly paused and spared him a glance. Victor continued gratefully. "I'd like directions to Doctor Campbell's facilities."

After she gave directions, Victor made the three mile walk across the township toward the colonial medical center. Its stylish exterior conflicted with the rest of the modest town. *Maybe he put some of his own money into building this place... wouldn't surprise me. Campbell is the kind of guy to give back to the community like that.*

Smiling, Victor strode up to reception despite the wary look of distrust he received from the woman behind the desk. Her painted lips pursed into a frown.

"Good afternoon, I'm Doctor Victor del Toro," he introduced politely. "Is it possible to speak with Doctor Campbell?"

"Do you have an appointment?"

"No, but I'm an old friend. He asked me to drop by whenever I was in the sector so here I am. Would you kindly inform him that I've arrived?"

The woman skimmed her fingertips over a floating hologram pad. The thin glass glowed orange beneath her touch. "Doctor Campbell is currently in a delicate procedure."

The hairs on the back of his neck prickled. "I'll wait." Victor forced a thin smile and demonstrated his refusal to leave by claiming a seat in the lobby. The receptionist watched him with watery blue eyes, distrust swimming in her gaze all the while. They became embroiled in a bitter staring contest that lasted for a half hour before she caved and tapped a few buttons on her monitor.

"Doctor Campbell, you have an eager visitor from the Royal Navy here to see you at your earliest convenience." She paused, presumably to listen to Campbell respond from the other end of the link. "He claims to be Doctor Victor del Toro. Yes, I will inform him."

Victor pretended to hold interest in the news feed scrolling across the wall instead of jumping to his feet.

"Doctor Campbell will be out shortly," the receptionist relayed with a cool smile on her plastic face. Everything from the flawless arch of her immaculate eyebrows to her sculpted chin and nose advertised Campbell's work. He'd always had a fantastic talent for reconstructive and cosmetic surgery, which he put to work on scarred soldiers.

"Thank you."

Heavy footsteps announced his friend's arrival. Doctor Campbell had always been a heavy man but his time out of the Navy had added weight to his already bulky frame, especially around his middle.

"Victor, you should have called ahead," he said, offering out his hand. Perspiration dotted his brow along his hairline.

"I did. Or I tried anyway." Victor put on a smile and shook Mathias' hand. "Since we passed this way along our route to the next port, I wanted to stop in and say hello, as you *asked*." He added a touch of passive aggressive emphasis to get his point across.

The pudgy man's nervous chuckle grated Victor's nerves. "So I did…" his voice trailed off and he cleared his throat. "I wish I could show you around, Vic, I really do."

The hated nickname drew a wince. "The Jemison will be here a day at least. I can return tomorrow if that's better. I'm really looking forward to seeing your work."

"I'm afraid that won't be possible."

Genuine puzzlement creased Victor's features. The man before him was a far cry from the colleague and friend he remembered. "Anything I can do to help take the load off while I'm here, Mathias?"

"That's kind, but unnecessary. The fact is, I'm heading off to the neighboring colonies tomorrow to see private clients, so I really do need to get back to my packing. Don't want to forget anything."

"Do you need a hand?"

"No, no. I have it covered, thanks. Next time, all right chap?"

"Next time," Victor agreed, cheeks aching from the stiff smile he forced himself to maintain.

***

"I tell you, it was dodgy." Victor shrugged out of his jacket and tossed it over his arm. "The whole place gave me the creeps."

"Lieutenant Shahid Amir stepped off ship for a time and returned with some troubling observations." Ethan rubbed his chin. "Lockhart, too."

"Something's not right, Ethan. Campbell has always had a bad poker face and that hasn't changed. I had the distinct impression he was hiding something. We aren't wanted here, and my war buddy asked me to leave. He had no interest in showing me his greatest life's work, when half a year ago he couldn't wait for me to see."

"So what are you asking?"

"Send a small team back in with me."

"Granted. If they don't want us here, well, they'll just have to sod off and accept that we're the ones with the firearms."

Ethan never pushed his weight around and typically believed in allowing colonies to handle their own affairs. For him to take such a heavy-handed approach could mean only a single thing: the governor had rebuffed his warning of a very real danger. If the leader of a colony disregarded his warning and failed to keep the Empire's citizens safe, it became a priority of the military to take prompt action.

"Give me an hour to call United Command. I want to make Admiral Novak aware just in case this encounter goes tits up."

"Fair enough."

Their tactical response team received the go ahead in less than an hour. This time they took a small shuttle directly to the hospital helipad.

After the events on Athena, Lopez took over as pilot for Rogers and left the group without a communications expert. Eager to return his boots to actual combat, Trevor volunteered to fill the vacancy and Victor supported the appointment. They counted on his psychic abilities to provide an edge, a predictor against the unknown.

"DuPrie, when we get inside I want you to monitor the main entrance. Ears open. I'm sure they'll have some things to say."

"Yes, sir." The activation of Saskia's natural gene ability blended her into the slate gray shuttle background. Within seconds, her highly specialized armor had adapted to her camouflage. She moved alongside them outside while appearing to be little more than a barely visible heat wave shimmer in the air.

Wide-eyed civilians watched them enter the building and approach the receptionist with the phony customer service smile.

"No need to call for Doctor Campbell," Victor gave the same receptionist a thin smile. "Go ahead and buzz us in."

If the woman had ideas to argue, she never followed through on them. Her pale gaze darted to the various weapons and soon the security doors flashed green. Three guards met them halfway down the hall.

"Gentlemen, stand down." Daniels grinned at the men. "Royal Navy. We're here with the full approval and authority of the United Command."

It's like he's almost hoping they'll put up a fuss, Victor thought with a shake of his head. To their credit, the guards backed off and allowed them to pass unhindered.

"Something doesn't feel right here, Commander Daniels."

"What do you mean, Lockhart?" Daniels asked in a low tone.

"I can't put a finger to it. It's just like... *everyone* is hiding something." Trevor shook his head and cast a wary glance around the sterile interior. "And... the background noise is excessive. Too much of it for so small a place and what they have listed on their patient registry." He raised both hands to his temples and shut his watery eyes, clearly afflicted with one of his migraines.

"We'll keep an eye out. Are you going to be okay here?"

"I'm fine, Doc. Which way is his office?"

Victor gestured down the hall. "It should be down this way. He always liked to be back by the labs."

"You didn't meet him in his office before?" Zoe asked.

"No, and that was another tip off. He made me wait in the lobby and came out to me."

Six rooms lined the hall, but Victor spotted a patient in only one of them. Nothing they had seen so far indicated any surgical or time-consuming procedures. *Whatever has been keeping Mathias busy, it's not his normal patients.*

"Hold up a minute. It's this way." Trevor stopped by a door marked as a restricted area. "I know the office is down the hall but... this ominous feeling, it's coming through here."

Victor hesitated, but he trusted in Trevor's abilities.

Daniels led the squad through the door and down a single staircase that emptied into a green-lit corridor. Each of the four rooms they passed housed a mechanical rig as lavish as Victor's surgical theater on the ship.

Where the hell did he get all of this? Certainly not on the Empire's budget. He can't afford it either.

"There's blood on the floor," Zoe muttered. Her enhanced sight picked out obscure details the others missed.

"Raines!"

Daniels knocked the smaller marine to the floor and threw up his arm to block the security laser aimed at her back. The beam cut through his armor and seared his skin, filling the hall with the smell of burning hair and skin. Zoe rolled to her back on the floor and took out the machinery with two well-placed shots.

"Here, let me look." Fairchild moved to the injured commander's side and inspected the wound. "It's not deep and it's cauterized at least."

"Are you okay?" Victor asked quietly while helping Zoe up from the floor. She nodded, but the doctor left nothing up to chance. A bio-scan assessed her condition and confirmed that she'd emerged unscathed from the incident.

Trevor searched the wall for an access panel and hooked his computer in. "It was operated remotely. Someone clearly doesn't want us snooping around."

Victor's fingers tightened into a fist at his side.

"Can we expect more tricks like this?" Zoe asked. She supported Daniels' arm while Fairchild wrapped the injury.

"I can try and hack into the system," Trevor offered. "If we're lucky I can gain all remote control, or at least lock out any other consoles like this."

"Do it," Victor said.

They lurked behind him in the chilly hall while Trevor toiled at the device. Anxiety bubbled in the pit of Victor's stomach and drove him to pacing.

"Done. I've disabled all the doors and security. There shouldn't be another surprise like this. The room at the end is the only one in use."

"Let's go say hello then," Daniel grunted.

Frosted glass on the door blocked their view of the room within. Daniels put his hand on the knob, made a silent count to three then slammed the portal open. Zoe, gun out and extended, rushed through first with Abernathy a step behind her. Daniels followed with the rest of the marines and then Victor and his medics.

"Oh my god…" The nightmarish scene scorched itself into his mind and turned his stomach.

It wasn't a medical laboratory; it was a chop shop. Fairchild appeared green in the face and Trevor backed out of the room entirely.

The pain must be excruciating for him to feel. Victor didn't envy the psychic's ability.

A cold corpse lay on the examination table. The young man, barely out of his teens, showed extensive cybernetic modification -- but most of the components had been removed, leaving yawning holes in their place. A shallow pan of pink-tinged solution lay to the side of the corpse on a metal tray, filled with gore-covered cybernetics. Three more bodies were laid out on cold tables at the back of the room.

Mathias Campbell stripped off his bloody sani-gloves and discarded them into the bin. Wise enough to understand the gravity of the situation, and that his guards wouldn't be coming to his aid, he stepped away from the table with his hands raised in a gesture of surrender.

"Victor, I wish you had listened. You should have gone."

He didn't think, he acted. Victor crossed the room and caught Campbell across the face with his fist. Cartilage cracked and blood splattered from the man's hooked nose.

"You were supposed to help people. You took an oath to do no harm!" Victor raged at him, punctuating the harsh words by striking Campbell in the mouth. The force cracked a tooth and scraped Victor's knuckles, but twice wasn't enough, and he quickly had to follow suit with a third. No amount of physical violence seemed large enough to wipe away Campbell's evil.

The other marines stood back and said nothing. No one spoke or admonished Victor for the loss of temper.

"What do you have to say for yourself?" Victor demanded. "Why would you do this to your own patients? To anyone? Answer me!" He slammed his fist into Campbell's mouth again, dislodging another tooth in the process. He shook the heavy set doctor who no longer deserved the title. A doctor was a person who healed; Victor held a killer in his hands.

"It all seemed so right. The research will save countless lives. You don't understand, Victor. They have power. They promised to help us–"

"How in the bloody fuck is this help!?" Victor raised his fist but the other man shrank back and screamed.

"Don't hit me again, no wait, wait! I can give you information. I can tell you anything."

"You're going to do that anyway, whether you want to or not," Trevor spoke up quietly from the doorway. "You pathetic bastard."

"They brought research and medical necessities that we needed. We were forgotten by the Empire and left on our own here! Your Empire abandoned us."

"Of course they brought medical research, they experimented on innocent civilians."

"I didn't know… I didn't know, Victor. Please. You must believe me." Campbell sagged in Victor's powerful grip. Bloodied spittle trickled from his mouth. "They brought prisoners at first. Murderers. I thought… I was doing what we talked about! I thought we would make new discoveries to advance science. To help people with debilitating brain injuries."

"And then what happened?" Zoe asked. She pointed toward the young man on the table. "He doesn't look like a murderer or a prisoner to me."

"They blackmailed me. I didn't have a choice! I would have lost my license if I didn't continue."

Victor shook him again. "That's your excuse? Nothing justifies this depravity. Who are they, Campbell?"

"They're–" Campbell's facial muscles tightened and twitched. He arched his back and stiffened without warning.

"Campbell?"

"Oh shit," Daniels swore.

The man didn't respond. A shake began over one side of his body and then the convulsion gradually spread. The doctor collapsed to the floor and seized, his arms locked against his body until he finally stilled.

Zoe touched Victor's arm and wordlessly drew him back. His limbs shook, indignation and fury taking firm hold.

"They must have put a chip in his head," Victor said numbly. He touched Zoe's hand to signal he was all right, and then he knelt beside the corpse to run his bioscanner over Campbell's head. "They cooked his brain remotely. Whomever this enigmatic 'they' happens to be."

The hydraulic laboratory door sealed shut with a sudden slam, its lock clicking into place. Above them, small nozzles that resembled a fire extinguishing system began to emit a barely audible hiss.

"Masks!" Fairchild called the warning, prompting them all to don their rebreather masks.

"DuPrie. What's happening?" Daniels asked over the comm.

"I killed the receptionist. She began punching a bunch of buttons at her desk. I believe she fried your friend's noggin and sealed you in."

"What about the guards?"

"I put them down, too," Saskia replied nonchalantly.

"Can you unlock the doors? She's gassing the room."

"This is a little foreign to me, but I'll try."

Within seconds, the gas began to flood through at an exponential rate until a heavy cloud filled the air. Whatever Saskia did, it worsened it.

"Goddammit! Trevor, can't you do anything?" Daniels demanded.

"I'm trying!" Trevor found the nearest console and jacked in with his personal rig. A brilliant green user interface expanded to surround Trevor, alive with flashing symbols and numbers.

Clueless about hacking and overrides, Victor stood by as helplessly as the other soldiers.

"This stuff is burning my skin. What is it?" Daniels demanded.

"No idea, but we're going to need one hell of a decontamination if we make it through this," Victor muttered.

"Trevor, hurry!" Fairchild cried.

"Doin' the best I can. I'm in the system, lass. Just a moment."

The doors flew open and gas spilled into the corridor. They didn't waste a second. Once they fled the room, Trevor contacted the Jemison to relay their findings. Ethan was furious.

Apparently the city council had attempted to pull a fast one to force the Jemison to vacate the planet, citing legislation written by Parliament. It allowed freely founded colonies the rights to live peacefully without military and government interference as long as they acted within the law.

"They're certainly not acting within the laws of the Empire here. That's why they want us to leave, sir. We'll hold it down until you arrive," Trevor told him. "Once the room is clear, we'll begin our investigation." He ended the transmission and turned back to face the squad.

"Well?" Daniels asked.

"The Jemison is sending reinforcements to lock down the facility. The Bridewell is en route, too, to pick up anyone we arrest. Estimated time of arrival is midday local time six local rotations from now," Trevor relayed. The Bridewell operated as one of three prison ships in the United Empire.

"Good." Once the gas cleared, Victor reentered the room and sat at a medical terminal. "Here, have a look."

He pulled up the screen into a 3D display for Trevor's perusal. "They were playing around with concepts I never even conceived. Nanofiber filaments spread through the frontal lobe.

"Most of these corpses are children, mate. Why children?" Abernathy asked. He and Fairchild pulled a sheet over the young man on the table.

"The preadolescent psychic brain is incredibly malleable and plastic, and neurosurgeons once believed they could recover from many more traumas than an adult," Victor said. He didn't move from his seat at Campbell's work station. He had to read it all. He needed to. "We had a theory once, but we dismissed it… I thought. I never imagined he could do this."

"It's disgusting," Zoe said. "Hurting kids. Using them like this."

"There are few things lower than harming a child," Victor said darkly. He closed his eyes and tilted his head back to breathe. His heart pounded frightfully fast and the world around him shimmered. He blinked through his blurry vision and inhaled a few deep breaths.

"I'm going to leave Chang, Fairchild, and Abernathy here with you, Doctor," Daniels spoke up. "The rest of us plan to clear this facility."

"Go ahead. I'll remain here. I need to get this sorted."

A week later, reinforcements arrived from the Empire, but by then, the Jemison's crew had figuratively whipped the details out of most of the so-called villagers. They were all employees and actors, hired by a faceless corporation no one could name. When Trevor and Nisrine prodded them with psychic mindscans, it proved they were telling the truth. They were paid to do Campbell's bidding, and to occasionally fly off the planet to abduct more victims.

Most of the original inhabitants of the settlement were long gone, used as experimental fodder in Campbell's grand scheme. A probe determined that the two outlying colonies had no idea about the atrocities committed in their sister community. Many families received closure at last and mourned the loss of their own children – those whose care they had entrusted to Doctor Campbell, their sole medical provider. Records showed six months of questionable deaths and sicknesses.

The combat squad discovered three dozen victims in a prison block beneath the clinic and with a little unnecessary investigation, they surmised that those dirty and malnourished survivors were next in line to visit the table. Half of them originated from Athena. Five survivors turned out to be the only remaining colonists from the lunar colony of Loki 4.

Victor's investigations made him heartsick. The total number of experiments in the system painted a gruesome portrait spanning back well over a year. Campbell kept meticulous notes but he failed to include his employer's identity.

They were still out there, and he intended to find them no matter what.

CHAPTER 18

Almost three weeks overdue, the Jemison arrived at her next port on fumes. Engineering didn't discover an insidious fuel leak until it was almost too late, and the department looked forward to receiving help from the technical experts on Elora's local military space station. Doodson Tide's synchronized orbit around the planet Elora allowed easy access by shuttlecraft between ships and the surface.

The Jemison limped into her dock, where she would remain until the necessary repairs were made. Everyone on board eagerly awaited a lengthy stay, desperate to wash away the horrors of Kantarn.

Elora's tiny shuttleport occupied a carved mountainside cliff. Since water covered 93% of the planet's surface, creative engineering utilized land space to the maximum potential without disrupting the natural flora.

Initially, Victor had intended to call off his visit to the planet, but Ethan strictly forbade it. "Take a break from this ship and refresh your brain. You won't crack this if you're dead on your feet, mate. You're not a machine."

Victor arrived on the planet first and stepped outside into the balmy air. Pink sand beaches spanned as far as the eye could see, contrasting against the turquoise waters. Jutting spires of rock speared up from the ocean, as familiar to him as his own hand.

A strange sense of melancholy struck him. It was expected, which was the precise reason he'd wanted to arrive alone without Zoe alongside him. He needed a moment to soak it all in.

He hadn't visited Elora in nearly three years, not since Ylona left her birth planet in favor of dwelling in a human settlement on Albion. With him. She'd moved with him into a home in Gloucester, lavishly tailored to her unique aquatic needs. During the funeral, he couldn't bear to face her parents, too consumed with his own guilt. Deep down, a small part of him still expected to see them waiting to greet him on the beach.

Time dwindled and people passed him as they headed on their way, but Victor remained where he was, his gaze held to the horizon.

"Ready for sunshine, frozen drinks, and snorkeling?"

Victor nearly startled out of his boots. He jumped and swung his gaze around to focus on Zoe. "Huh? Yeah. Yeah, I'm ready."

Her dress became the distraction he needed. The rich teal color stood out brightly and suited their paradise setting. The vibrant hue complemented her dark hair and caramel skin.

They took a romantic beachside stroll and enjoyed the peaceful atmosphere. Without a rush to reach their lodgings, the couple chose to travel a rambling path through the tropical coastline.

Zoe tilted her face upward, her delighted expression bathed in sunlight. "I know the lamps in the bio-farm and medical are supposed to mimic this, but nothing beats the real thing. I could sit out here for hours just soaking it up."

"It was like this at home in Paradiso. I remember the sun always seemed to be shining, and the summer rain made for the best time of the year. As a child, I'd just stand in it."

"Back on Tallulah, I used to run out and play in the puddles during a rainstorm, but that usually ended with a day or three in bed afterward."

"You're more than welcome to dance in the rain now," he quipped cheerfully. He paused to kiss her beneath a flowering tree. Purple and golden leaves as long as Victor's arms shaded them briefly from the sun, while heavier ground flora provided concealment from the other tourists. "Are we going to come back to swim after check-in?"

"Not right away if I can help it. I don't really want to share you." She often teased by tossing his words back in his face, which had the desired effect of making him laugh. "The sunbathers are already out in force," Zoe explained, her eyes twinkling with amusement.

Their walk cleared his head and allowed him the chance to relax. Ethan had been right to insist. Not only for himself, but for Zoe's sake as well. She deserved the R&R just as much.

"C'mon, our room should be ready by now."

Pacifica Cove maintained only two surface structures. The remainder of the sprawling city spanned underwater.

The first settlers had come to the world as a scientific expedition full of oceanographers and their families. The native Elorans, curious and unafraid, had come out to greet them. It marked the very first interspecies friendship in human history, and Pacifica Cove was born. The Elorans helped them build a suitable habitat beneath the waters and since that day the city had grown to support more than the initial research team.

After checking in on the upper level, they took the scenic stairwell to the ocean floor. Zoe flit from one window to the next along the way, bright-eyed wonder on her face as she pointed out one ocean creature after another. An enormous jellyfish skated by, gelatinous tendrils gliding behind it with luminous bulbs at each tip. It glittered in shades of vermillion and teal, contrasting colors that made Zoe's mouth fall open.

"I take it you've never visited the Cove before?"

"No, my friends always wanted to stay in Atlantica, so I never came down this way." The northern hemisphere settlement provided an abundance of eye-catching activities for visitors who preferred parties over relaxation, a literal den of sin tucked away in the chilly waters.

"There's a marauder crab." A dog-sized, soft-shelled crab worked diligently at hollowing a colorful, rainbow lump of coral. "They wear pieces of coral for shells, but they're known for evicting other creatures from inhabited structures and prefer that over an empty dwelling."

"Seems like more work. Why would they rather fight for one?" Zoe crouched beside the glass for a closer look at the muddy brown crustacean. It froze, completely aware of her attention.

"No clue," Victor admitted. "Maybe the theft makes the house more appealing."

Without further warning, the crab struck the glass with one claw.

"Holy crap!" Zoe startled and fell on her rump in the middle of the hallway. Her fingers instinctively went for the non-existent holster at her thigh. Weapons were highly restricted on the planetary surface. The peaceful Elorans disdained them, so only a small number of human security personnel kept arms locked in strategic points for emergency purposes.

Chuckling, Victor offered both hands to Zoe and pulled her back to her feet and into his arms. "I considered warning you, but that's the best part."

"I was right about you at our very first meeting," she grumbled as she soothed her dress back into place. "Sadist."

Victor grinned. "They're one of Elora's intelligent forms of life and loathe to be seen naked. Come on. Our room is this way."

"I will get you back for this," she promised without any heat. Fingers entwined, Zoe cast a last glance back at the crab then nudged Victor to continue down the hall.

"I think he liked your dress," he teased.

"Ha! Well, if he wants it he'll have to fight you for the honors."

Their playful banter helped Victor to brace himself for the next wave of nostalgia. It struck as he led Zoe down the familiar corridors. He'd met Ylona at Neptune's Garden, the only high-class restaurant in the city, where she served meals to lonely diners who declined a table to sit at the bar. At the time, Victor was one of those lonely men, too embarrassed to take a table for one, and absolutely bewildered that the lovely Eloran had seen his heartache and wanted to comfort him.

Ylona had touched him ever so gently, and conveyed all of her concern in a single mental caress of her mind against his thoughts. They chatted for hours after the end of her shift.

"We're this way," he told her. The transparent walls of the public areas darkened to opaque shades in the hotel's residential area. Guests were assured privacy.

He let them into a room at the end of the hall, and Zoe gasped in surprise at the sight awaiting them.

Light from above the ocean surface shimmered in fantastical patterns over the exquisite king-sized bed, while multi-colored fish swam in school formation, undulating their slender bodies in the underwater paradise.

"It's lovely, isn't it?" he asked softly. With longing, he gazed at the graceful creatures opposite the glass. Coral formations served as privacy screens for the room's occupants and homes to bottom-feeding creatures. He dropped his overnight bag and crouched near the glass to watch a scuttling sea-spider pursuing an emerald feather worm. A larger shrimp-like crustacean struck from within the hollow coral and caught the spider with its many segmented pincers. Its double pairs of eyestalks watched them through the glass.

"The fish, yes. That thing… not so much." Zoe knelt down beside him to watch. "Is it going to attack the glass, too?"

"No, he won't do anything to threaten you. You're too large. Come on. You have to admit it's sort of beautiful, even if it is nightmare fuel. They'll let you hand feed them."

"As much as I enjoy our lab sessions, I'd really rather not lose another limb."

"You're not a particularly brave Royal Marine," Victor teased.

Zoe shot him a dirty look.

"I'm only joking. You'll see plenty of them once you're snorkeling off of the coast." He moved to the in-room bar where a bottle of wine waited in an ice sculpture carved to resemble a crashing wave.

"I'd really like that. Gosh, this room is gorgeous. You didn't spend a lot, did you?"

Victor grinned at her and returned to popping the cork free to pour them each a glass. "Don't worry about what I spent. It was worth it to have time alone with you." As he poured, Zoe snuck behind him and wrapped one arm around his waist. Her cheek pressed against his shoulder blade, her breasts a firm presence at his back. Her body heat soaked through his thin t-shirt, a comfort in the cool underwater hotel room. He almost overfilled the first glass.

Whiffs of peach and subtle oak enticed him to sneak a sip. Sweet, effervescent bubbles tickled across his taste buds, and then Zoe snuck her other arm around to steal the glass from his hands.

"Since you're the guest, our next destination is up to you, my dear. What would you like to do? Dinner? Dancing?" With three nights promised to them, Victor had no desire to waste a moment of their leave from the ship. In his head, he planned dozens of possible activities from water-skiing on the coast to hiking in the jungle terrain.

193

"Umm... well." Their bodies parted as Zoe eased away and tilted the glass to her lips. She emptied it in a few sips and plucked the bottle from his hands to set both aside. "Do you *like* to dance, Victor?" Zoe stepped in close. "Or should I be in fear for my toes?"

"I've taken lessons in over a dozen styles of dance dating to the 1800s, hon. I think your feet are safe." Zoe's lips parted and her brows raised. "My ex was a bit of a twat when it came to determining the use of our time away from the ship," Victor explained.

"Maybe we should be worried about *your* toes then."

"Nah, I'm used to it. We stopped taking the lessons when the instructor always pulled me to the front as an example to the rest of the class. Hannah didn't like that I outperformed her."

It was the beginning of the end, and it was the catalyst to Victor realizing no amount of effort brought her happiness. Their split came days later during the two-week leave on Elora, where Hannah insisted he accompany her while she met a famous native instructor for overpriced lessons. They fought and spent the second week in separate hotel rooms. Then he met Ylona.

"C'mere. Let's see if you're completely a lost cause."

Apparently, he was as patient a dance instructor as he was a doctor. He led her through the steps and never fussed at her graceless shimmies, but he also never missed an opportunity to gently make fun.

"You wanna sway your hips smoothly, hon. You'll hurt someone doing that. It isn't a fight."

"Are you sure? Dancing seems to share some of the kata movements they like to teach us." Zoe's impish smile shined up at him.

"For the love of... I'm not going to body slam you into the carpet. Maybe if I were Daniels..."

After the first half hour, sweat beaded his brow and dampened her dark bangs. They laughed together when her overstepping footwork landed on his toes, and he fought the urge to kiss her each time their movements brought her in close. He taught her to bend her knees and to flow with the music.

Zoe had a body made for dancing, with tireless, athletic legs honed by training. He lived for the whisper of her dress against his trouser legs and the way she molded against him just right.

Thoughts regarding her physique culminated in the expected result, stiffening Victor to a state of unbearable arousal.

"Victor? Am I tiring you? You have a funny look on your face…" Zoe's voice trailed off. The firm presence pulling his pants tight told her for him.

Moments ago, he'd swept her up and down the room, convincing her to relax all the while. It was pure irony that he became a tightly knit ball of nerves in her stead over something so natural as his own masculine reactions. "I'm fine, Zoe. I was thinking."

"A quid for your thoughts?" she queried softly. The smooth glide of her fingers ventured up his neck, breaking his skin out in anticipatory goosebumps. Warm color tinged the apples of her cheeks and her eyes gleamed.

Victor turned his head slightly to avoid meeting her eyes. His tight chest restricted the oxygen in his lungs. "I don't want to disappoint you. Goddammit, Zoe, I've tried. I don't want to ruin a good night." If only his body cooperated with his mind and didn't shatter their intimacy with a stressful panic attack.

Her hands framed his face, drawing his anxious gaze back to her face. "Victor, love, breathe," she soothed. She waited until his attention refocused on her. "You haven't disappointed me. You've *never*, not once, disappointed me."

"You've never asked me what happened."

Her thumb swept the curve of cheek. "I have some ideas from what you've said and from what I've seen, but it's your story to share when you're ready. I'm not going to force you to tell it. I know what that's like all too well."

"You're the best thing I could have ever asked for, Zo. The best thing to come into my life. And I want to tell you. But not now. I want to make love to you, and I want to spend the rest of this night with you in this room."

Zoe's breath hitched audibly. "I can't think of anything I'd rather do than be here with you."

He struggled against the desire to have her right then, right there, to unfasten his pants and discover the heat of her body's natural embrace. Her sweet kisses provided the reassurance he needed, renewing his damaged confidence.

"As sexy as this get-up is, you need to get it off, Zoe," he mumbled against the corner of her mouth.

"Unlace me?"

"With pleasure."

Victor tugged at the complex knot securing her tightly laced bodice. "How do you women get into these? Did it take all five of your bunkmates to tie this?" he jested. Harmless jokes helped to cover his own apprehension. After a few gentle plucks of the laces over her back, the snug garment loosened from her midsection.

"One of our most ancient secrets," she replied mysteriously.

"To be honest, you're amazing no matter what you wear, but I actually expected you to disembark in boots and pants," Victor said.

"You said you never saw me in a dress and… I wanted you to…" The dress slipped down over her shoulders and fell to the floor around her feet. She twirled for him to showcase the entire package and the peach lace accenting her curves.

"My beautiful little rebel," he murmured appreciatively, awestruck by the delicately sexy garment.

"I'm glad you approve."

One after another, buttons flicked open beneath Zoe's agile fingers. Her hand delved through the opening before his pants had a chance to make it over his lean hips.

"Tomorrow we're going shopping."

"Huh? Shopping?" With his mind drowning in lustful thoughts of every sexual fantasy he'd had since their first intimate night, he could barely focus on her actual words. "Why?"

The answer came on the sound of ripping fabric. Zoe's right hand fisted in his shirt and yanked, tearing the cotton like tissue. If anything, her dominant display made him more desperate to have her.

Despite her pretty undergarments, Victor craved the sensation of flesh against flesh, and nothing would satisfy him until the last scrap of peach lace hit the floor. Afterward, once they were both bare, hands free to roam and fingers able to reciprocate eager fondling, they moved toward the bed until the mattress hit the back of his legs and Victor found himself abruptly sitting on the edge.

Zoe straddled him. Her fingers traced a wandering journey that began at his taut abdomen and worked their way upward over his pectorals, drifting through the fine hairs scattered across his chest. Her hands remained in constant motion, exploring without the hindrance of clothing.

"I don't... I don't like to be on the bottom."

"Then you don't have to be," Zoe whispered against his ear. Without another word, she surrendered the top position and drew him down with her to the bed. Victor lowered easily atop her, settling his body against receptive curves. Her legs fit perfectly around his hips. Beneath him, Zoe made no judgment and set no expectations. Her affectionate gaze tilted up to him with desire and absolute patience in her golden eyes.

His lover's experience and overactive imagination guided them through several positions, each one more colorful and entertaining than the last. Zoe's gentle guidance made him feel alive again, easily restoring the vitality lost during his year of mourning.

"Hey, Zoe?" Victor murmured afterward as they lay in a sweaty sprawl across the enormous bed.

"Hmm…yeah?"

"I'm glad you're my patient."

The very cybernetic talents Ylona encouraged him to train and develop had introduced Zoe, the new love of his life, into his world. His Eloran wife had saved him from loneliness even in death; she'd given him Zoe.

"Me too."

At the end of their lovemaking, Victor suggested a shared shower. They washed each other tenderly beneath the lukewarm spray. And then they laughed like children when Zoe took off with both towels and forced him to chase her to recover one.

Later, when Saskia messaged Zoe to relay news of a party in Atlantica Cove, they ignored the text to stay in. They had all of the party they needed with each other.

CHAPTER 19

"Trevor invited us along for a hike and some parasailing. His online lady friend made him promise to get some fresh air in the outside world."

"Good for Flidais. Still, as much as I adore Trevor's company, off and online, I don't know if I want to share you today either," Zoe admitted.

"A private hike then. We'll catch up with him tomorrow."

More than a dozen paths led from the most popular tourist attractions, winding into the overgrown thickets and jungle flora. All the hot spots for the traveling population centered around the planet's habitable land mass. Three miles of trekking through the lush growth was enough distance to escape civilization, and afterward, the landscape treated visitors to an abundance of natural growth. Waterfalls, quick-flowing rivers, and trickling caverns were only some of the other wonders Victor had found over the years. He'd gladly share them with Zoe. Skinny-dipping with her in some freshwater stream became his next priority.

They enjoyed a five-mile morning hike through the tropical terrain, ensuring their privacy away from the more adventurous crew members. Curls of steam rose from a hidden hot spring where Victor coaxed Zoe out of her clothes with minimal effort. To make new memories of a planet already close to Victor's heart, they made love again on the leafy shoreline where the sand had bled away into dense and silky foliage.

Eventually, once their racing hearts calmed and they felt up to the task of returning to civilization, they bathed in the pristine water and returned to the carefully navigated path. Zoe only got them lost once when Victor put her in charge of the holomap.

"You could have said there was a cliff there."

"It was on the map," he said with a laugh. "I thought you were being adventurous. I'm all for taking the climb down if you are."

Zoe swatted him.

They celebrated their return to civilization with lunch at a beachside cafe. Cuddled side by side on a wide hammock, they shared a colorful salad of local fruits and a plate of double-tail prawns stuffed with marauder crabmeat.

"What's this one?" Zoe asked, curiously holding up a piece of fruit for Victor's inspection. Tiny pink seeds dotted throughout the rounded, canary yellow slice.

"Sunfruit. Try it. They're only harvested for one month of the year here. The Jemison arrived at the best time, really. Three weeks ago when we should have pulled in this wouldn't have been ripened enough for picking."

"Mmm, wow." Zoe eagerly dug through the bowl for a second piece. "It's tarter than I expected but yummy."

"If you want sweet, try this instead." He offered a bumpy, slightly soggy grey berry, not bothering to hide his chuckle when Zoe warily eyed it. "I promise it tastes better than it looks. I asked for this specially. Local secret."

Zoe leaned in and took the fruit from his fingers with a teasing nip. A quizzical look crossed her face which quickly morphed into a pleased smile. "Okay, how have I never tasted this before? It's like liquid sugar laced with… is that wine?"

"I told you, a local secret. The Elorans ferment the berries after plucking. You miss a lot when you take liberty in Atlantica," he teased.

"We need to buy a bottle or five."

"Already ordered three to be sent to our room. Anything more and customs won't allow us through."

"Yes, but if *you* get three and *I* get three, then we have six," she replied with a sage nod.

"You're wise beyond your years," Victor teased, brushing a gentle kiss across her lips.

Beachside lunch for two was followed by a trip through the colorful market stalls. Every time a ship pulled in, the natives, both human and alien, set up a weekend surface bazaar to peddle their wares. The latter preferred to trade for physical objects over galactic currency.

An aqua-skinned Eloran lured Zoe over with an assortment of carved sea stones. The crystalline rocks littered the ocean floor, polished to a satin finish by years beneath the water.

"Look, it's one of those crabs." The decorative carving masterfully depicted the vain crustacean with an ornate shell of fan shaped coral.

"As ugly as the little blighters are on the outside, their interior polishes like mother of pearl. This was carved from the inside of his bottom shell," Victor explained, much to the Eloran woman's surprise. She clapped giddily and nodded, sending her sleek waves of green and pink striped hair bouncing over her shoulders.

Native Elorans lacked the capability for human speech. They communicated through a series of sounds and inhuman vocalizations that carried beneath the water to express emotions. Among their own kind, they conveyed deeper meanings and thoughts through physical contact. Sometimes they shared the psychic experience with humans.

"Really?" Zoe's eyebrows hiked upwards. "It's actually pretty and it'll be a nice reminder of our visit, even if you did laugh at me."

"Your little shriek was adorable. Well worth the two seconds you glowered at me."

Zoe rewarded his teasing with a kiss then shooed him off to look around while she bartered for the keepsake. A wandering pace through the stalls lightened his pockets and wallet, exchanged for his favorite soap and a few local sweets. By the time he caught back up with Zoe, she was carrying a new woven basket full of her own purchases - and the rest of her belongings from her purse.

"Let me guess. She traded your bag for the crab."

Zoe beamed up at him and Victor ducked his head to kiss her dimples.

"She did, actually, but then she threw in a basket. I think she must have understood my worry about making you have to carry everything."

"What can I say? They're a considerate people. As for you…" Victor peered down at her collection of goodies. "I can see that you're an impulse shopper."

"What? Okay, so I want my own seasilk sheets," she fussed. "Yours spoiled me."

Victor grinned. "And all of that?" He gestured to the polished coral trinkets, bracelets, and glittering shells. Bright jewels shone from the surface of a unique hair comb crafted from a coral shrimp's tail.

"The bracelets are for my sister," she defended. "Well… most of them anyways. And… oh fine, I'll put some of it back."

"It's your purchase, Zo. Ignore me, I'm only taking the piss out of you again. Enjoy the time away from the ship," he coaxed her. Otherwise, he'd be forced to return and purchase the very things she removed from her basket.

"Honest, I'm being good. I didn't even try to stuff that dress in. I had no idea the Elorans wove such pretty silk."

"They don't. Elorans only began to wear clothing when the first human settlers came. They do it for our modesty. Get the dress. You'll regret leaving it once we're in flight."

The crisp ocean breeze was alive in the air, infusing every woven article with the smell of the saltwater.

Lingering traces of it clung to Zoe's skin, along with the fragrance of a native citrus she'd dabbed against her throat. Victor breathed it in and set his cheek against the top of her head.

Zoe made her final purchase of the evening and returned to him with an airy, semi-translucent fabric fashioned into a strapless, knee length dress. Multiple layers of the gold and green material maintained modesty, but fluttered into an asymmetrical gauzy hemline against her thighs when she held it up for his approval.

"It'll look great on you," Victor said.

"You don't think it's too short?"

"Uh. No?"

"My dad would call it scandalous and my brother would feel compelled to duel you for daring to escort me in such a shameful state," Zoe told him.

"I take it that your region of Tallulah is rather…" A war of humor versus horror raged in Victor, divided clearly over the matter of her admission. *What the hell kind of family am I about to get myself attached to?* "Backward then?" he finished awkwardly.

"It's rather old-fashioned, yes. Some of the newer cities, like where Daniels hails from, aren't quite so traditional."

"I see. And they've reinstated dueling. That's always grand. Do I need to purchase a revolver to practice my draw and aim?"

Zoe chuckled. "It's not as bad as some places. Astreya, for example."

"I suppose you've brought this up for a reason and I'm to be accompanying you home during leave?"

"Oh…" Her gaze dropped and she tucked the ends of her hair behind her ear. Since their first meeting, Zoe's hair had grown out almost two inches. "Victor, I left home to escape all that sort of stuff. I wouldn't drag you there unless you wanted to go."

Their wandering path toward the resort slowed and eventually came to a halt. Victor turned Zoe toward him with a hand to her shoulder. "Do you want me to go home with you?" he repeated.

"I think my sister Merrilyn would like you."

"How long has it been since we met? Five months? Six?" Victor smoothed a disobedient lock of hair away from her brow. "And almost as long since we began dating. Meeting your family seems like the next logical step. I don't mind."

"Maybe when this is all over, if you still feel that way, we can plan a trip," Zoe compromised as she linked their hands together. "C'mon, I'm ready for our little private bubble again."

"Fair enough."

Zoe flopped down on the bed the moment they returned to their room and set their souvenirs aside. "I didn't think it was possible, but you've worn me out with your outdoor escapades."

"Are you so certain of that?" Victor asked, feigning his most lecherous expression. A crooked finger from Zoe was all the encouragement he needed to join her on the bed and strip away her clothes.

They didn't stop until true exhaustion held them captive. Once they sweatily collapsed on the sheets, they twined their limbs and snuggled close to trade kisses and affectionate murmurs.

"I never would have guessed there was a randy teenage boy inside of you waiting to get out."

"A tired boy now."

Curled together, sleep came easily. Victor enjoyed the nights Zoe spent with him on the ship and always slept better with her at his side. Their time alone on Elora was no different.

A persistent beep pulled Victor from pleasant dreams. Ignoring the summons didn't work and only threatened to wake the woman at his side. His comm fell to the floor on his first attempt to grab it. He shifted away from Zoe's warmth and swept the device up. A text communication waited for him.

Victor stared down at the message and swallowed back his conflicted feelings. Oblivious to his inner turmoil, Zoe lay sprawled in the bed beside him. It was time to stop running away and face his past. He touched her shoulder lightly and shook her awake. "Zo?"

"Hmm? What is it?"

"I need to go handle something. Will you be okay here for a bit?"

Zoe had already stretched out, taking over the warm spot he left behind. "How long?"

"A couple hours, tops."

"M'kay," she mumbled drowsily. "I'll go lay on the beach and wait for you then."

Victor leaned down and kissed her nose. "I promise I'll make it up to you."

***

The meeting took place in the underwater restaurant attached to Victor's hotel. Elaborate decor sculpted from unique marble, pearl, and other precious metals employed use of the best features from Eloran and human design. They were a friendly culture, and while they prohibited the desecration of their beautiful world, the natives had aided the humans in the construction of their own underwater colonies, protected by glass domes. The two cities, Pacifica Cove and Atlantica Gulf, were proof that the two species could peacefully coexist.

Victor traveled down two flights of stairs and crossed the hotel grounds until he reached the restaurant. He passed several Elorans on the way, as the hotel employed both species in its staff. They chatted in their own tongue and the two friendly creatures waved to him in passing. He may not have remembered them, but the recognition was visible in their slender, pale faces. He smiled courteously in passing and waved.

Ylara didn't waste a precious second. She threw herself into Victor's arms and hugged him tight. Her affection caught him by surprise.

"Ylara?" She smelled like the ocean. Like Ylona. Her daughter had resembled her greatly in life, from skin the color of a twilit sky down to the sleek strands of bicolored, purple and ivory hair spilling down her back. He hugged her tightly, unconcerned with the press of her damp skin against his pristine dress shirt. A thin, frayed skirt of seaweed and kelp clothed her lower half, adorned by beaded embellishments, pearls, and tiny shells that glittered in the candlelight.

Eventually, Ylara leaned back and held him at arm's length with her hands on his shoulders. Her smile revealed a few dozen tiny teeth set in two tidy rows. The slender woman stood eye to eye with Victor, as the Elorans were a tall race with builds varying by their climate preference. The Elorans of Pacific Cove, like Ylona and her mother Ylara, possessed aquiline features and graceful, elongated limbs. Her flesh felt like seal's skin beneath his fingertips, damp velvet to the touch. Their cold water counterparts carried an abundance of insulating fat beneath thicker arctic fur. Victor once joked with his wife and showed her photos of Earth's extinct manatees.

You look well, Ylara said to him, her voice a mere whisper that slid through his mind. Victor never quite came to understand how it worked, and whether she knew the language, or if the magic of her psychic prowess translated it for her.

"As do you."

I did not think you would come. Her fingers delivered a reassuring squeeze.

"I'm sorry, Ylara. Coming back, it's been hard in a way."

I understand.

"Well then… shall we?" Victor asked nervously. He offered an arm and escorted her toward the hostess who led them to a small table where they settled near the window view to the ocean.

Ylara took his right hand in her left. *I tried many times to contact you, Victor. You have become a stranger.*

Remorse filled his heart and flushed his face until Victor ducked his head to sever eye contact. He studied the tiny script on the menu instead.

As if sensing his discomfort, Ylara quickly leaned across the table and touched his cheek with her other hand to guide his attention back to her huge, midnight blue eyes. *I am not upset with you, Victor. We have missed you. Most of all, we have wanted to know if you are well.*

"I am."

You hide something from me.

The beautiful Eloran matron took both of his hands in hers. Victor's fingers trembled between her webbed digits.

With no idea what to say, he blurted out exactly what was on his mind. "How could you possibly desire a meeting with me when Ylona is dead because of *me*? I killed her, Ylara. Me. If I hadn't deployed again she'd be alive now."

She had no words, but Victor experienced the full range of her emotions. Sorrow, loss, and compassion – but no condemnation. He sensed her movement but didn't lift his gaze until she slid into the neighboring seat and pressed her cool, thin lips to his cheek.

"I miss her so much. There isn't a day that I don't think of her," he confessed quietly. His eyes burned until he blinked back the stinging sensation.

We never blamed you. There are many worlds in this galaxy, each one filled with its own dangers. Ylona knew that when she left our home, but you were worth the risk to her. You showed her a world beyond Elora, Victor. There is no shame in that. Oron and I lived for our daughter's stories of Albion and your people. He will be disappointed that their hunt cost him the opportunity to reconnect with you. You are missed dearly.

"She told you stories?"

Many. She told us she once answered your door for the postman without the pretty clothes you bought for her.

Victor chuckled. "She frequently forgot to don anything at all. I would find her in the garden without a single stitch. Our neighbors were scandalized."

They chatted for hours over a shared meal, as was Eloran custom. A large platter with a single seared fish and raw sea vegetables dominated the center of the table. The crisp taste of Eloran sea apple complimented the succulent orange fish. Fond memories of family dinners at her parents' table led him to pick out more of Ylona's favorites from among the assortment of green spears and flowering ocean buds.

Eventually, Victor remembered to check his watch. "Christ. Where did the time go? I should get back, Ylara. I… Someone is waiting for me."

She perked up quickly and a big smile spread over her face. Eloran smiles were disconcerting for some humans, but Victor had long grown used to them. *You have taken a new bondmate?* she asked.

"I have," he answered slowly, uncertain despite Ylara's delighted expression. "Her name is Zoe."

Will you allow me to meet her?

Victor stared across the table. He blinked a few times. "You would like to meet her?"

She must be truly wonderful if she has earned your heart.

"She is exceptional," Victor agreed.

May I meet her?

For some reason, the sincerity of the request took Victor back. All of his knowledge about their generous culture hadn't prepared him for experiencing her goodwill firsthand. "I… well yes, of course you may, Ylara."

He paid the bill and offered an arm to escort his mother-in-law to the upper level of the underwater resort.

A sharp chirp and flashing red light from his communicator interrupted their idle chatter along the way to the surface. Victor groaned and played the urgent text.

Trouble?

"It's an emergency recall from the Jemison. Something's happened."

The same message passed over the city's announcement system. "All hands, return to the Jemison immediately."

"I'm sorry, Ylara. I have to go."

The woman raised her hand to his jaw and smiled up at him. Her lips brushed his cheek and a final whisper skimmed his mind. *Keep safe and return to us. Do not stay away so long again. We have never stopped loving you, Victor. You will always be my son.*

He took her kind words with him and rushed to his room.

CHAPTER 20

Decontamination burned sometimes. Zoe's eyes still stung when she emerged to a world of orderly chaos. Enlisted personnel ran back and forth, accepting their new commands and preparing the Jemison for takeoff.

"All combat personnel, report to your supervisors," the executive officer announced over the public channel.

Zoe pushed her way through the heavy crowd and quickly visited her berth to change into uniform. Afterward, she descended to the armory and found the rest of the squad had already gathered in the adjacent shuttle bay.

Their nervous faces revealed what she had already guessed. They were all still in the dark.

"You know anything about what's going on?" Saskia dropped down in the seat beside Zoe. "Did your boyfriend say what's up?"

"No. We weren't together when the call came in so I haven't seen him." *Not since his date...* Zoe sighed and clasped her hands in her lap. Now wasn't the time to think about what she saw at the hotel. She trusted Victor too much to doubt him over one incident.

"About Doctor del Toro..." Fairchild began reluctantly. She glanced away from Zoe to sever eye contact swiftly. "I heard some sneaky rumors when we were boarding the shuttle."

"Like what?" Saskia asked before Zoe had a chance to open her mouth and protest.

"Well, Radha told everyone on the deck that his lust for xenophilia must not have ended and that he broke off your relationship."

"We didn't break up!" Her sharp protest failed when her voice cracked.

"She saw him with an Eloran. At dinner." Fairchild rubbed her arm awkwardly. "Sorry, Zoe."

"You should never take rumors at face value, Beth, you know that," Zoe admonished. "I think I'd know if he broke up with me. He even sent me a text when the recall occurred to make sure that I was all right. He got all of our things."

"Zoe, love. It isn't your fault if he fancies aliens. Pox on him for hiding it behind your back," Fairchild continued as she laid a sympathetic hand on Zoe's shoulder. "I'm certain that there's more to it than this."

"Than him being a bloody cheater?" Saskia asked in disbelief. "Honestly, Beth, you should be ashamed of yourself for even suggesting that he's cheating! Don't listen to her, Zoe." Fairchild opened her mouth to protest their friend's censure but the doors hissed open.

"Listen up!" Daniels strode into the shuttle bay where the marines waited. "The Jemison received a distress call from one of our own in this very system. We will arrive at the coordinates in fifteen hours. I want all of you back here rested, geared up, and ready to go in twelve."

"Aye, Commander."

"Raines and Abernathy, I want you both in the armory for the next hour. DuPrie, make sure Lackley has things in hand on the cannon. Lopez, get the pre-flights done on the shuttle. Everything needs to be ready to go. The rest of you, report to your bunks. We can't afford for any of you to be less than your best."

Everyone dispatched as ordered. Zoe welcomed the work to keep her mind busy.

"Any idea who he meant?" Abernathy asked across the workbench.

"No. From the sound of it, I'm guessing they received a Royal Marine distress code."

"Huh."

Preparation for missions involved a full inventory check on all squad weapons and gear. Zoe and Abernathy had the dubious honor of guaranteeing that everything was in working order.

"Hey, I'm going to go check in with Saskia a minute. One of her clips is missing. I bet she left it in her vest again."

Abernathy waved her off, focused on the weapon in front of him. "Bring back some coffee, would you?"

"Yeah, sure thing."

She needed the walk to clear her thoughts. Fairchild's words played through her mind, accompanied by her own observances on Elora. Indecision followed her into the lift. Zoe's fingers hovered over the selection for medical but she decided against seeking Victor out. *He'll be busy, and I have a job to do,* she rationalized. *We'll talk tonight and... and I know he'll be honest with me. He told me his Eloran lover died.*

The internal pep talk renewed her courage. Victor wasn't an unreasonable man. He was a good man, an ethical and dependable man. He wouldn't make love to her and turn to the arms of another woman – human or Eloran – without letting her know his feelings had changed.

As expected during war time, she encountered a busy main battery. The room teemed with offensive specialists and technicians charged with the maintenance of the ship's guns.

"Where's Saskia?" Zoe swept her gaze around the room. Lackley was squeezed between two power panels adjusting a series of resistors.

"She stepped out to get some coffee," Lackley replied. "The cannon is off by two millimeters and I have no clue how it happened. I just calibrated this damn thing."

"Okay, thanks. I'll go see if I can catch her. You want me to send her back with anything else?" Zoe asked.

"More coffee."

"Popular request today. I'll let her know," Zoe laughed and stepped out of the enclosed space.

The entire ship shuddered. Alarms screamed their warnings and bright red emergency lights glared from every corner. Zoe stumbled to the right and hit her shoulder against the wall.

"Breech detected in level 3. Breech detected in level 3," Jem announced over the ship's system.

Another explosion rocked the ship. The sirens maintained a steady, deafening alert that spread from corner to corner of the Jemison. The very floor beneath Zoe's feet vibrated with the hum of energy.

"All hands to the shuttle bay. The Jemison is currently under at–" The sensual female voice abruptly stopped mid-sentence and died. The emergency lights flickered.

"What the hell is going on…?" Zoe continued forward with one hand braced on the wall.

She climbed down the access shaft with only emergency lights guiding her. Another quake shuddered through the ship and the tube went pitch black. The explosion knocked Zoe's grip loose and she fell several feet before she snagged the rungs with her biotic arm and caught herself. The alarms dimmed in comparison to her beating pulse. She clung tightly to the ladder and waited for her trembling limbs to still before continuing down.

When she crawled out of the access shaft into the hangar, Zoe stumbled over a motionless shape on the floor. A shape with a bullet hole between his wide-open brown eyes, beneath neatly gelled black hair.

Lopez. "No!" she cried out, touching his still warm face. He hadn't been dead for long. "Raines to Medical. I have a man down in the hang–" Zoe cut herself off. Something moved in the corner of her vision, something familiar and colorful. To her, the vibrancy of Saskia's genetic ability always looked like dozens of sparkles in many different hues.

Zoe slowly stood.

"Saskia. I know you're there. I *can* see you."

The splicer stepped out of the shadows and dropped her camouflage. "Toss your communicator here," she ordered, her gun aimed at Zoe's unprotected chest.

Weaponless, Zoe did as instructed. She pulled her comm from her wrist and tossed it. The slim band skidded across the floor and hit Saskia's boot. The woman promptly crushed it beneath her heel.

"I didn't want it to come to this, Zoe."

"Why?" She gestured toward their fallen pilot. "Saskia, what are you trying to do?"

"No one else has to die. Step back and walk away. Let me leave in peace," the genetic shifter told her in a calm voice. The tone chilled Zoe and ran icy fingers down her nape.

"You killed Lopez. *Why?*"

"He locked me out of the bloody shuttles. I could have been far away from here by now, but it's taken me every second to unjam what he's done."

She would have killed him anyway for witnessing it. He must have known what would happen, Zoe thought. She swallowed back the forming lump in her throat. A nearby console glowed with a combination of green and red lights. *The shuttles are still offline. She's trying to override it.*

"Did you also take the engines and A.I. offline?"

"A necessary price to guarantee my freedom from this farce. A Commodore whose chief concern is his cock, and a government that doesn't care about the people beyond its closest borders. I found a new cause to serve, Zoe. You can come with me."

Zoe stiffened. "Excuse me?"

"Come with me," she said again. This time she lowered her gun to her side. "You'll have the best cyberneticists at your disposal. Think about your future. Come with me."

Behind her, one of the shuttles began its startup routine. The engine hummed to life. Zoe's time was running out.

"That's treason."

"So what?! It's a small price to pay. What did they teach us at United Command? Sometimes, a little sacrifice is required for the greater good. Don't you have a wee sis in cancer treatment? She could benefit from their research, Zoe," Saskia pleaded to her. "They could have fixed her by now and allowed her to live a normal life."

"No… Victor said–"

Saskia shook her head. "Don't make me laugh. Del Toro is a brilliant tool, but he won't take the steps needed to further his work. How can you possibly put your faith in a man who's already dishonest with you?"

The barb stung, but Zoe refused to be baited. Saskia had defended Victor against Fairchild's earlier insinuations. Bringing him up now struck her as a desperate move.

"Saskia, you sabotaged the ship and now we're under attack."

"They came for me, and the moment you allow me to leave, the attack will end. Don't force me to kill you, too. You're the perfect candidate for their work, Zoe. Don't you understand that we're working for a cause willing to improve this galaxy?"

"They're murderers, Saskia! You saw with your own eyes what they've done. They're abducting innocent children and subjecting them to torture. If you're with them, I'm not letting you get on that shuttle."

"So be it." Saskia lifted her arm and leveled her weapon at Zoe's heart.

CHAPTER 21

When Victor arrived at the medical bay, technicians had already received their assignments from Hart. They rushed to and from the stockroom to gather necessary supplies and made portable first aid kits. O'Reilly arrived out of breath, bearing an armload of nanite core gel. It was the base of almost all medicinal products that went into the field. It served as the binding glue for bio-stitches and anti-toxins.

Victor's hands began to cramp, so he stopped to sweep his fingers through his hair in frustration. A visceral headache pounded behind his eyes, but too much work remained to take a break. "Hand me another pack, O'Reilly. We'll need about…"

"I've kept count, sir. We require one for every man aboard the ship and five for every medic. This marks ninety-three."

"Victor, can you tell us what we're walking into?" Hart finally demanded.

As the leader of the medical department, Oshiro had another task ahead of him. It became Victor's duty to lead preparations for deploying their combat medics into a possible battle situation. And he didn't believe in leaving his men in the dark. "All right," he agreed quietly. All eyes fell upon him. "I don't think there's any harm in telling you what's happening. Due to the severity of the situation, it's to the benefit of everyone to remain completely aware. We have a possible hostage situation involving a marine thought to be killed in action."

"Who?" Davis asked curiously.

"Hamish Lockhart sent a Royal Marine distress signal to his brother while we were on Elora."

"No shit?" Hart was the first to blurt out.

"Three hours ago Jem picked up an emergency distress signal from him and patched it to Chief Lockhart. He confirmed its authenticity. We're looking at the recovery of a man who has been missing for five years and subjected to the unknown. We need to be on our game."

"Holy shit... I always thought he was a decent fellow," Hart said. She shook her head in pity and resumed her work at the station. "You have a thousand doses of halergen left in quantity, Doc. You're getting low."

"What do we have as a substitute? Do we have any kinderal?"

Before she could answer, a quake tore through the Jemison and tossed bottles of antibiotics onto the floor. One shattered and the others rolled out of sight beneath the table.

"Shit," Victor swore under his breath. "What was that?"

"Breech detected in level three," the ship's artificial voice announced. "Breech detected in level three."

"Level three is engineering," Victor muttered.

"All hands to the shuttle bay. The Jemison is currently under at–"

The glowing nimbus of color surrounding the PA system speaker dimmed and sparked out.

"Jem?" Hart called out.

"And now we've lost the main ship console," Davis said. Her brow furrowed in concern. The lights flickered and died, but the backup power generator activated and restored power to the medical wing.

"Never mind that. I think Jem tried to warn us of an attack," Victor said.

Trevor skidded into medical. His flushed face glistened with perspiration. "The lifts dropped offline. I can try to get them goin' again with the access panel in here."

"Do it," Hart said. She abandoned the lobby workstation and left it open for his use. "Fairchild, take O'Reilly and get down to engineering. They're bound to have injuries."

"You'll have to use the maintenance hatches," Trevor called over. He pried off the wall panel and pulled out his datagram to access the electrical module. A dozen red and green lights winked on and off, indicating a disturbance in the system. "It's goin' to take me a few moments to get this sorted."

"Got it!" The two medics grabbed emergency kits and headed out.

What if this is planned? The terrifying revelation crossed Victor's thoughts, running his blood cold with fear. In all his time in the military, he'd never encountered a similar situation before. Attacks on the Empire's ships simply didn't happen. "Do you think this is connected to our mission objective?" Victor asked.

"I hope to God it isn't, Victor. He's counting on us, and I'll tear anyone apart who stands in my way. If… if that is Hamish out there sending a distress signal, we've got to retrieve him, aye?"

Victor set a hand on his shoulder. "Aye, mate. And we will. Calm down and do your job. Focus."

Trevor nodded. "Thanks. I'm just… after thinking he was dead for all of this time, for him to send our special code… It's got to mean that it's him, doesn't it?"

"We'll find out. Daniels will have the assault squad ready for the retrieval by the time we arrive."

Victor's personal communicator shrieked to life. "Raines to Medical. I have a man down in the hang–" Zoe's voice cut off abruptly before she could complete her message.

"What happened? Did communications drop?" Fear made Victor's lungs squeeze like a vice constricting his ribcage. *Not Zoe. Maybe her link dropped. Maybe systems are down across the board.* His breath shook and his heart rate increased despite his attempt to maintain focus. Oshiro had taught him methods to remain under control, but for a moment they failed him. He was terrified of losing her.

"Shit," Trevor swore. He left the panel and crossed to the medical terminal. "No, comms are still up and running, but Zoe's is inactive. I can't get a link to it."

Victor lingered behind his friend, practically lurking over Trevor's shoulder. "We need those lifts back up. I can't evac wounded without them." *Or get to the hangar to Zoe.*

"I'm doing everything I fucking can, Victor. Let me breathe! I know you're worried about her, but I can't rush this."

When given a man with a gut wound, Victor knew exactly what to do to prolong and save his life. Place him in front of an open series of connectors and power couplings, and he was all thumbs. He grabbed emergency gear while Trevor feverishly worked at the panel.

The green light above the lift in their hallway blinked on. Trevor slammed the access panel shut. "Done."

"Hart, report to the Commodore. Let him know the lifts are up and we have an issue down in the shuttle bay."

Victor and Trevor rushed out. With the lifts operational they arrived on the lower decks within a minute. The Jemison rocked beneath another assault.

"Shit. Looks like the pirates." Trevor directed Victor's attention to one of the small viewports in the hull. "I recognize the build… That's the flagship of the Black Jackals. Where the hell did they receive those kinds of upgrades?"

"What do you mean?" Victor asked.

"That's a bloody military cannon."

"Probably scavenged off a ship…" Victor's voice held uncertainty. To the best of his knowledge, no vessels in Her Majesty's Navy had fallen to smugglers.

"Face facts, Victor. If they scavenged a military cannon off a ship, that means one of ours was lost in battle. Have you heard reports to that effect?" the man asked grimly.

"I know. We'll consider those ramifications later. Right now we need to get to Zoe."

The passageway took them directly down to the hangar. The double doors remained dark and unresponsive, but that was the least of Victor's worries. The sight through the window chilled him.

"What in the hell is going on in there? Why is Sassy holding a gun on Zoe?" Trevor asked in bewilderment. "Christ, that's a body on the floor!"

"Zoe!" Victor banged on the glass.

His arrival drew Saskia's attention to the viewing portal. Zoe capitalized on the distraction and flicked a tool at the woman's hand and charged. Victor held his breath, a helpless observer to the chaos beyond the unbreakable partition. The weapon discharged the moment it struck the floor. Sparks exploded off the nearest shuttle and left a charred, circular dent in the metal.

"We should have taken the maintenance shaft. Shit!" Trevor swore.

"Can you hack into it?"

"Already on it," Trevor muttered from the dataport beside the door. "With the ship offline…"

The two physically skilled women in the hangar exchanged blows, matching strikes and kicks. As a cyborg, Zoe had strength on her side, but Saskia weaved in and out of the fight like a cobra. She lacked Zoe's heavier muscle, and for every punch that the brunette landed, her adversary seemed to deliver two. Saskia was lithe, slender, and frightfully swift.

Daniels had trained her well.

Blood slipped down Zoe's chin, leaving a crimson trail. She shrugged it off and maintained her guard.

Come on, baby. You can do it, he rooted from the sideline. *Take her down, Zo.*

Victor had learned from experience that Zoe hit as hard as any man. She hadn't struck him with her cybernetic arm, but he spent an entire evening icing his jaw to alleviate the swelling after sustaining a blow from the left during a training session. Apologetic kisses and soft laughter had helped ease the discomfort.

"Trevor, what's taking so long?"

"Workin' as fast as I can, I swear to you. I have to get into the wiring to disable the magnetic locks," he explained distractedly. His concentrating expression dissuaded Victor from questioning him further.

The anxious doctor waited beside the door with his surgical laser in hand. A year ago, he'd been completely helpless when news reached him of the ECF Orlando suffering losses during a meteor storm. When he learned that the water supply lines burst and that his wife's H2O tank had drained on the floor during transport, Victor hit rock bottom. Despite all efforts by the flight attendants to keep her moist and comfortable, despite other passengers donating their glasses of refreshment, she had suffered an excruciating death – and he hadn't been there to help her.

Not Zoe, too. Please. He wouldn't survive another loss.

Saskia bore Zoe down to the floor, but the latter managed to gain the upper hand. The two marines flipped across the hard, grated ground. Zoe bloodied Saskia's face until the woman kicked her off. Her opponent lunged for her gun but Zoe caught Saskia by the ankle and tripped her back to the ground. Bloodied spittle flew from Saskia's mouth, indicating she must have bitten her tongue when her chin hit the floor.

"Got it!"

The magnetic lock on the door released. Both men rushed into the bay to find their comrade on top of the situation. Literally.

"Traitor!" Zoe slammed Saskia's face against the floor. "Fucking cow!"

"Zoe, it's over. She's out." Victor pulled Zoe's struggling form off Saskia's limp body right before Daniels and Abernathy swept in with drawn weapons. "Get some restraints on DuPrie. I don't know what happened yet, but Lopez is dead and she had a gun on Raines," he called to them.

"Lopez caught one right between the eyes... Holy shit. She murdered him," Trevor breathed from where he crouched beside the corpse.

Lights blazed above them and returned to functional status.

"The ship has returned to online status. All services will resume shortly. Please standby," Jem's calm voice announced shipwide.

"C'mere. Let me look at you," Victor murmured gently to her.

While Daniels handled Saskia, Victor led Zoe aside to check her over. One of the medical teams arrived but he waved them off. Sometimes, Victor preferred to do the work over delegating authority to anyone else. Zoe was worth that time.

"She broke your nose." Saskia had also gashed Zoe's forehead, but it was nothing a few nanites couldn't set right. He drew his penlight and swiftly assessed her for lingering effects from the fight. "Pupillary reflex looks fine... how's your head?"

"She killed Lopez," Zoe whispered instead.

"I know, Zoe. But how are *you*?"

"Hart to del Toro. We need you in medical. Creswell lost footing in a maintenance shaft and jarred an abductor cable in his left cyberleg pretty terribly during the fall. I'd wrench it back in, but I'm likely to fubar the entire thing, mate. We need you."

Victor paused. He turned his face toward the link pinned to his lab coat. "We have injuries in the shuttle bay, Hart."

"Go. I'll be okay," Zoe urged him.

"Zo…"

She smiled fleetingly and squeezed his hand. "Creswell needs you."

So do you, Victor thought. Zoe's arm was fine and the rest of her injuries could be tended to by any medic. Creswell required a cyberneticist.

"I'll check in on you when I'm done, I promise."

His professional behavior lapsed long enough to kiss her brow. Leaving Zoe behind in a state of need pained him beyond words.

With systems back online, the Jemison engaged engines and began evasive maneuvers. Victor had felt uneasy with the previous stillness of the ship and took reassurance from the familiar thrum of power coursing beneath his feet.

Medical personnel moved back and forth between patients, tending to those injured during the attack. Wounds ranged from mild bruises to second degree burns. Victor and the other doctors had their hands full.

"Stay away from that viewport, Hart. It's small, but if movies have shown me anything, it's that we should never leave a blasted thing to chance," Victor told her.

"Agreed," Oshiro said from the mouth of the corridor that led into their open lounge. He and Davis approached from the examination rooms.

Hart reluctantly stepped away from the small window. A few other members of the medical team nervously shot glances at the translucent portal to the world beyond their ship. Occasional bursts of cannon fire lit the open void of space like a thousand stars all combusting at once.

"How's our traitor?" she asked Oshiro.

"Properly secured under an armed guard in the treatment room," he replied.

"Hogwash is what it is. The bint hobbled our ship, killed one of our men, and now we've got to play nice with her?" Davis demanded.

News on a ship spread like wildfire. Saskia's arrival under guard in medical had started an entire slew of rumors and accusations. It didn't take long for the story of her betrayal to make the rounds.

Victor shook his head. "Trust me. She won't find anything nice about what happens to her next, once our ship is in the clear."

"Yeah? What's happening, Commander. What can you tell us?" Fairchild asked eagerly. "You've always been straight with us."

"Yeah. About that. I don't actually know what's happening next. With the commodore on the bridge directing the battle, I'm honestly in the dark, too."

Their expressions deflated. Just as Victor opened his mouth to apologize for his lack of information, Jem's voice blasted over the public channels, "Red alert status has ended."

Hart sagged in relief against him. He leaned against her in return.

"Thank God. I've never been in an actual battle before. That was terrifying."

"Very," Lil agreed quietly from her work station. The young woman didn't show her fear, but Hart had glanced at her often enough to indicate that she picked up on her emotions.

"Now I'm going to the viewport," Hart announced. She and Davis fought over it. The result of their squabble was that both women ended up cheek to cheek, peering through the small window into the outside world. The Jemison used its tractor beam to anchor and draw the deactivated ship toward them.

"They'll board the ship," Oshiro stated calmly. "We must be prepared for more injuries."

A doctor's work was never finished.

CHAPTER 22

Rendered completely harmless, Saskia lay upon an examination table with little more than a modest sheet covering her. Medical staff had secured her safely with restraints.

"How long do you suppose she's been on their side?"

"Impossible to tell," Ethan replied to Victor. The man crossed his arms against his chest. "I want to throttle the little bitch for what she's done, but we're waiting for Nisrine to begin the interrogation."

"Hopefully we will receive answers for this travesty," Oshiro said. The older man shook his head and quietly observed.

"How's Raines?" Ethan asked suddenly. "She's earned herself a promotion as far as I'm concerned, stopping this traitor before she escaped."

"Lil patched her up and sedated her to ensure she got some rest before we arrive for the mission. She's fit for duty, if that's what you're asking," Victor said.

"No, I simply meant–"

The doors hissed open and cut Ethan off, heralding the arrival of their intelligence officer. Nisrine approached the CO with her chin held high. Her reddened, puffy eyes told the story they already knew.

"You good for this, love?" Ethan whispered to her. His blue eyes searched her weary face.

Nisrine nodded and turned away from the three officers.

"As you won't willingly give over the information we seek, it appears that I shall have to retrieve it all myself." Nisrine strolled up to the table.

"You can't do this to me. There are bloody laws prohibiting–" Saskia struggled against her restraints.

"You seem to forget something, DuPrie. You're a traitor and this is my ship. A good man is dead because of you," Ethan spoke out in an even voice. "You won't receive an ounce of pity from us."

The ship had sustained heavy damage during the space battle, but Lopez's death remained the priority matter. Ethan valued people over property.

Unfortunately, Saskia didn't feel the same way.

"This will not hurt *me* a bit. I cannot say the same for you." Nisrine lowered both hands to Saskia's head and cradled her face with both thumbs against the traitor's cheekbones. Nisrine anchored her head in place and prohibited any movement.

They all knew when the real work began once Saskia's terrified shrieks began to reverberate through the room. She thrashed on the examination table and her pupils dilated as her memories were rifled through.

The use of telepathic abilities lacked pretty physical effects to mark Nisrine's progress; she didn't glow, shimmer, or appear any different while invading Saskia's mind. Instead, they were treated to the spectacle of the psychic victim convulsing and screaming while Nisrine calmly leaned over her without loosening her grip. "Good. I hope it hurts. I hope it hurts badly," Nisrine said.

Victor involuntarily shrank back a step.

Nearly twenty years ago, as a new candidate for the Naval Academy, he and a dozen other of the Empire's finest had each spent a half hour with the school's psychic.

He didn't remember her name anymore, but he would always remember her face and the pitying look in her eyes when her hands lowered from his cheeks. He remembered that she had excused herself and taken a tissue to dry her eyes, and that she'd called an end to the psych exams for the day and resumed them the next morning. Like Oshiro, she never reported what she saw to the top brass. There wasn't a doubt in Victor's mind that his past would have disqualified him from serving as an officer.

"Are you able to get anything from her?" Victor asked hesitantly.

"Plenty."

Ethan dropped his voice low and whispered to Victor, "She isn't killing her, is she?"

"I don't believe so. Though I think there's always a risk of brain death whenever a psychic goes into an unwilling mind like this," he replied.

"She is the one who took Hamish Lockhart," Nisrine reported. "There is a clear memory here of stalking him during his patrol. Attacking. She dropped his body for others to pick up."

"That means she's worked for the enemy at least five years. Perhaps six" Victor said.

"What about the people directing her movements. Who are they? Who's responsible for this treachery?" Ethan asked.

"This woman," Nisrine spat the word with vehemence, as if she had another description in mind. "She informed Jarvis Crane of patrol routes, allowing him to keep ahead of us.

Ethan grunted. "That bloody tosser wasn't even on board. Bastard must have fled prior to the assault, but we do have his second mate's corpse in the freezer. What else do you see?"

"She reported to the leader of her cell, Doctor Mathias Campbell, and she killed him when you were too close. She is the one who attempted to gas you on Kantarn."

"Shit," Victor swore under his breath. "I didn't want to believe he was that high up."

Ethan clapped a hand to his shoulder. "Is that it, Nisrine? There has to be someone higher."

"Nothing. Her mind is particularly resilient when it comes to identifying her superiors. Either she remains unaware of their identities or she has been conditioned to conceal them. I can continue to delve deeper, but it may kill her this time." Nisrine's hardened gaze remained on the woman in her hold.

"Do it."

"Do we want to risk losing her?" Victor spoke up suddenly to his friend. "I want the information as badly as you do, but…"

"I know. Do no harm," Ethan muttered.

"Nisrine is one of the best in her field when it comes to retrieving mental data. If she is unable to do it safely, no other psychic can," Oshiro said. The man frowned. Like Victor, he didn't approve of Ethan's methods. "But the possibility of loss is great. We are not the ASR, Ethan. Please. Let us have a traitor to release to the prison ship when it arrives."

The Soviets wouldn't have hesitated to vegetate one of our own, Victor thought bitterly. As much as he despised having to call an end to it, risking Saskia's life so deliberately would make them no better than their enemies across the galaxy.

"Fine," Ethan agreed. He waved a hand. "Get her to the brig in a paper gown only, but take that back once she's secure. I want two female officers at her cell at all times."

Saskia's history as a highly trained and deadly field operative meant Ethan didn't plan to leave anything to chance. Victor didn't blame him. He'd watched Saskia pick a lock with her fingertip once.

Saskia's head lolled to the side after Nisrine released her. Hart moved in and guided the quaking psychic away without prompting.

"Oshiro gave her an injection to destabilize her abilities. She won't be going camo any time soon either, but we colored her arms with medical dye just in case," Victor said.

"Brilliant. All right, I have to go write some reports. I hate this bloody part of my job."

Victor sympathized. "Can't believe we also lost Roswell."

"Lovely marine. I know. Fastest shot on the bloody ship, too. That's why she qualified for the boarding party. It'll be impossible to replace her. The same goes for Lopez, beyond their duties."

Losing a member of the crew was never easy and Victor could only imagine the deeper loss Ethan felt as the commanding officer. He clapped his friend on the shoulder.

"We'll get who did this, Ethan."

"Yes. We will." Ethan drew in a deep breath. "Go on now and check your bird."

"She's asleep remember? There's too much work to do, and too many injured."

"No, you are going to rest. I need you fresh for this mission, Victor. Check on Raines to ease your worries then hit your rack. That's an order. I'll see you in ten hours."

He's right. I did the same thing to my medical team not even an hour ago. "Ten hours. We'll get our guy back."

If they made it in time.

CHAPTER 23

Zoe's sedation denied Victor the chance to speak with her. By the time she awakened and reported for the mission, the Jemison was less than an hour away from its destination.

I'll talk to her after we rescue our marine.

He returned her uncertain smile and sat beside her on the shuttle during its somber descent. The dense jungle landscape claimed most of the planetary surface and restricted the squad's options for a landing zone. They chose the facility's rooftop shuttle pad for its close proximity and practical position.

Without wasting a second Daniels kicked open the roof access door and the marines spilled into the facility, moving as a cohesive unit once they breached the property. They had a single mission: to safely retrieve their lost comrade. Hamish Lockhart had to be somewhere in the building.

"Movement on level two," Trevor reported. He paused in the middle of the corridor and lowered his shotgun to one side. The other arm extended in front of him. "I can feel them... They're directly beneath us. Six... no, seven."

"Do you feel your brother?" Victor asked.

"No."

"They may have protection against psychics on their lower levels. It wouldn't be the first time we've seen those tactics deployed to protect company secrets," Daniels said.

Trevor nodded. The hope remained in his bright green eyes.

Daniels and Zoe took point. The group rounded a corner in the hallway, coming up on two uniformed security officers.

"Weapons down and hands up!" Daniels bellowed.

"Don't shoot!" The panicked officers threw up their hands. The man and woman each wore a Taser on their left hip.

"We didn't do anything," the woman shouted. "Please don't shoot."

"Holy shit. Royal Navy? What's going on?" another confused voice shouted from the lobby.

Five more security officers emerged from a surveillance room. Once they saw the guns leveled at them, they also put up their hands.

"Any one of you wanna tell us what happened here?" Daniels asked as he stepped forward.

"We wish that we knew," one of them spoke up.

"The scientists packed up in a hurry. First, they put out an alert about some experiment escaping the laboratory. They had us out there in the jungle looking for it, but wouldn't tell us shit about it," another guard said.

Victor and Trevor exchanged looks.

"Did they reclaim their experiment?" Victor asked.

One of the guards shook his head. His pale face, along with the fluttering heartbeat Victor picked up on the bioscanner, indicated his words were true. "Not that we know of. They started panicking after three hours. Said the tracking equipment was shot to hell. Apparently, their science project killed a couple of us down in the lower levels. Next thing we know, they're loading up on the shuttles. Took off without us."

"We're stranded here," the female security guard said.

Daniels raised one hand to his communicator. "Daniels to Commodore Bishop. The facility has been abandoned. No sign of Lockhart yet."

"We really don't know anything," the male guard repeated.

"Find out if they're telling us the truth, Chief. Raines and Abernathy, clear the rooms on this floor," Daniels ordered.

"Gladly, sir."

Trevor confirmed the veracity of their claims in under two minutes. The security officers were too afraid and confused to pose a threat.

"The back rooms are clear," Zoe reported, coming back into the hallway. "There's no one else here."

"Did you find anything?"

Zoe nodded. "Papers. A few tools. If these guys weren't here to tell us what happened, I'd say the place was ransacked by pirates."

"They must have cleared out before our arrival. The laboratory offices are empty," Abernathy added.

Daniels deployed the team in pairs to sweep through the remainder of the facility. The security officers who had been left behind voluntarily confined themselves to an empty office and stayed out of the military's way.

"If they departed in a rush, then they left DNA evidence. We'll get a forensics team in to perform a full sweep and try to discern some identities from that," Victor said.

"Sirs," Davis spoke through her commlink. "I found a surgical room in the lower level and two corpses. Looks like a marine's work."

"O'Malley and I found living victims in the adjoining building, Commander," Williams spoke up through the communication channel. "It looks like Campbell's clinic. We have a lot of malnourished and scared people."

"Do what you can for them until we can secure the building," Victor replied.

The marine commanders rendezvoused with Davis in the basement level, where they found her crouched above a corpse with another body sprawled nearby. Both members of security wore cutting-edge armor, and their holsters were fitted to protect specialized guns.

Daniels whistled. "I know the model that belongs in there. The guys upstairs didn't have anything like this," he pointed out. "I'd put money on it that the main level guards are nonessential staff, and these are their loyal security squad members."

"Of course. They kept a couple poor sods aware of their illegal studies in the event that something of this nature were to occur. Fat lot of good it's done them." Victor shook his head.

"He killed these two… See the broken neck? Took their pistols after that, I think. Both of them have empty holsters," Davis pointed out. "There's a third body in the next room, but it was stripped of everything but his boots. My guess is that our guy took him out first and snagged his uniform, then came up on these two without so much as raising an alarm."

"I'll be damned," Daniels muttered, impressed.

"Hamish was always one of the best operatives on any ship. Maybe… I want to try something. If the body hasn't been dead for long, maybe I can see the last thing to cross this man's vision," Trevor said.

"Go for it," Victor encouraged him.

Trevor crouched beside Davis and took in a deep breath. With both hands against the cheeks of the corpse, he turned the security guard's face toward the ceiling and leaned above him to make direct eye contact. What took seconds for the observing marines must have felt like the passing of hours for Trevor. He took his shaking hands away and dropped heavily back onto his behind.

"It was Hamish. He's really *alive*."

"We knew that all along, mate. Come on. Let's go find him now." Victor leaned down and pulled Trevor up to his feet again.

"You don't get it, Victor. I *saw* him. Right in front of me…"

They waited until he re-gathered his wits and recovered from the psychic experience then Davis pointed out the trail of carnage for them to follow. It led to a locked door requiring a security clearance.

Trevor viewed the map briefly. "It's the only way out of here," he muttered.

"Can you hack it?" Zoe asked.

"Sure I can," Trevor knelt beside one of the fallen bodies and pulled an identcard from the man's pocket. "Or I can swipe this and get out faster."

A world of jungle flora awaited them on the opposite side. Less than twenty yards from the door, a network of plant life obstructed their path, created from dense vegetation and twisting red leaves.

"How are we going to find anything in this?" Daniels demanded.

"Hell if I know. Perhaps if we divide into–"

"Here!" Davis cried. Her call came from the edge of the growth. "Right here. Someone came through this way barefoot. You can see a heel indent in the soil. The ground is still soft."

"Good catch, Davis. Where'd you learn to track?" Daniels eyed her thoughtfully.

"My dad used to take me hunting before I joined up with the Navy. Showed me a lot of things," Davis replied. "He went this way. No wonder no one found him... It's thick. To our benefit, though. He crushed a lot of the flora when he ran through. Poor bloke's probably scratched to bloody hell."

"And scared," Victor remarked for Trevor's sake. "Let's try not to draw pistols. He's armed and we don't want to offer him any reason to fire at us before he recognizes our colors."

Trevor shot him an appreciative look, which he returned with a smile. Their path took the group deeper into the jungle where the ground squished beneath their feet and became boggy from the atmosphere's excessive rain patterns.

"There. He tripped over that root and fell down on one knee here. Heavy bastard, isn't he?" Davis commented. She glanced at Trevor doubtfully before they proceeded forward.

Without warning, a shot glanced harmlessly off the helmet protecting Victor's head. As a result, every marine ducked and moved into defensive positions with their guns drawn.

"Don't shoot!" Trevor yelled. He jumped forward with his arms out. His firearm landed in the brush as he broke ranks and ran forward.

"Lockhart, no!" Daniels called after him.

It was too late. The psychic delved into the thick foliage, pushing forward while calling his brother's name.

Sweeping heavy branches out of his path, Victor broke through the thick growth a second later to find Trevor in a standoff with an armed man. With the exception of a few physical details, Trevor and Hamish were similar in every way. The latter no longer had hair, as it had been shaved away, most likely during some recent procedure.

"How do I know you're who you claim to be?" Hamish demanded.

The gun shook slightly in Hamish's hand as he backed away from the approaching marines. Victor held out one hand, begging caution. Despite his cool and calm appearance, his heart hammered inside his chest.

"No one move. Give him a moment. Put your weapons away," Victor ordered. "You too, Daniels."

"Do as he says," Daniels ordered. Everyone lowered their guns but remained on alert.

"Hamish, I'm your brother. I'd never do anything to hurt you."

"Prove this isn't another test. Tell me something only Trevor would know."

"When we were six, you shoved another kid face down in the mud for knocking my ice cream cone out of my hand. Da' was upset about the trouble it caused, but mum praised us behind his back and said we should always count on each other."

Hamish's hand wavered. As the seconds ticked by, it appeared as if he might drop the weapon. "I can't trust that. I can't trust any of you. They've been in my head... they know everything. This is all a lie. You only want to drag me back to that room."

"Read my thoughts, Hamish. You'll see the truth."

Hamish's bleak expression was one Victor knew well. His weary features displayed open despair and loss of the deepest kind.

"I can't," Hamish whispered. "They took it from me."

Trevor stopped in his tracks, and the placid mask he wore for the sake of his brother finally cracked. "Big brother, let me help you. Please put down the gun."

Hamish shook his head again and took another step backward. "They like to play games. You're not real."

"They're gone," Victor spoke up gently. He stepped forward slowly with Trevor, only to pause when Hamish's muscles stiffened. The tension spread down his arm to his trembling hand. "How do you feel about leaving this place, Hamish? Would you like to see the Jemison again?"

"I'd like to go home. I want to return to the Jemison again," Hamish admitted. His eyes flicked back and forth, giving him a close resemblance to a trapped animal. He tracked their movements, missing nothing, always watchful and alert.

"What do you have to lose?" Victor asked softly. He grazed Trevor's hand with his knuckles. *I'm going to distract him so that the rest of you can take him down, mate. Tell Fairchild to sedate him. Have Zoe and Daniels secure him.*

He'll shoot you. He's a caged animal right now, Victor. Don't do it.

I won't allow him to strike anything vital, Victor thought. Their mental conversation occurred in the span of a second.

Victor made his move and lurched forward.

"No!" Hamish practically shrieked. He squeezed the trigger as if by reflex, with the barrel already trained on Victor. The impact knocked the doctor backward and shattered the plate of his combat armor. It punched him down to the bone.

Gritting through the pain, Victor sat heavily on the ground and fetched a secondary tranquilizer from his personal medipack. His instincts were rarely wrong, and his intuition told him that Fairchild would need another dose soon.

"We're trying to help you!" Zoe grunted.

Zoe pitted the strength of her cybernetic arm against Hamish's weight to pin him down from one side. Daniels and Chang took him from the right and practically laid their bodies across his torso to secure him to the ground. He bucked wildly, a traumatized victim behaving beyond his own control, and drove one of his knees into Daniels' side. The Commander grunted out in pain.

"Now, Fairchild!" Daniels ordered.

Fairchild dove in and jabbed the auto-ejecting tranquilizer against the outer aspect of Hamish's thigh. As she slammed it home, it cracked and the needle snapped.

"No good!" Fairchild reported. "He's got cybernetic muscle weave beneath his skin."

"Catch!" Victor hurled the second toward her. "Inject it into the jugular!"

"I won't go back there!" Hamish yelled, maddened. He threw an elbow back into Chang's face, shattering the demolition grade polymer faceplate.

"Holy shit! Cybernetic arms, too!"

Hamish's larger size and superior reach granted him the advantage in the fight, but Zoe moved faster and with more flexibility. She threw her weight against him and wrapped her arms and legs around the downed man in a full body hold.

"Stick him already, dammit!" Zoe cried. Hamish struggled in her grasp.

"Daniels, secure him from the right," Victor barked out. "Raines has it handled on her side."

The injector pumped Hamish with milky fluid, and then the true fight began. He buried the soles of his feet against the ground and shoved. If not for Fairchild clinging to him like a toddler, he might have overpowered the combatants pitting their strength against him.

"Hold him until it works!" Fairchild screamed.

Between the combined efforts of the marines and the potent mix of sedatives, the fight slowly drained from Hamish Lockhart. He feebly pushed and shoved until his eyes rolled back and his jaw became slack.

None of the soldiers pinning him dared to move.

"Is he out for good?" Zoe grunted, wedged halfway beneath the heavy man. She tried to shove him off but barely managed to nudge him an inch. "How the hell much can one guy weigh?"

Daniels helped pull her out. "Damn, he's strong as an ox," he muttered.

"Sort of glad you put us through the ringer on the mats, Commander. Longest ground tussle of my life," Chang complained. The man sagged against a tree while Davis tended to his bleeding face. Jagged shards from his shattered faceplate were embedded in his skin. Luck had been on his side since both of his eyes remained intact.

Victor grunted from where he sat on the ground. While they were occupied with Hamish, he began his own field dressing. Applying it one-handed took more skill than he anticipated.

"Here, let me help."

"I've got it. Raines, you see to Hamish."

Zoe ignored him in favor of kneeling down to pull at the shredded remnants of his shoulder piece, revealing the dark blood soaking the uniform beneath it. "Let me help you, your hand is shaking. Here, I can—"

"I fucking said I've got it," he snapped, jerking from her.

She flinched at the reprimand and dropped her hands. "As you say, sir."

He regretted his harsh tone immediately. Unfortunately, there was no taking it back. While Hamish and Trevor counted on them, they would have to cast aside their feelings; he needed an obedient marine, not a lover.

Cool logic didn't change the way his stomach twisted in turmoil, and Victor knew if their positions were reversed, he'd have done the same thing.

CHAPTER 24

Zoe reclined on her bunk and gazed up at the ceiling above her. A poster collage of her favorite family photos decorated the former bland grey surface. She may not see eye to eye with her parents, but she still loved them deeply.

"Sergeant Zoe Raines, there is a message for you from Commander Victor del Toro," Jem's voice informed her in a perfect, breathy sigh.

Zoe jerked her attention toward the speaker aperture located in the corner of the room. "Go ahead and play it, Jem," she replied to the ship A.I.

"Report to my office in medical, Sergeant Raines. Now."

Shit. The usual warmth in Victor's voice was absent. She hardly recognized the stern tone.

"Uh-oh," Angela muttered. "What did you *do?*"

A shake of her head discouraged her bunkmate from pressing further. Zoe hastily slipped back into her uniform, heart pounding. She had a solid guess what he wanted to talk to her about. Before heading out, she dampened her fingers and ran them through her hair to tame the disheveled strands.

Victor's office door took on an intimidating presence, one she steeled herself against with both palms pressed over the cool surface. Once her racing heart calmed, she knocked.

"Come in."

Zoe stepped inside, muscles tense. She closed the door behind her and stood at attention in front of Victor's desk.

She focused on a spot over his shoulder because she couldn't meet his dispassionate grey eyes.

"You wanted to see me, sir?"

"Would you like to tell me what you were doing down there, and why you disobeyed my order?" Victor demanded.

"I saw our medical officer bleeding out and struggling to treat himself." It came out before she could tame her tongue. Victor wasn't amused.

"I must be mistaken. I wasn't aware of your medical training, Sergeant Raines."

Zoe opened her mouth to speak but quickly snapped it shut. She swallowed back her protest, stomach churning. It wasn't the first time she'd been subjected to a reprimand or stern words from a ranking crewman, but it cut deeper coming from him.

"It's recently become apparent to me that we've surpassed the point of maintaining a professional relationship."

In her heart, she'd always known there'd come a time when they were no longer able to work together. She nodded in silent agreement.

"There's also no room on our squad for a marine who can't follow my orders. I've put in notice to Commodore Bishop requesting your immediate reassignment to another team."

His words carried the same effect as dousing her with a bucket of ice water. She was numbed initially, and then furious, the anger sweeping through her until the heat of it reached the top of her ears. "Permission to speak freely, sir."

The momentary loss of his stoic expression indicated Victor's surprise. Once the surprise faded, he nodded and leaned back in the seat.

"With all due respect, *sir*," Zoe said, "But if you have a problem with me being on this team, then *you* need to deal with it. Yes, I tried to help you instead of tending to

Hamish, but did my actions hurt the team? Pulling rank on me like this is crap."

"Is that all?"

She swallowed back another bitter retort and nodded. "Yes, sir."

"You're dismissed, Sergeant. We'll speak later outside the office."

Zoe snapped to attention, turned about face, and strode out without another word. She didn't trust herself, even if she had the breath to speak. Without looking, it felt as if every eye in medical followed her on the way out.

She made it out the department's door before the first tears slipped down her cheeks. The pressure building in her chest released as a choked sob which she quickly attempted to smother by ducking her head and covering her mouth with her hand. The path ahead of her became the least of her worries, right up until she sped around a corner and bounced into a solid wall of chest. The most muscled chest she'd ever seen beneath an officer's uniform.

"Raines?"

Kill me, now. Please. Running into the CO, literally, seemed like the worst sort of luck on top of a day gone so horribly wrong.

"What's wrong, love? What can I do for you?"

"Nothing, Commodore," she rushed out, face warming to a feverish temperature. "I'm so s-sorry. I should have been paying attention."

"Toss the formalities into the rubbish for a moment. Now what's wrong? What have I missed?"

Zoe shook her head, wishing she had a hole to crawl away into. If it was possible to die from shame, she'd be a stone cold corpse at his feet.

"It's n-nothing, sir." Another sob escaped her lips.

"We'll have a jaunt through the bio-farm then. Come on. I'm told by one of my officers that it's the cool place where all of the kids like to snog these days. Let's go have ourselves an eyeful."

Commodore Bishop left her little choice in the matter. His hand settled on her back between her shoulder blades, guiding her down the passageway.

He even offered her a handkerchief. The gentlemanly gesture caught her by surprise.

"Take your time."

His kindness opened the floodgates. Zoe couldn't stop her tears, so she focused on not blubbering. *Get it together, Zoe! No way you can cry to the CO. Not about this.*

Numb, Zoe was dimly aware of passing trees and carefully tended rows of vegetables. She focused on her breathing and pulling it back in like a proper marine.

"Are you feeling better now?" Once she nodded, he continued. "Perhaps this is too personal to ask, but would you kindly tell me why Victor's requested for your transfer? I'd like to hear it from you first."

Great. Zoe twisted the damp square of cloth between her hands and drew in another deep breath. "I didn't follow an order, sir," she replied in a carefully measured tone.

His features softened and for those seconds, Commodore Bishop wasn't the hard-ass commanding officer of the ship, he was any sweet, fatherly figure showing concern for a person in his care. "I assure you, Sergeant Raines, I haven't asked out of duty to a friend. You have my word that nothing said to me here will condemn you or return to the doctor. What order?"

"I…" she blinked, spilling another tear down her cheek. "The marine we were sent to find, he shot him, sir. After assisting in taking him down, I went to check on Vic–Doctor del Toro. He was wounded and… and looked as though he was having trouble. I offered to help and he told me he had it and to assist the other members of the squad. I tried to help him anyway. As I saw it, sir, our doctor was wounded and there were plenty of others on top of the situation with Hamish for the moment."

"The poor sod didn't dress you down in front of the rest of medical, did he?"

"Doctor del Toro called me to his office, sir, to address my insubordination. He was right to." *Doesn't make it hurt any less.*

He punched in something on his personal datagram. A subtle beep from her badge indicated a change in her duty status. "Good. Go clean up and lay in your cot for the day. I'll handle our mutual friend. As a squad leader, it's up to him whether or not you'll remain on the team, but I *will* offer my recommendation to rethink his request."

"Thank you, sir, but you don't need to do that. I didn't mean to trouble you." Zoe offered the handkerchief back to him.

"Keep it. I've got a thousand of them for the enlisted." The commodore strode away.

Zoe remained beneath the trees a few minutes longer, wondering if she'd be forced to choose between the team she loved and the man she treasured.

CHAPTER 25

Victor loathed invasive neuro procedures most of all. Arms and legs were basic performance modifications, but none of those were potentially life-threatening issues. If he botched a job by misplacing a cybernetic leg's nerve connection to the hip socket, no one died. He simply opened the patient's incisions and tried again.

The human brain required absolute precision to a degree beyond human capabilities. Doctors like Victor relied on virtual enhancements, droid-assisted surgery, nanobots, and software protocols to perform necessary neurosurgeries. For that reason, and that reason alone, he had no intention of physically delving into Hamish Lockhart's skull. And thanks to the blueprints and work left behind by Mathias Campbell, he wouldn't have to. An hour of exploration with the NORI machine told him everything he needed to know and confirmed the blueprints in Campbell's database referred to Hamish.

Fairchild dabbed Victor's brow with a cloth while he made the incisions with his surgical laser. Anxiety beaded his forehead with sweat, almost to the point of distraction. One wrong move could activate Hamish's internal defenses and instantaneously detoxify the sedatives from his bloodstream. One miscalculation in their dosage estimations would be enough for Hamish Lockhart to awaken from his drug-induced sleep. They didn't want that happening.

"He's so bloody complicated. Never seen anything like this," Victor muttered as he opened a window into the cyborg's chest. The layer of synthetic skin peeled away to reveal Hamish's metal-plated bone structure. Plasteel-laced bone guarded his interior organs, most of which appeared to be improved or replaced. They had practically hollowed him.

"As you can see, they've augmented roughly 60% of his skeletal structure with a reinforced periosteum. Both arms are prosthetic with reinforced shoulder joints."

Davis took her position at the opposite side and assisted with holding the small incision open. His sternum split open down the middle once unbolted and pried apart, designed for easy access.

"Overhead lights: swivel fifteen degrees starboard, thirty degrees downward," Victor commanded the surgical theater's artificial intelligence. "God, would you look at this, Oshiro." The micro-camera on his tools projected a live-time feed on the monitor to the other doctor observing on the other side of the glass. "His heart has a complex filter to separate the cybernetic lipids from his bloodstream. You see, humans need blood, but blood clots in cybernetic parts. Causes blockages. Hamish doesn't have to worry about that."

Or plenty of other things, Victor realized. The boy was an anomaly, constructed piece by piece to such a degree that more machine existed than man. At the very least, the ratio was close.

"According to the notes from Campbell's files, they added a failsafe. If I remove it now, that's one less concern to trouble us later," Victor muttered.

"His vitals are holding steady. The suspended microparticles seem to be holding the sedatives in his system," Lil reported from the side of the room. Her sole job was to keep Hamish under.

"All right, I'm going in."

A series of leads connected to Hamish's heart, wiring him like a ticking time bomb. First, Victor snipped the signal relay. Someone out in the galaxy held Hamish's life in their hands, and Victor would be damned if they ended it now. Second, he cut the feed from the electrical current along with its backup supply to be absolutely safe. Victor performed the operation as dictated by the manual until the sadistic cardioverter was no longer a threat to Hamish's life. He dropped the sinister device into a metal tray O'Reilly held.

If I didn't get that hunch about Campbell, this wouldn't be possible. I'd be floundering in the dark and this entire thing would have gone tits up, he realized.

It took less time to close Hamish up than it did to open him. In ten minutes, Biosutures and medical grade glue restored him to near-perfect condition. Their patient was none the wiser, but his medical staff only relaxed once they returned him to observation status.

"Do you have that thing cleaned up, O'Reilly?"

"Right here, sir."

The round device looked like any other pacemaker at first glance. They worked off a kinetic power source, converting movement from the beating heart itself to keep their charge. This one had been heavily modified to release a lethal shock and to slay its wearer, but once it was rinsed clean of blood and oily residue, Victor saw the detailed electronics encased in the protective clear case.

Victor set it beneath a magnifying scope and brought the image up on screen.

"Did it serve an actual practical purpose?" Oshiro asked. "Will he be all right without the simple pacemaker, that is?"

"I don't think he'll require one," Victor replied, turning the medical tool slowly beneath the scope. "All we can do now is monitor him. If he does, we can put one back in."

"One that will not kill him on a whim." Oshiro sighed and shook his head. "To see them take something designed to prolong and assist life, then subvert it to such a cause."

"I know, Yuki. Power and money appear to have corrupted these doctors."

"Ah, there, is that what you were looking for?" On the screen, the enhanced image showed the small details the human eye alone would miss. A small series of numbers were etched into a chip on the cardioverter next to a faded pictogram. Oshiro magnified the image further. "It looks as though they tried to acid wash the serial away."

"Yeah, but they couldn't all the way without compromising the integrity of the chip itself. This logo looks vaguely familiar, too."

Oshiro stepped over and touched his hand to Victor's back. "Go. You will need fresh eyes to solve this, Victor, and you have been running on fumes."

"But—"

"No excuses. You have your own wound to tend to and Hamish is safe now. O'Reilly can take this down to Intel and let them research it."

"Right away, Doctor."

Victor sighed. "Take it directly to the lieutenant, O'Reilly. No one else. Ask her to please find out all she can about it and its manufacturers."

"Will do, sir."

While Hamish remained in hibernation under Oshiro's watchful eye, Victor retreated to his office and tended to his own needs after pulling up a chair to a small mirror. He removed his scrub top and peered down at the jagged line of staples. Sloppiest work he'd ever done on himself, and he didn't know whether he had Zoe to blame for the distraction, or if his hand had shaken as much as she claimed.

"That looks like shite, Victor. Did you allow a local monkey to stitch you up?" Ethan announced his arrival with a joke at his pal's expense.

Victor grunted and continued to pluck the staples out of his shoulder. "It's not that bad. It was barely a flesh wound," he replied. "The bloody tosser fired a shatter round at me. It's a piece of armor that punctured my skin - not the bullet. Didn't puncture a blood vessel." He dropped the final staple into the tray and sagged in his seat.

"Ah, I see."

The two, simple words carried an entire load of connotation behind them. Victor sighed.

"What do you want, Ethan? Hamish is stable, and I'll be back to work as soon as I finish this. I actually planned to call you down once I reviewed the surgical exam."

"You work too hard, but in this instance I understand. Still, that's not why I've come. I wanted to see if you were serious about this transfer request. A bit dramatic isn't it?"

Victor paused with his back to his friend. Ethan knew how to read him as well as Oshiro did, and that meant that he had to keep it cool. "Are you officially questioning my judgment, Commodore?"

"Maybe. Or perhaps I'm simply trying to get a better handle on what happened."

"She disobeyed an order. When lives are stake, every order counts. I can't have a member of our team playing favorites," Victor said evenly.

"Of course you can't. But, and I want you to think back carefully, did you give an actual order? Or did you just not want any help? You doctors are always a stubborn lot."

Victor stiffened. "I gave a very clear order to attend to the man we landed to rescue. She ignored it."

"According to Daniels' report, Zoe is the one who pinned him down after he shot you. Seems like he was well attended." Ethan spread his hands. "Look, Victor, I know how hard onboard relationships can be. Why the hell do you think I avoid entanglements?"

"Yes, and then you behave like a randy, ill-bred canine the moment we disembark from our ship. Not to mention your online behavior."

Ethan grimaced. "Right, well, there is that, too. But it's more than just avoiding any sort of preferential treatment. You can't swing too far the other direction either. If it had been anyone else on the team, would you be requesting a transfer?"

Ethan hit a nerve. To avoid responding, Victor resumed cleaning his wound with a topical agent. He drew up a dose of pain reliever and reparative gel, and injected it directly into the partially closed wound. "I made the right decision," he finally answered when Ethan stood by staring at him.

"So… if I put her on the boarding team are you going to be useful, or are you going to be pacing the medical wards like a caged drake? I refuse to waste her talents in the armory."

"Maybe I've decided to end it and follow my commanding officer's lead, you bloody hypocrite."

"By all means, go make the woman cry. Then you'll be in your cot doing the same bloody thing by midnight, you wanker. Once this mission is complete, I'll support whatever you choose… but I want you to know this, Victor: your Eloran is gone, but you've got a fine woman right here who cares as deeply. Don't ruin it. Don't chase her away because you haven't the slightest clue about how to handle a shred of authority. You, most of all, know how much you deserve happiness."

Groaning, Victor ran his fingers through his hair and leaned forward against the table. "I hate when you talk sensibly. Go diddle one of your online playmates and leave me be."

"I'll enjoy some downtime once you and the Lockharts are settled. How is he?"

"I removed the device from his heart successfully and intel has their hands on it. He burns through sedatives like nothing I've ever seen though. Lil had to keep a constant stream going to hold him under for the surgery."

"A poor reaction to the drugs you think or something deeper?"

"Not sure yet but I'm pretty sure it has nothing to do with the meds. The initial drugs became ineffective before we returned to the Jemison but he didn't wake up. He has a lot of security precautions, and I'm sure that one was intended to neutralize sedation and drugs." Victor stood up from the chair and pulled his shirt on again. "C'mon. I'll take you to him since you're here."

Victor stepped over to the patient room. Hamish lay upon a hospital cot in a simple gown. His bland, emotionless stare focused on the wall opposite the bed while Trevor sat beside him.

"Trevor?"

The conscious twin scrubbed at his face with the heel of his palm quickly to dry away the moisture on his cheeks. "Oshiro let me in a minute ago after they finished the cleanup. I had to see him in case he wakes up. You know?"

"No need to explain, mate, you're fine. But would you come into the office with us for a wee bit? I'd like to review the results of the examination and surgery with you both. I promise, if he shows any sign of waking, we'll come right back."

Oshiro joined them in Victor's office as well, where they settled in seats and nervously prepared for the worst.

A digital video replayed the events via high definition projection, transforming the doctor's personal office wall into a macabre picture show. In three hours, they reviewed twelve hours of Victor's hard work with scanning equipment and ended it with his surgery.

"Using the intel retrieved from Campbell's system, I managed to locate and disable a kill switch sutured into Hamish's heart. It can't threaten him now, but it was the least of his troubles. He also has extensive brain modifications."

"Is it beyond your scope of ability?" Oshiro asked Victor.

"I've never operated on anything this complex in all of my studies. I don't know how he survived brain wiring to this extent. Hell, I'm still trying to piece together how some of these parts work. All right, look there."

"The amygdala?"

Victor nodded to Oshiro. "Yes. I believe that could be to blame for his bland affect. They installed a chip–"

"Speak English, Doc. Please," Trevor pleaded, cutting in.

"The amygdala is the… you could call it the control center for human emotions," Oshiro explained.

"And many other things," Victor confirmed. "Memory, aggression, our sexual orientation. Everything that makes us a feeling human being resides there."

"So they've done something to Hamish's… amygdala. That's why he's zoned out?"

"Yes. Until we can rule out any remote control and compulsion, we'll have to maintain strict IV sedation, Trevor. I don't like doing it, but it's the only way," Victor said. "It's too great of a risk to allow him to awaken on his own."

"But he was awake. He *talked* to us," Trevor said.

"I know. The most that I'm able to discern at the moment is that there's some sort of remote leash on him, for lack of a better term. Without their control signal in range he's set to automatically hibernate.

"Like a rig," Trevor said. "I understand, Doc."

The twins had been perfectly identical prior to Hamish's disappearance five years earlier. Thanks to the traces of scar tissue marring Hamish's body, no one would ever mistake them for each other again, even after his hair returned to its normal length and style.

"Will he be… himself again?" Trevor asked the magic question on everyone's mind.

Victor practiced honesty at all times with his patients and avoided even the minutest falsehood if possible. Glancing at the video again, he rubbed his chin thoughtfully. "I think so. When I threaded the cam into his abdomen for a look at the installations there, I noticed some adjustments made to his internal organs to make room for additional hardware. Nothing we can't regrow in time with cloning. It's his brain that concerns me. I can't access the interior braincore software without the code. If I try, I run the risk of frying his brain."

Trevor's expression fell and all signs of hope evaporated from his wistful features. "So… you're saying that my brother's going to be a vegetable for the rest of his life?"

"Far from it. We have the best intelligence agents in the United Empire tracking down information," Ethan assured him.

"Thank you, sir. I just… How are we going to find anything?"

"Tech like this came from somewhere, Trevor. Nisrine has the fail-safe device I removed from Hamish's heart. She's tracking down all leads on the logo etched into it."

"Thank you, Victor. All of you. I… I couldn't even bear to write home to mum. I can't tell her about this until I have good news."

"Now you do. Tell her we've found her boy and that the doctors have sworn to do everything in their power to help him recover."

If I can help it, that woman will be talking with her son by this week's end.

***

Jem's usual music serenade crescendoed until it roused Victor from his sleep. His grumpy protests while attempting to roll over and hide his head beneath his pillow failed utterly in making the noise go away.

"Lieutenant Shahid Amir requests a conference at your earliest convenience to discuss recent findings regarding Hamish Lockhart."

"And you decided to wake me up? How long has it been?" *Jem's worse than a mother hen.*

"Her request came an hour ago, but I determined six hours was insufficient rest and allowed you to remain asleep."

Victor groaned and rolled to his back. *Allowed. God, what I wouldn't give for five more hours.* Victor wasn't entirely sure which had exhausted him more; his stern confrontation with Zoe, the tedious twelve-hour examination, or his talk with Ethan afterward.

A quick shower and a fresh change of uniform later, he made his way up to the restricted halls where the intelligence and operation departments were housed. Jem provided a dim trail of blinking lights to Victor's destination.

"Please come in," Nisrine invited after his knock. She adjusted the black veil over her hair, which led Victor to wonder if she lowered it when in the privacy of her office or room. He had never seen her without the traditional garment associated with her people. "Did you get enough rest?"

"A few hours, yeah. Thanks." Victor crossed to the desk and practically collapsed into a chair. "What have you found?"

"The first logo actually led me to Hephaestus Tek. You'll recall them from Athena. The base of the device was their design; a common pacemaker and quite harmless."

"But this has been modified." He plucked up the small piece of tech from a glass dish.

"Yes. And from that I picked up images and impressions of its makers."

She swept her hands over the desk to send the other screens away, then manipulated one to a larger size. A gold and black icon dominated the upper left hand corner, depicting a double helix within an upraised robotic arm. She swiped down and zoomed in on a small picture of a researcher in pristine white scrubs. "This is what I saw. Only they wore tight hoods too, to cover their hair and necks."

"DNAturals." Victor read. "Wait, I recognize the name. They pioneered the nanobot technology for vein restructuring. Like what Zo– Sergeant Raines has equipped in her arm."

"Yes, and they have developed other technology for the Empire as well."

"Do you think it's an inside job? We know about DuPrie and Campbell, but are there many others above their rank who were working with them? How far could this possibly go?"

"I will not know until I sift through their financial records. If you and Doctor Oshiro are willing, I would appreciate a list of equipment and tools required to maintain such cybernetics. As well as any other unique requirements pertinent to these operations."

"Absolutely, I can have that to you within an hour."

"Commander–"

"Victor, remember?"

Nisrine bowed her head. "Victor, there was something else I picked up while handling that. Something that disturbs me."

"What is it?"

"I felt pain. Hamish was awake, I think, for many of their procedures. *Aware*," she clarified with particular emphasis.

"That's common for a craniotomy," Victor explained. "In order to safely navigate the brain you need your patient to be able to respond to you."

"Yes, I know, but they did much more. I received the impression they kept Hamish awake for more than what was necessary."

Victor stiffened. "You mean he felt it. They didn't sedate him?"

"I believe so." She looked away and folded her hands together. "They wanted him awake during the limb replacement. Someone missed a nerve connection during the first surgical procedure, which cost them time and money to correct."

"We never conduct nerve grafts while a patient is awake. It's too painful a procedure."

Disgust twisted his belly into a cold, hard knot, and then an overactive imagination pieced together a detailed portrait of Hamish's five years in captivity. Pain. Torture. Madness. If some part of him did remain alive beneath their programming, they faced a large chance of discovering he was no longer the man Trevor and Ethan remembered. He would be lucky to have a shred of sanity.

"Did you know him before this?"

"A little. He was best known for his pranks. Silly, harmless things."

"He ever get you with one?"

Nisrine shook her head. "No. We were not well acquainted so he never targeted me. But I remember him." A faint smile curved her lips for a brief moment. "He always had a book in his hands."

"A few months from now, I want you to tell me that he finally caught up with you. I hope it's a good prank."

It's going to be the best prank he's ever pulled off if I have anything to do about it. I'm going to do everything I can to recover this man's mind. No one deserves what happened to him. They did more than take his body. They raped his soul, Victor realized. He'd spent countless hours and very little sleep since Hamish's rescue, determined to bring him out of a vegetative state.

I have to do this.

CHAPTER 26

The intelligence department worked nonstop to sift through everything in the Empire records on DNAturals. The small technological corporation held a few exclusive contracts with the Navy but the bulk of their work was independent.

Without contacting United Command, the CO laid in a course for the third habitable planet in the Eloran system.

Zoe spent a hectic hour in the armory ensuring everything was in top notch condition for the team. *Might as well go out on a high note,* she grumped to herself.

Daniels cleared his throat. "Sergeant Raines."

"Yes, Commander?" She looked up from her pack, tense and ready to accept the next twist life threw at her.

"Good luck on the boarding team. It sucks to lose you now, and for what it's worth, I'm sorry to see you go."

I guess that means it's official then… Her attempt to dredge up a smile failed dismally. "Thank you, sir."

"Don't suppose I can convince you to stay, can I?"

Zoe arched a brow. "I wasn't aware I had a choice in the matter."

"Didn't you request a reassignment?" The easygoing smile dropped from Daniels' face. "What's going on?"

"Raines!" a voice barked out from behind her.

Zoe's spine stiffened. Ever since the end of their passionate vacation on Elora, every act between them – whether initiated by Zoe herself or Victor – appeared to place their relationship in further jeopardy. Nothing seemed stable anymore and with a comatose patient on his table, they lacked the time to talk as desired.

Daniels glanced past her shoulder then back down to her apprehensive face. A supportive pat on her arm accompanied a quietly muttered, "Shrug it off." He moved past her toward the shuttle.

Alpha squad, led by Daniels and Doctor Matthews, had already loaded. Zoe was due to join them in the rockskipper at any minute. Meanwhile, Chief Nwosu, leader of the demolitions experts in Bravo Squad, shouted orders to his team about their equipment.

Apparently, Bishop didn't plan to leave anything up to chance. The Jemison planned to deploy their fighter pilots and their heavy bombers to accompany the marines on foot.

"Raines," Victor called again. "A moment please."

Is he going to kick me off in front of everyone?

She turned around to address him. "Commander del Toro, how may I help you, sir?"

Victor wore his scrubs. During the mission briefing, Daniels told them Doctor Matthews planned to fill in for the man during the mission. Some of the others were thrilled about seeing the so-called vampire in action, but Victor's absence left a small hole in her heart.

Is he staying back for Hamish's sake, or is it because he lost control… because he can't serve with me anymore?

"Don't 'sir' me right now, all right? I know you're upset at me but… we can talk later about things after the mission. About what happened." He drew in a deep breath then squared his shoulders. "I came to perform a brief maintenance check on Creswell since this is his first mission on the team. Thought I'd have a look at you as well."

Maintenance check… That's a first, she thought. His professional demeanor prompted her to do the same despite the hollow ache it caused. *We were never ever this stiff and formal with each other even before the dating began.* "Of course."

Zoe shrugged off her tactical coat and offered her right arm out for his inspection. He palpated tenderly along the nerves beneath her synthetic skin.

"How's that feel? Any discomfort?" he asked.

Victor's touch was no different than the very first day they'd met in his examination room. He lit her skin on fire, covered her in goosebumps, made her weak in the knees, and every other known cliché associated with love. Deep down, she had become absolutely terrified that she'd only ever have physical contact with him again in a professional capacity. That Elizabeth and Saskia were right.

"No. Everything's been tip-top since you fixed my wrist the last time."

Satisfied, he released her cybernetic limb. Her overactive and hopeful imagination felt him caress the back of her hand ever so gently before ending contact. "You give them hell, Z–" The conflict showed on his features. Maybe he wouldn't say it, but what she wanted more than anything at that moment was to hear her first name from his lips. Not a title. Not her surname. Zoe. "Take care down there, Zoe."

With her wish granted, Zoe darted in and stole one last kiss, slow, intoxicating, and absolutely unprofessional, while their fellow marines prepared for battle. She took pleasure in the dazed look on Victor's face when she leaned back to gaze up at him.

"Hey Raines, time to buckle up!" Daniels called over.

"I have to report in. Good luck with Hamish. We'll take out that signal, no matter what it takes."

Victor's fragile smile provided minute reassurance. Saskia and Fairchild were wrong. Radha was wrong. And that was all that mattered.

"I'll be waiting for you."

***

"Are you nervous?" Daniels asked.

"No." The shuttle ride offered the chance to clear her thoughts. She had to force herself to shake Victor from her mind, knowing that even the minutest distraction could be deadly. *I can't afford to make another mistake.*

"You'll be fine." Daniels clapped her shoulder with his heavy hand. "Go in hard on your last mission with us."

"All due respect, sir, but I figured you'd be glad to be rid of me," Zoe admitted frankly.

Daniels' mouth curved up in a half-smile. It was an expression Zoe rarely received from the hard-faced officer.

"A few years back when I was still new to being an officer, I had a young kid under me with a brand new set of arms. Put every quid he'd received with his recruitment bonus toward them. Hell, I still remember the model. The P-69 LeadBuster. Supposedly impervious to every modern-day round."

"I'm guessing not so much…" Zoe's voice trailed as her mind envisioned the worst outcome.

"Yeah. He got killed. Ran into a hot zone and that was the last we saw of him alive. We were up against a cell of terrorists from the ASR with armor-shredding rounds." He paused. "Like the one that almost took out del Toro. Stupid but brave thing to do."

"The doctor can handle himself," Zoe said while keeping her gaze directed to the rifle sitting across her lap. "So the kid with the arms. You think he did it because of the upgrades?"

"I think so. Yeah. I've seen a lot of recruits dive into battle thinking their upgrades will win them the fight.

"Well if it makes you feel better, I didn't ask for mine."

"I know." Daniels leaned his head against the wall behind him and closed his eyes. "For what it's worth, I'm sorry for misjudging you, Raines."

"I'm sorry for hitting you in the balls."

"Nah. I deserved it. Del Toro made sure I knew it, too."

Zoe shifted on the cold metal bench. Davis, Abernathy, and Chang occupied the seats in the rear of the shuttle. Their newest addition, Creswell, sat between O'Malley and Jefferson. Fairchild was alone, enduring a self-imposed alienation ever since she and Zoe had argued over Victor's public behavior. The woman gazed out the window in silence.

Elizabeth hasn't been the same since Sassy... since that bitch turned on us, Zoe realized. Guilt lanced through her briefly. Throughout all of the drama since their return from Elora, she'd neglected to realize her friend was hurting.

Too pissed at her for the comments against Victor. Too childish to speak to her first. Zoe sighed and turned her attention to the window.

"We're entering the planet's atmosphere," their pilot shouted over one shoulder. He flicked a few buttons on the dash above his head and glanced back. His fresh-faced enthusiasm didn't lighten Zoe's spirits, but she made a valiant attempt to put on her brave face. "Get ready to haul ass out there. I'll trail you to provide gun support."

It wasn't the same without Rogers or Lopez. Zoe mourned their respective losses. The former would return to the Jemison within a year after his recovery, physical therapy, and adjustment to his cybernetic leg was complete. Lopez was gone forever.

"Raines, you know the drill. Get a gun on that door and cover our drop."

Zoe leaned out the shuttle door with her rifle at her shoulder. One by one the rest of her team leapt the five foot drop to the ground. Doctor Matthews landed like a cat, without a sound. The others followed her with less grace. Zoe unclipped her safety line and made the drop last. Her feet hit the pavement with a thud.

Their target was in the outer limits of a bustling city. The humans, reluctant to share a planet with the water-bound Elorans, had cultivated and terraformed a rough piece of rock into a green paradise.

Then they killed it anew with their industry. During the descent, the squad's shuttle had passed a great manufacturing plant that belched clouds of dark smoke into the air.

In the lead, Matthews darted in and out of cover as they made their approach to the building. DNAturals Laboratories was spelled out in large letters across the brick front.

"Holy shit, she's fast," someone muttered.

The doctor darted up behind a roving security guard, and the man hit the ground before he ever realized he was in danger. She jabbed a tranq against his throat.

Zoe fired at a second guard when he rounded one of the outer structures. A dart utilizing the same tranquilizing agent embedded in his skin. He fell without raising an alarm.

"Alpha leader, this is Bravo. The facility rear is clear."

"Copy that, Bravo. Alpha moving in," Daniels relayed in a low voice over the comm. "Masks on, everyone."

Their commander pulled a sphere from his belt and activated the small device. After a silent count to three, he opened the door a fraction and rolled it inside. Trailing wisps of smoke immediately began to leak out. Daniels waited five more seconds before bursting through the door.

"Get down! Anyone who remains standing after this warning will be put down," Daniels roared into the smoking office. The facility's lobby had already dissolved into panic, but through the fog, half a dozen unarmed civilians could be seen sprawled on the floor in search of fresh, untainted air.

With her mask firmly in place, Zoe glanced over the interior. "Down!" she called to a receptionist who seemed divided between lying down or standing again. The woman quickly threw herself belly down on the floor, choking and sobbing all the while.

"Keep your hands where we can see them, arms out in front of you, palms up. Chang and Williams, secure them all."

"On it, sir!"

The squad stormed the room and spread out while the two marines bound and secured the harmless civilians. They proceeded forward with caution.

"Located a map detailing the fire escape route. Data uploaded to our links," Creswell stated. "Building is three floors with two sublevels.

"Which way to the server?"

"Signal is originating below us, sir," Creswell announced.

"You know, for once, I'd like to find all the bad crap on the top floor. Or in the pretty courtyard," Davis muttered in complaint.

"Bravo team," Daniels spoke into the comm. "Lobby is secure. Alpha team proceeding to the objective in the sublevels. Move in and assist securing the building."

The floor immediately beneath them contained empty equipment labs. Shiny new prosthetic parts lined shelves and racks in neat rows. They cleared each space then took the stairs down to the bottom level.

A lone guard stood watch in front of a door at the end of a long hallway. Matthews offered him the chance to surrender. He wasted it by raising his firearm.

A second later, she had planted a knife through his sternum. The facility guards were neither heavily armored, nor prepared to defend against military forces. He dropped the gun when he staggered back, and then made a futile attempt to grasp at the weapon protruding from his chest. Upon release of the handle from her hand, the blade had glowed with heat and streaked through the air as a red-hot projectile. It had seared into his body without releasing a drop of blood.

Davis picked the gun up from the floor before they proceeded into the basement laboratory. Its expansive floor spread for several yards in either direction, filled with sleek, silver, waist-high towers. The impeccable server room housed at least a dozen machines.

"What the hell… Whoa! Whoa!" A man in a white lab coat threw up his arms and stumbled back from a wide desk near the entrance.

"Down on the floor," Zoe ordered, training her gun on the man.

Creswell holstered his weapon and moved to the impressive computer banks. The touch panels lit up beneath his hands. "Ask him for his password."

"You heard the man." Zoe finished patting down the technician, securing his wrists behind his back. "What's your login?"

"I don't have one, I swear."

"You work here and you don't have codes?"

"Look, I don't have the access codes. I'm just a junior technician. I come down every hour to check the temps."

"He's telling the truth."

Daniels turned his gaze on the officer beside him. "How do you know?"

"His body language and his fear are a dead giveaway. He's terrified. I can smell it," Matthews replied promptly. "I will take him up with the others and coordinate with Bravo. They should be completing their pass through the upper floors."

The doctor hefted the man up as if he weighed little more than a child. He quivered, tripped over his own feet, and only kept his footing thanks to Matthews' secure hold.

"Jemison to all teams. You need to find the remote link and disable it, ASAP." The commodore's voice came over the comm line with intermittent static.

"What's going on, sir?" Daniels asked.

"Hamish is going crazy. They activated some sort of programming and he hauled ass out of Medical. He knocked Jem offline, hell if I know how, and shorted out our engines. Everything is going to shit but it's worse than anything DuPrie did to us. It's like… we're under a cyberattack," Trevor filled them in.

"You *are*," Creswell corrected him. "I could be wrong, Chief, but… I believe he could be hacking it by thought. You'll never defeat him."

"He's going to vent the entire ship if you don't do something! Our sedatives aren't working. Hart and del Toro shot him with over a thousand CCs of the good shit."

Daniels paced the room anxiously. For the first time since her arrival to the Jemison, Zoe saw fear in his eyes.

"Okay… I'm in the main system. Download in progress. Hot damn that's a lot of info."

"I'm looking through your video link now. These are 250 exabyte servers," Trevor spoke into the communication channel. "Standard for cyberware corps. It'll take you fifteen minutes to nab that much data on your equipment. We don't have that kind of time!"

"If he's acting out of sorts, that means someone must have control of him remotely. Help me try to find it," Creswell pleaded.

Trevor and Creswell put their heads together and broke down each vital objective into tasks to defeat the threat head-on.

They failed. No matter how they attacked the signal and attempted to trace it to the origin, it rerouted and wormed to another point in the building.

Zoe's palms grew damp as she listened to the back and forth between the techies. Hacking and computer software were beyond her knowledge, but she understood the stakes if they failed. Her friends, her crewmates – everyone aboard the Jemison was in danger. Including Victor. The thought tore her up inside.

"I can't get anywhere close to the command signal," Creswell called over, sweat soaking his blonde hair. His fingers flew over the holographic display, but no matter what he tried the screen flashed red. "It's beyond the scope of my ability."

"If you can't shut it down, we won't have any choice but to kill him." Commodore Bishop's grim voice took over the line. Killing Hamish was the very last thing that any of them wanted.

Trevor became very quiet. At first, it seemed he had left the communications line entirely. "Pull the power. It's a long shot, but it's the only thing left that may work. Knocking out the facility's power will kill the interlink with the satellite. If there's someone there controlling my brother, they may lose access for a brief period while reconnecting to the next signal relay."

"Over here." Leaping up, Creswell moved to a large power generator on the opposite wall. With Abernathy's help, they unsecured the front paneling and began work on the inner lining.

"What if there's a backup?" Daniels asked into the line.

"Let's hope there isn't," Victor replied. The sound of his voice, strong and even, flooded Zoe with relief.

"Last connection and… got it. Right, let's see what we have here." Creswell pulled the shielding panel off. The inner core glowed with pristine white light. Zoe turned her face aside and squinted.

"Damn it all! That's a Valkyrie conduit." Creswell threw the panel aside in frustration. "I don't know how to deactivate one of these without causing some serious damage, lads. We'll be better off blowin' the entire building. It'll save the Jemison but lose everything here."

"We need that data for our fellow marine," Zoe said.

"There isn't enough time to evacuate the lot of you from the facility, Creswell. Find another way to do it. Lockhart, can you walk him through a safe method for powering down the… whatever the hell he called it,"

Ethan asked. "We're on borrowed time. Hamish depressurized the cargo bay."

"It's a Valkyrie conduit. They're overpriced cubes of white matter," Trevor said. "They become unstable energy when disrupted. The only safe method for powering it down is to hit the deactivation switch. It's going to take half an hour to go cold. Minimum."

Thirty minutes they no longer had at their disposal. Twenty-five minutes after the Jemison depressurized and its 447 inhabitants became cold corpses.

"I'm sorry, Trevor."

A single gunshot echoed over the line. The report of Ethan's large hand cannon silenced the communication link of all chatter.

"Shit," Daniels said, raising one hand to his face.

"Oh no." Fairchild's hands flew over her mouth. Davis moved over and squeezed her shoulder.

Like everyone else in the room, Zoe waited in strained silence, willing the sick sense of dread to go away. They were too late and now a good man was dead. A man who counted on them all.

"Shit! He's not down." The communications link became filled with panicked shouts and cries of warning from Victor and Trevor.

Three successive shots followed. Hart screamed for Ethan to run.

"Take it down, now!" Trevor yelled. The comm line died to static.

Daniels took aim at the power panel with his gun.

"Are you feckin' crazy?" O'Malley yelled. "You shoot that and you blow us all up!"

"My family is up there!" Abernathy exclaimed. "I can't... we need to do what we can. I've got a little boy up there, and he's only four. Four bleedin' years old. I'll die before I let anything happen to those people."

"He's right. We have to get that power source out somehow," Daniels argued. "We knew what we were getting into when we came down here, and the way I see it, none of you have a better idea."

"That's true," Davis agreed. "It's us or the ship. We have civilians. Our fellow service members have their families on the Jemison on our residential deck. It has to be us."

Lose the ship or sacrifice ourselves. Is that all we have? For Zoe the solution seemed so simple.

"Commander, tell him I'm sorry."

"Tell who – Raines, what are you doing?" Daniels tried to snag her but Zoe's arm was stronger, allowing her to jerk from his hold. She didn't stop to think or reevaluate her plan.

Zoe plunged her right hand into the open power box and closed her fingers around the miniature star. White heat encompassed her fist, but her cybernetic strength dislodged the power source from its setting. The optimistic side of her expected to feel no pain, believing it would scorch through the synthetic nerve endings too quickly for her to feel it.

She was wrong.

Her fist combusted and the fire spread, a flash of lightning traveling her synthetic skin and melting the metal skeleton beneath. The remains of her hand resembled an aged candle left in the sun. The acrid odor of cooking flesh and hair filled her nostrils.

It was a hundred times worse than the accident that mangled her flesh and blood arm years ago. An inhuman scream tore from Zoe's throat but her uncooperative bionic limb refused to release the conduit.

Somewhere to her right, a marine screamed, "Do something! Get it off of her!"

It sounded like Fairchild. Her good friend Elizabeth, who she'd never have the chance to forgive. She should have made amends on the shuttle. Hugged her one last time.

"No! Get away from her," Creswell shouted. "Everyone down now!"

The disrupted valkyrie conduit pulsed, dimming and flashing multiple times. It stuck fast to Zoe's disfigured hand and white exploded before her eyes.

CHAPTER 27

"Need to talk?" Trevor asked him quietly.

Victor shook his head. "I'm fine, mate. Keep your concern for your brother where it belongs." *The last thing you need to hear right now are my foolish relationship woes*, he thought.

"You're also my friend. The funny thing about concern is that it can focus it on many different things, aye? Are you worried about Raines?"

Victor nodded stiffly. "Feels silly. I shouldn't allow my personal life to distract me from the job. Your brother requires 100% of my attention, and yet, here I am. Thoroughly distracted."

"I wouldn't want you working on my brother if you were an unfeeling clod. You're an amazing doctor because you've got your heart and you feel," Trevor said gently. "It's… weird. Since he returned, I can sense things more clearly. It's not how I felt during our childhood, but… It's like he's almost here again." Trevor gazed at his twin. They both occupied the pair of seats in the observation room, watching over Hamish as he rested in a state of apparent hibernation. Like a sleeping rig set to conserve energy.

"He's in there. Nisrine is certain of it, so you aren't alone, and you're not imagining it. We're going to free him from their control and punish everyone responsible for this."

Trevor nodded. His green eyes drifted back to Victor. "And Raines is going to come away from this safely, too. You love her, you know. I can feel it whenever the two of you move beside one another. It's like an arrow straight into my senses. I used to envy you."

"Trevor…"

"You have a good thing here. You know… I thought I'd never want another woman after Tara pulled her bullshit. Used to think that little tart was as good as it gets. Our child dies and she mourns Rosie by sleeping around. Didn't think I'd ever move on. Maybe that's why the only dating I've done happens to be with an anonymous avatar in an online videogame."

"I've seen you with Flidais. Perhaps you're not together in person, but whatever you have is real," Victor cut in.

"Maybe. Maybe I'm using it as a crutch to avoid taking my life forward. Who could say for sure? I don't even know her real name. She could be married for all I know."

"Have you tried asking?"

"No." Trevor chuckled and rubbed his neck. "My big brother… he'd be laughing at me right this moment. Asking why I'm so afraid. Our mother has Japanese and Chinese ancestry, and she once told us that our people held a belief a long time ago that was picked up again on Xiao's southern continent where she was raised."

The poor bastard… he's petrified, Victor thought. He humored Trevor's rambling brain, using it as a distraction from the fears that troubled them both. "Yeah?"

"Aye. I was born first. By your standards, that makes me the older twin. Not so in her homeland. The twin born second is the older twin who graciously allowed their weaker sibling to be born first."

"Really? That's an interesting way of looking at it. So he's always looking out for you then if he gave you the 'grand' honor of leaving the womb first."

"Yeah, I guess he did. When Rosie died, he burned all of his leave time to get me on my feet again. Had been saving it, but he used it for me. Didn't think twice about it. Doesn't matter what I needed, he was always there for me.

All my life." Trevor rubbed at his face to dry the tears glistening on his cheeks.

"I've got a pair of trays for the two of you from the officer's galley," Hart called from the doorway. "Come sit with me and eat. It's lonely out here," she claimed, infusing a hint of light-hearted warmth to her voice.

Victor passed him a nearby tissue box. "Sounds like a good brother. Come on. Let's get some food into you before you pass out. You'll be no good to him when I have him awake if you're passed out in the next cot, mate."

Trevor resisted at first, but with Victor's insistence, he left his seat. The human brain required food as fuel to thrive, and as a psychic, Trevor needed a larger quantity than most others. Missing a meal could be the difference between a crippling migraine that landed him in his bunk for a couple of days, and staying coherent to help his twin.

Both men settled at the medical station's counter alongside Hart. To Victor's left, a floating monitor detailed Hamish's vitals, providing assurance that the patient remained stable. Two identical trays awaited them, some sort of creamy casserole with a heavy serving of noodles, two palm-sized pork meatballs, steamed veggies, and slices of cheesecake.

Victor regarded the casserole on his plate with mild interest. It was a shame he had no appetite to do more than pick at his meal. Trevor appeared to eat on autopilot, putting his dinner away without appearing to enjoy it.

"Feel better?" Victor asked at the conclusion, once they were both pushing around crumbs from the cheesecake served as the evening dessert.

The heavy dose of fat and carb-based calories restored some color to Trevor's face. "A little, yeah. It's just… I can't lose him again, Victor. I want to tell mum that we found him and that he's gonna be all right."

"We're going to do everything we can, Trev–"

The translucent glass holographically presenting Hamish's vitals lit up like a holiday display, casting hues of green, orange, and yellow from its surface. The numbers changed to indicate his racing heart rhythm and rising blood pressure.

Victor pushed his tray aside and quickly brought up the terminal display.

"What's happening?" Trevor demanded.

By appearances alone, Hamish seemed normal and no different than any other man in his early thirties. He rested peacefully with his eyes closed, but his chest barely moved.

"I don't know. Everything seems normal here. Let's have a look then," Victor muttered. Upon leaving his seat, he received a better view of the adjacent observation room once Jem defogged the opaque glass. The ship's infirmary was equipped with a fantastic observation bay located beside the medical staff's front office station. Any nurse or member of the crew could peek in on a whim.

"He seems okay," Hart whispered, as if Hamish could hear her through the solid wall.

Hamish bolted upright in the bed.

Equipment crashed to the floor and the IV stand tipped. Hamish's movement from the bed pulled the lines from his body and released a trickle of blood down his medical gown.

"Oh shit!" Trevor stared through the glass. "What the hell's he doing?"

"Jem, seal Observation Room One," Hart quickly ordered.

The magnetic locks activated and secured Hamish in the room. His fists slammed against the door, a repetitive hammering that threatened to dent the metal.

"Hamish, stop." Trevor attempted to reason with his brother over the intercom. "You're safe now on the Jemison, just like I promised."

Another loud bang on the door was the only reply. Hamish's dispassionate features remained stony without any flicker of acknowledgement.

"I don't think he hears you, Trevor," Victor said in a low voice. "Look at him."

A third strike against the door yielded the same failed results. The barrier held and kept Hamish contained.

"He looks soulless," Hart whispered.

Hamish moved away from the door and crossed to the observation window. His blank stare unnerved Victor but it was Hamish's punch against the glass that worried him most.

"Um… will that hold?" Trevor backed away.

The next strike answered the question. It splintered the thick pane's interior layer, creating a network of fine cracks spread out across the buckling glass.

"Jem, evacuate medical!" Victor's cry sent up the alarm. "Security to medical!"

The window shattered with the second punch.

"No one here wants to hurt you." Victor raised his hands up, palms out, and placed himself between his patient and the door.

Hamish grabbed him, displaying reflexes augmented by one of his new pieces of cybernetic gadgetry. His fingers were too strong, likened to individual bands of steel curving into Victor's skin. The throw hurled Victor halfway across the room where he crashed into Hart like a bowling ball scattering pins.

"Are you okay?" Victor asked in a groaned breath. Pain registered, sending twinges of agony across his back, but he didn't have the time to acknowledge it and mope on the floor. Fire spread throughout his shoulder and pulsed down his arm. It had to be dislocated.

"I'm fine," Hart replied. "But what the hell! I thought you said he was turned off."

"Get the tranq gun!" Victor shouted at her as they struggled to regain their footing. "Something changed. Shit!" he swore. Despite his combat training, Victor had no intention of taking on a cyborg. One well-aimed punch could shatter a man's skull.

Hamish wasn't merely his patient now; he was a lethal weapon in the hands of their enemy. Divided between his duties as a doctor and his desire to keep the crew of the Jemison safe, Victor hesitated to take further action.

"Get the tranqs!" *What do I do? What can I do?* Victor wondered. Needing both arms at full working capacity, he gritted his teeth against the pain then wrenched his arm into the shoulder socket again.

Hart slammed a case on the desk surface and unsnapped it to reveal their stash dedicated to hostile patients. He loaded a cartridge into a gun while Hart did the same. For a noncombatant, her aim was good; the dart sank into the meaty portion of Hamish's posterior where he lacked metal augmentation.

"Nice shot," Victor commented. His dart nailed the cyborg in the throat and injected its bounty of fluid.

Nothing happened.

"Bridge to Medical. What the hell is going on down there?" Ethan's voice cut through over the comm system.

"Hamish Lockhart awakened from his hibernation. He's no longer responding to sedatives," Hart reported back.

"Security is on the way and so am I."

"Copy that, sir. We'll follow his movements," Hart replied, grabbing two field kits. She followed Victor out into the hall. Hamish strode with purposeful steps ahead of them, making his way unhindered through the ship corridors.

"Shit, he's getting in the lift." Trevor shoved a hand through his hair. "Jem, can you hold him in there?"

"Negative, Chief Lockhart. He has overridden my lockout commands," Jem replied in her sultry tone. "Destination: Engineering Deck. I have issued evacuation protocols."

"He can cause all sorts of trouble down there." Trevor muttered.

"Jem, can you slow the lift down?" Hart asked. The A.I. provided no response.

Trevor swore. "He deactivated her. Crap. I should have expected that."

A thousand scenarios floated around in Victor's head, none of them good. "Do you think he could destroy the ship? I'm not familiar with the workings down in Engineering."

"I…" Trevor looked sick, and a thin sheen of perspiration dotted his brow. "I don't know. I don't think so, but… it's possible."

A five man security team caught up to Hamish in the passageway outside engineering. Victor, Trevor, and Hart arrived via the lift in time to become spectators to Hamish's brutal assault. The last man flew over the cyborg's shoulder, slammed mercilessly to the hard deck with a technique that wrenched his shoulder from the socket and snapped the bone. His shock baton rolled uselessly away from his limp fingers.

Oblivious to his pursuers, Hamish stepped over the groaning man without batting an eyelash, intent on reaching his destination.

"Mum taught us judo," Trevor said in a rush, "but I've never seen him move that fast before."

"It's the upgrades." Victor said, equally shocked.

"Go on, I'll oversee all of this," Hart said. She knelt down to assist the security officer with a broken arm. Victor crouched nearby and retrieved his baton.

The two men trailed Hamish as far as the main engine room. At some point prior to her deactivation, Jem had evacuated the crew members assigned to the space.

"What's he doing?" Victor asked.

Hamish held position in the control room, his palm against the computer console. His expression remained as impassive now as it had when he first awakened in medical, like a wandering sleepwalker unaware of his actions.

No, not a sleepwalker. It's like he's not even there. He's a puppet.

"What the bloody hell is happening on my ship?"

Ethan's furious voice jolted Victor from his thoughts.

"He's interfaced with all the Jemison's systems, sir," Trevor answered. He was crouched down with a panel pulled from the wall and his diagnostic hologram hooked in. Streams of data flowed across the open space above them. To Victor it all looked like gibberish.

"Unacceptable." Ethan scowled and pulled his personal firearm from the holster at his thigh. "We go in there and we get him out."

"If we go in there, he'll attack," Victor argued.

"If we don't go in there we risk the safety of everyone on this ship." Ethan replied, as grim as Victor had ever seen him. "He's done something to Jem and is mucking about in *my* ship's systems. I want to know why."

"What if we shoot the console? Destroy it?" Victor suggested. He understood the stakes and he was certain Ethan didn't want to take extreme measures against Hamish, but he would if he needed to. As the commanding officer the ship came first before a single man's life.

"He'll just go to another and you risk causing an explosion in the drive systems. He picked his spot well." Trevor's fingers flew across the holographic interface. "God he's fast. By the time I manage to block him he's opened two more pathways."

Ethan frowned, shook his head, and opened a line to their surface squads. "Jemison to all teams. You need to find the remote link and disable it, ASAP."

"What's going on, sir?" Daniels asked

Ethan gestured for Trevor to pass on the details regarding Hamish's damage to the ship and systems.

"They'll find it," Victor assured his friend quietly while Trevor was busy working with their planetside team.

"I hope you're right about that, Victor. If they can't we'll be left with only one option."

Take out Hamish, by any means necessary…

Trevor pulled up another screen on the panel and Victor shifted aside to grant Ethan more space to oversee what was happening. A gritty image from Creswell's helmet occupied the upper left corner of the feed. Part of him had hoped to catch sight of Zoe.

"I'm looking through your video link now. These are 250 exabyte servers," Trevor said. "Standard for cyberware corps. It'll take you fifteen minutes to nab that much data on your equipment. We don't have that kind of time!"

"If he's acting out of sorts, that means someone must have control of him remotely. Help me try to find it," Creswell pleaded over the line.

The two techies put their best ideas out and tried several different methods to hack the planetside systems. Most of the jargon between them flew right over Victor's head so he didn't even attempt to make suggestions. Their bleak tones and colorful swears were more than enough to convey their failed attempts.

The footage wavered as Creswell moved positions. Victor's heart constricted when he caught a too-brief glance of Zoe in the video.

If anything happens… if they fail or we do… my last words to her weren't what they should have been. Hindsight always carried clarity. *I should have told her I love her.*

"No! No, no, no." Trevor slammed his hand against the wall. "Hamish started the depressurization process in the cargo bay."

They had five minutes before the Jemison became a floating tomb.

"I'm sorry, Trevor."

A second after his somber apology, Ethan squeezed the trigger as Trevor cried out a plea for him to wait. It was no good. The bullet tore through the air and snapped Hamish's head backward after making impact. The man tumbled to the deck and lay on the ground without even a single twitch.

Hart sobbed behind Victor, one hand raised to her mouth. To his other side, Trevor broke down into tears. Just like that, it was all over and there wasn't a single thing Victor could do about it but sigh in defeat. He lowered one arm around Trevor's shaking shoulders while the commodore strode forward and crouched down beside the motionless body.

"Christ…" Victor muttered. "I'm sorry, mate… we did everything we could." Something, or rather the lack of something, caught Victor's eye. He turned his head toward the unmoving cyborg again to stare. *Wait. There's no blood. There should be blood all over the floor. That should have taken off the top of his skull.* "Ethan, get away from him!"

Victor's warning came too late. A split second after he voiced caution to Ethan, Hamish's fist shot up toward the commodore's face. Ethan staggered back, narrowly avoiding a blow to his chin. "Shit! He's not down."

Hamish moved too quickly for Victor's mind to register what happened. A fist hit Ethan's ribs, and then he was airborne. The back of the man's head struck the hard ground, but he never lost control of his pistol.

"Ethan, no! Get out of there!" Victor called to him.

The gun raised to fire three more point blank rounds at Hamish's chest. One missed outright, the second clipped him uselessly in a metal-enhanced rib, but the third carried between the bones into actual biological matter. Despite the blood spilling from the circular bullet wound, Hamish never uttered a single sound. Nothing changed.

"Take it down now!" Trevor yelled to the surface team seconds before Hamish severed the connection. With no alternative, the psychic sprinted forward and hurled his own body at Hamish to distract him from murdering their leader.

Victor activated the shock baton in his hand, igniting a sizzling arc of electrical current at its tip. The weapon proved a useful tool despite its simple and archaic design, especially against violent patients. Against cyborgs with older, unshielded equipment, the baton could be devastating. He wasn't counting on it to knock Hamish's electrical systems offline, but he did hold on to the hope that it would knock him out.

Before Victor was able to get in close enough, Hamish swung around with a heavy punch. The doctor barely avoided the strike with a quick sidestep. Victor touched the live end of his baton to his attacker's elbow but Hamish shrugged it off without any outward reaction.

He's not going to stop until he's dead or the person directing him drops control. The realization was sobering.

Hamish landed a glancing blow across Victor's shoulder which almost made him lose his grip on the baton. He grit his teeth, fingers tingling with a pins and needles sensation, and drove his weapon against Hamish's thigh. The cyborg's knee buckled then an invisible force thrust him away two yards. It had to be Trevor.

"Trevor, catch!" Hart called.

Another shock baton arced toward them. Trevor caught it out of the air and took advantage of Hamish's brief display of weakness. Both of the twins were equally skilled in martial combat, a plus in Victor's favor when it came to taking on his opponent.

Hamish avoided one strike after the next, weaving in and out despite Victor and Trevor's joint effort to take him down. They narrowly blocked his attacks with their weapons, but Victor lacked Trevor's agility, balance, and telekinetic ability. Hamish's fist came dangerously close to splitting open his head until Trevor spun a roundhouse kick that knocked his brother off the mark.

Damn, they're both so bloody quick. Victor had never trained with Trevor before to see him in a combat situation. It quickly became evident Victor could have never stood against Hamish on his own.

Trevor's baton struck Hamish in the lower spine. He arched his back but inevitably recovered seconds later to sweep Trevor's feet out from beneath him. With murderous intent, he crouched above his twin and raised Trevor's head by a handful of hair.

Seeing his chance, Victor leapt forward and extended the prod toward the back of Hamish's head, touching the arcing prongs to the base of his skull.

Hamish dropped Trevor, keeled over on his side to the floor, and didn't move. This time Victor was positive he would remain that way. At least for a little while.

I hope… Now to get him secured.

Hart beat Victor to the punch, producing a set of medical restraints from her field pack. "See to the big boss, Victor, I've got this," she told him.

"Lockhart," Ethan groaned from the floor. "Get in the system and shut down what he did or we won't be around to save his life."

"He's already on it." Victor assured him. "Be still, mate. You won't be breathing easily for long if you try to trot back to the bridge with fractured ribs."

"Who's trotting?" Ethan's chuckle swiftly turned into a pained wheeze.

Hart kept guard over Hamish, out of his reach with her Taser in hand. After everything they'd witnessed, they didn't trust the wrist restraints to slow him down if he regained consciousness.

"Decompression sequence aborted," Trevor relayed. "Communications are up. I'll get Jem back online in a few minutes."

"Are we back in contact with our teams?"

"Not yet, sir. Scanners show there was an explosion in the facility. Looks like it was contained to the lower level."

Victor's fingers stilled against Ethan's chest. A chill crawled down his spine and his pulse quickened, a sudden sense of dread overcoming their recent triumph in subduing Hamish.

"Hold on," Trevor spoke up suddenly. "Incoming message on the back-up channel." He switched through the frequencies until a familiar voice crackled to life over the static.

"Jemison, this is Creswell. Requesting immediate emergency trauma response. I repeat, immediate emergency response."

Ethan's attempt to rise was put to a quick stop by his protesting ribs. The pain, combined with Victor's restraining hand, kept him on the floor.

"Victor, I need you to stay here with Hamish. Hart, get a full team together now and whatever extra marines you can fit on the shuttle. I'm not losing any more people. Not today."

CHAPTER 28

"Wounded incoming."

The medical ward doors opened in conjunction with Jem's verbal announcement, admitting the rushed and loud arrival of the response team. Nothing prepared Victor for the sight that greeted him once he stepped from the room where Hamish was restrained under heavy sedation.

No, not Zoe.

It was always a possibility while serving on a military vessel. Husbands and wives disembarked from the ship all of the time to serve on combat missions, but they usually came home intact. The losses suffered recently by the Jemison were unusual occurrences in an age when the military guarded the galaxy with an iron fist. That was especially true during peacetime while the Empire held an unwavering treaty with the Soviets. There hadn't been a true war in a decade.

"Victor, we need you!" Lilibeth called out. A second gurney floated in behind the first, bearing Daniels' limp form.

Both units displayed the vital statistics of their occupants in a real-time holographic display projected above the heads of the floating gurneys.

"Administer two CCs of cybex sulfate in a liter of saline to her. Now!" Victor had never been the doctor who shouted orders at his staff, but he became that man in an instant. He moved alongside the grey-lift stretcher during Zoe's transfer to the surgical theater, where he and Davis brought her to rest upon the operating table.

By the graces of adrenaline and stimulants, Victor remained on his feet for another seventeen hours. She coded twice on the table but was revived by a tenacious team of doctors and medical assistants.

I won't lose you, too, Zo. I can't. I won't go through this again.

He worked above her to the point of exhaustion, personally applying aerosolized replacement skin after removing damaged tissue. A sense of unnatural focus came over Victor that guided his hand with superhuman dexterity. By the end of it, he could barely tell anyone his name, let alone power down his surgical laser. Hart had to pry it from his fingers and deactivate the tool herself after he slumped onto a stool beside the operating table.

"We will transfer her to a room," Lilibeth assured him gently. "Please. You are in our way." A tiny smile accompanied her words, smoothing away some of the grim mood.

Victor reluctantly stepped into the hallway while the two women clothed Zoe in a patient gown. Oshiro waited for him, open concern etched into his tired features.

"You should shower and rest, Victor. I will sit with her," Oshiro promised, pressing a small cup of tea into his hands. The fragrant steam wafting upwards was familiar, a family remedy Oshiro had pressed on him a few occasions in his lifetime. He accepted the cup then shuffled down the hall without a word.

I'll just get cleaned up and then I'll sit with her myself.

Victor washed his face, changed out of his scrubs in the locker room, and then settled behind the desk in his office for only a moment to enjoy the tepid cup of green tea. He was asleep before he set the empty mug on his desk.

***

Soothing notes from the strings of a cello gradually slithered into Victor's hazy consciousness. A few more minutes passed before the increasing volume pulled him completely from sleep to the dim interior of his office. The automatic desk chair had leaned back and tilted into a perfect incline. Someone had also sprawled a medical warming blanket over his chest. Cozy heat radiated from the double-insulated piece of material.

"The hell?"

"Good morning, Doctor del Toro," Jem greeted him. The office lights gradually brightened to their normal daylight settings.

Victor jerked upright in a panic only to realize someone would have retrieved him if Zoe had taken a turn for the worse. "What time is it? How long was I out?"

"Ship time is 0216. We allowed you to sleep for eight hours."

Despite the protesting of his back and sore muscles, he rose from the chair and tossed the blanket behind him over its arms. "Status on Zoe Raines?"

"Sergeant Raines remains in stable condition. All vitals are within normal limits."

"Status on Grayson Daniels?" he asked next.

"Commander Daniels has been released from medical," she relayed smoothly.

"Did we have any other major injuries from that skirmish?"

"Negative, Doctor. All further injuries were minor and treated by medical technicians."

"What's the status on Hamish Lockhart?"

Jem's silky voice took on a chilly edge. "Hamish Lockhart is awake and requesting your presence. Commodore Bishop is with him now."

"How is he awake? I didn't go into his braincore yet."

"Commodore Bishop would not allow Doctor Oshiro to wait until you awakened," Jem informed him. "With the blueprint Lieutenant Creswell obtained from the laboratory and my assistance, they were able to safely perform an emergency craniotomy to remove the guidance chip without causing further harm."

"How long did that take?"

"Less than one hour. Doctor Oshiro is an accomplished neurosurgeon. Hamish awakened only an hour ago."

The fine hairs on the back of Victor's neck rose.

Did Hamish recall anything about their frantic efforts to bring him down? Victor would find out soon enough. Without further hesitation, he shrugged into his lab coat and stepped into the hallway. His route took him past Zoe's room, where he peered in at her through the translucent observation window. Floating vitals with large green numbers confirmed Jem's assurances, so he sucked in a relieved breath and watched her for a while.

It's over now. She's going to pull through.

Once completely satisfied with watching the rhythmic rise and fall of her chest and stabilized vitals, Victor drew up her chart for a quick look. Good. Oshiro kept his promise. Hart and Davis were the most recent to enter and leave, maintaining a steady supply of Neurothol to eliminate Zoe's pain – and also keep her heavily sedated. He reviewed everything else on the chart and estimated another two hours until she awakened.

Someone had set the glass observation panel to Hamish's new room to 'privacy', transforming the clear glass to an opaque mirrored hue. Victor knocked first by habit prior to entering.

"Look who's up. You look a sight better, mate." Ethan offered out a steaming mug of coffee before the door even clicked shut. "By the way, you were drooling in your chair. Thought you should know."

The friendly taunting put Victor at immediate ease and diffused what he expected to be an awkward meeting. Hamish ducked his head shyly and focused on his hands, both of which were folded over his lap. The bashful behavior humanized him.

"Hamish, this man is Doctor del Toro. We've got him to thank for having you back," Trevor said gently.

"Hello, Doctor," Hamish said in a hoarse whisper. He barely made eye contact. His right hand raised briefly then lowered with a dull slap against his hospital gown covered thigh again. "Thank you."

"Call me Victor, please," he requested, while offering out a hand to the man in the bed.

Uncertain, Hamish glanced at his brother first for approval. When Trevor nodded, the older twin raised his hand to accept Victor's greeting.

"It's good to finally see you awake, Hamish. How are you feeling?" *He has excellent control for a fresh cyborg,* Victor noticed. Hamish barely gripped his hand for a shake and released it as quickly as possible.

"Like shit, sir. I... Trevor told me I hurt a lot of people here."

"You hit like an Imperial dreadnought, but I'll live. So will the others that you injured," Ethan said cheerfully. "I assure you, it's nothing I haven't felt before, mate."

Hamish didn't appear convinced or comforted by their assurances. "I'm guessing you all didn't come here to pat my hand and tell me it's all going to be okay. You have questions and military protocols direct you to hand me over to United Command. I'm not dumb. I know what happens next."

Victor glanced at Ethan. The Commodore looked too at ease, his expression too cordial if he planned anything of the sort.

"The HMS Bulwark is en route with an ETA of about seven hours. I'm not going to lie to you, son. They have orders to take you back to Command for treatment," Ethan said.

"Ethan. You know as well as I do that they'll subject him to weeks of questioning before he receives a bit of treatment," Victor said. "*If* he receives any at all."

"I know, but they think he's a risk," Ethan replied.

"I know he's dangerous. There's no doubt about that, and he's got cybernetics that don't exist on the market," Victor said defensively. Concern for the wellbeing of his patient overwhelmed his sense of reason. "But that doesn't excuse medical neglect. And turning him over without receiving help is exactly that – neglect. We can't allow them to take him."

"What if they lock him away again? Hide him?" Trevor's worry carried over in his voice and expression.

"Don't talk about me as if I'm not here," Hamish spoke up. "I know what they plan to do, Trevor. It's all right."

"Hamish–" Trevor began, only for his brother to swiftly cut him off.

"The doctor's right about it. I'm a weapon now, and that's all I'll ever be."

"No. You're more than a weapon," Ethan interjected. "Trust me, son, whatever they intended for you to be, they failed. The very fact that you are sitting here, apologizing and worrying about what happened under their control, proves that."

"Then we need to protect him. We owe it to one of our own to keep him safe when he needs us," Victor argued.

"Yeah, about that. As I was planning to say before you became Doctor Passionate and interrupted me," Ethan said, rubbing his chin. "I've sort of tossed the rulebook aside and taken some pre-emptive measures to guarantee Hamish's safety. Until we can ferret out this nonsense, I believe no one is to be trusted."

Doctor Passionate. Victor harrumphed. "I'm guessing you have a plan. So are you going to clue us in or keep the suspense?"

"Nisrine submitted an official report to the Royal Archives on Astreya. You know how they like to have everything in triplicate and stored on their tidy shelves." Ethan waved his hand in an absentminded gesture. "The head archivist took it upon himself to personally message and send over a copy to Her Royal Majesty, the Empress. She has requested an audience."

"What?" Trevor's eyes practically bugged out of his head.

"Your brother is getting a royal reception home," Ethan clarified. His wide grin reached smug proportions. "I'd like to see them sweep that away into forgotten obscurity."

"Does the Bulwark know that?" Victor asked, floored.

"I imagine they will shortly." Ethan's amused laughter filled the room. "You're not going to the Bulwark, Hamish. The Jemison will deliver you to Albion by Imperial decree. The flagship will escort *us*."

"I can't believe it." Trevor sank back into his seat again and stared at Ethan in wonder. "Thanks."

"No need to thank me. I'm only doing what's right," Ethan said.

Hamish's voice dropped to a slight whisper. "Is it going to be… public?"

Ethan's expression softened. "To a point, yes, but I think the Empress is a wise enough woman not to make a spectacle out of you. The important thing is that too many people in the upper echelons will be aware of your situation for you to be easily shuttered away again. The Empress is big on pomp and ceremony, so the media has been notified that a lost hero has been found."

"I'm not a hero," Hamish quickly spat out. He ran his fingers over his close-shorn hair. A couple of weeks had passed since the most recent surgery, but the remnants of his scars revealed the critical points of entry for their brain modification. Eventually, Hamish's hair would conceal them completely.

"You are," Victor gently said to him. "Thanks to your actions, over two dozen souls were spared from that laboratory. They're alive because of you."

"I don't know how I did it," Hamish said. "They routinely drugged me for ease of handling, or so they said. But that day I was clear headed for the first time in a long while."

"I think I know why," Victor said. "We also sedated you, but suddenly all at once, most of the drugs were cleared from your system. Their own tool became their undoing. Perhaps it isn't fully functioning or wasn't properly deactivated in the lab after one of their tests, but it saved you."

"Were you aware at all during your jaunt through the ship?" Ethan asked.

Hamish dropped his gaze to his lap again. The man lacked his younger twin's confidence, and Victor had to wonder if it was a result of the experimentation and his captivity. "In a way. Imagine you're in a hovercraft set to autopilot, but you're unable to deactivate the program. It takes you wherever it chooses, and you're merely there along for the ride."

"Trapped in your own mind…" Trevor's voice shook.

"Yes," Hamish whispered. "I don't know whether it'll help your investigation or not. I remember everything, but what I know may be useless to you."

"Any detail helps," Victor assured him. "No matter how minor it may seem to you."

"Okay. I'll tell you whatever I can before we reach Albion."

"We have a few days, Hamish." Trevor sighed in relief.

"Your brother's right, mate, there's no need to rush it all out now."

"Doctor del Toro," Jem interrupted. "I thought would like to be informed that Sergeant Raines is exhibiting signs of premature awakening."

The coffee mug in his hands slipped and only quick fumbling saved it from shattering against the floor.

"Go, Victor," Ethan told him. "You should be there when she wakes up. Trevor, Hamish, and I have this."

"Thanks, mate."

CHAPTER 29

Zoe awakened to a voice muttering above her supine form. Lifting her eyelids seemed comparable to bench pressing an elephant. A distorted view of the world greeted her, blurred beyond recognition.

"Ten more minutes, Ma," she slurred drowsily. Unable to focus, she closed her eyes once more and nearly surrendered again to the desire for sleep. The mutters promptly ceased.

"Zoe?" The voice didn't belong to her mother but her hazy memory failed to place an immediate name to the familiar cadence and timbre.

Fighting her heavy eyelids, Zoe tried again to bring the room into focus.

"Hey now, don't try to get up just yet." A hand pressed to her left shoulder and nudged her back against the bed, but Zoe didn't even recall trying to sit up. Her desire to remain awake warred with her body's need to continue resting. *Just a few minutes more.*

Victor's concerned face swam into her view, derailing her desire for more sleep. "What happened?"

"You almost died," he answered promptly. Exhaustion creased his scruffy face and made him appear older than his 39 years. "You've been asleep for hours since the surgery. Are you in any pain? How do you feel?"

Surgery. The word penetrated the fog and grounded her back to reality. She remembered unrivaled agony, the scent of burning skin and circuitry, and the deafening bang of a shotgun preceding the blinding light of an explosion.

Panic and fear seized her when she recognized the loss of pain, and that in its place she felt nothing at all.

"My arm. I can't... I can't move my arm." The realization struck her at once, a sobering truth that shook off the final vestiges of the sedative and replaced it with panic. Her pulse quickened on account of the adrenaline fueling her new sense of coherence. It took her back to memories she had tried desperately to forget.

"Zoe, breathe." Victor's cool fingers swept over her brow in a soothing stroke. "Your replacement will be ready and waiting for us at the hospital on Albion."

Get yourself together, Zoe. You'll have an arm. They aren't going to let you go without one. Those thoughts might have been comforting if she didn't recall what it was like to be a fresh amputee. She shoved back the dark recollections and focused on the soothing music playing in the background. The melodic cello, along with Victor's encouraging touches, calmed her racing heart and evened her breaths.

Gradually, the area gained clarity and allowed her to take in the surrounding recovery room. Each galactic cruiser kept four functional wards for the purpose of caring for injured soldiers, and at least a half dozen smaller rooms. She hadn't been moved to one of those yet, as evidenced by the size.

"What did you do to me?"

Victor drew in a deep breath. "We reinforced your ribs after we dug out the scattershot from the round Daniels fired at your arm. Lil synthesized new tissue for the second and third-degree burns while I reconstructed your shoulder so you'd be a fit for the new arm. Other minor repairs, mostly cosmetic."

Memories resurfaced of the military doctor on her old vessel, especially his avoidance of her eyes and the way he'd patronized her with a pat on the remaining arm, telling her a cybernetic limb would become her new replacement *one day.* Zoe spoke the misdirecting language of military doctors fluently, and when she read between the lines, it all became clear.

She was hideous – a one-armed freak with a face covered in burns. The insidious little thought slid through her mind and brought tears to her eyes.

"I want to see it."

"All right," Victor agreed quietly.

He reached up to grasp the holographic screen and redirect it toward her. It was meant for real time video conferencing from the sick bed, but since it wasn't connected to another screen it merely displayed Zoe's own face back at her. A shiny dressing covered the skin on her right cheek and jaw, fitted perfectly to the shape of her face. Another protective dressing curved down her neck toward her shoulder, where the remnants of Victor's surgical work revealed her bandage-wrapped stump. Due to the nature of her injuries, she wore no hospital gown, only a sheet for modesty and strategic application of gauze.

"And my ribs?" Her voice cracked.

Victor nodded in agreement. He peeled back the bedsheet tucked around her chest, and one by one he drew away the corner of the bandages. A dozen circular scars littered her torso from the waist to her right breast, joined by a crescent incision. She'd never wear a two-piece swimsuit again. Not now. Not unless she chose to withstand hours of surgical enhancement.

Blinking rapidly failed to soothe her stinging eyes, and despite all of her efforts to remain calm, a quiet wail shuddered from Zoe's lungs. Hot tears slid down her face and there was absolutely nothing she could do to stop them.

I'm hideous.

"Zoe–?"

"Go away," she sobbed. *He'll never see me the same.*

His chilly fingers lowered to her left arm, but they lacked the personal contact she had become accustomed to over the course of their relationship. He laid them upon her forearm like a doctor, her caretaker, but not the lover she desperately wanted.

"I said, go away!" she screamed at him, shrugging off the impersonal touch.

Zoe didn't want Doctor del Toro; she wanted Victor, the man she loved.

I love him, she realized with startling clarity. It was the one clear and rational thought in her otherwise drug-muddled mind. *But he doesn't love me. I'm just his patient now.*

"Zoe?" he questioned again. "I'll leave if that's what you really want, but I'd like to stay here with you. Please don't push me away. Please."

Words failed her, she couldn't get a single one past the lump in her throat. She turned her face away from him on the pillow while numbness spread through her whole body.

His fingers touched to her cheek but Zoe closed her eyes tight. She didn't want to see the disgust on his face. The pity. Another wracking sob shook her body, bringing a fresh upwelling of pain from her right side, as the shock of seeing her injuries and her emotional collapse burned through the remnants of any medications she may have been on.

"Don't shut me out." Tears were wiped away beneath the swipe of his thumb. "Do you want some pain meds? Tell me how you feel, Zo."

"Y-Yes please. What's going to happen to me?" Zoe finally managed to ask. Talking hurt, each breath akin to dragging glass through her throat.

Victor left the bedside briefly, only to return with a cup of water and a straw. He offered it to her, and she gratefully slurped it down until the straw pulled only air. "We're going to keep you in medical until we reach Albion." Victor administered the pain relief through her intravenous line.

"Okay," she croaked. Crying drained her of the will to do anything more than curl into a ball and go to sleep.

Eventually, the surgical and phantom limb pains began to dull, diminishing gradually until barely a twinge of her physical suffering remained. It only solved half of Zoe's problem. Despite all of the galaxy's medical advancements, researchers had yet to develop a painkiller to numb a broken heart. "Thank you."

"There's no need to thank me, Zo. Christ, I've never been so afraid in all of my life." Victor finally sagged against the bedrail and laid his brow against his arm. "You're going to be okay."

His palpable relief came as a surprise, contrary to what she expected upon awakening. "It's not okay. I'm... I'm broken. An ugly mess."

"You're beautiful to me no matter what, Zoe. You don't need me to tell you that. And you saved all of us. This entire ship has you to thank for it, and once you're up for discharge from medical, you'll see that."

What the hell is he raving about? "I don't understand."

"Gifts and cards have been arriving from the civilian deck since word went out about what occurred at the facility. Everyone on board the Jemison knows, Zo. Even the Empress wants to meet you." Victor took her hand and kissed her knuckles gently.

Who cared about the Empress? "But... you don't want me anymore," she whispered.

"Zoe..." Disbelief filled his voice. "Baby, no... why would you ever think that? Because of what happened in my office?"

It was only a small part of it, but Zoe nodded.

"That was work. I could never–" He cut himself off and leaned against the stiff back of the unyielding chair. "I overreacted by taking you off the team, but I never meant to imply we were over. Never. I've wanted to apologize since you left my office."

It was almost too good to be true, to believe that Victor still cared, but there was one more thing she needed to learn. "But I saw you on Elora. I saw you kiss that gorgeous woman."

Crushing silence fell between them. Victor didn't offer an explanation, and she didn't pry further. As far as she was concerned, the Royal Navy could discharge and send her home to her family where she desperately wanted to return.

"Why did you even bother saving me?"

His answer was instant and unrehearsed. "Because I couldn't bear to lose another woman I love. Because *you* were the one who gave me a reason to live again." His hands shook, the first indication that something was amiss. Victor's perpetually steady hands rarely trembled.

The answer stunned her. She'd expected something trivial and automatic on account of his oath to save lives. She'd expected flimsy excuses regarding protocol. "R-really?" A fresh wave of tears spilled down her face that she tried valiantly to dry against her pillow. All the fight in her died, leaving a soul-deep exhaustion in its wake.

"Zoe." He took her fingers between both of his hands and brought them to his stubbled cheek. "I intended to bring her to meet you that night, but the recall interrupted my plans."

"Who was she?"

'She's… You would call her my mother-in-law. My *deceased* wife's mother," Victor clarified.

Mortification flushed her skin warm with color. She moved to reach for him, but her dominant arm was gone. "You never said…" *Married to an Eloran? I didn't think that was even allowed.*

"She sent me a message while you were asleep, asking if I had time to spare for her. She saw the military shuttles at the dock. Whenever one would come to Elora, she would write to me and ask if my new ship had come to visit."

"Why didn't you tell me?" She couldn't hide the thickness in her voice.

"I was afraid of losing you. You've come to... to mean so much to me, and... and I didn't think I could bear if you judged me."

"Victor..."

"All the while that I served on the Glenn, I heard every joke there is about interspecies marriage. I had been the butt of everyone's humor from my old CO to my fellow medical officers, all because Hannah couldn't accept what happened and that I couldn't be what *she* wanted. Ylona was the first woman to... This is ridiculous. You don't want to hear this," Victor groaned into one palm and abruptly ended their confessional. "Look, get some rest, Zoe. All right? I–"

"That's just it. I do." She hesitated, but pressed on with her next thought. *Now or never, Zoe.* "Is that when you decided you wanted to die?"

"Yeah," he admitted, lowering his gaze. He smoothed his fingers through her hair, tidying a few errant strands. "This isn't the best time to air my dirty laundry. I'm also your doctor. I should be caring for you now instead of making a fool of myself."

Zoe took advantage and grabbed his hand. She held it to her undamaged cheek before he could move out of reach, unwilling to end their contact. "Please stay. I just... God, this is going to sound so childish, but I just wanted a hug. Anything. I thought you didn't, you know... want me anymore." Her voice faded with her admission.

"You're the only woman I've wanted since Ylona died. The *only* one, Zoe." He paused and attempted a strained smile. "I thought I'd be feeding you medicated protein paste with a spoon by now, not pouring out my heart to you."

Hope had flared bright with his first words, easing the tight knot in her chest. She turned her face and kissed his palm before releasing her tight grip. "I'm an idiot. I'm sorry."

"I… didn't know what I'd do if I lost you, too."

"Takes more than an exploding conduit to get rid of me." Fresh tears spilled from her eyes to accompany her wobbly smile. "Just… talk to me from now on, okay?"

"I'll tell you whatever you want to know. No more secrets. You mean the world to me, Zoe."

"What a pair we make, huh? Like one of your classic movies. I thought that I'd not been… enough."

"You are more than enough." He brought her hand to his lips and kissed her knuckles, then closed his eyes and suppressed the nearly unperceivable shudder in his shoulders.

"Will you stay here with me?"

"There's nowhere else I want to be."

AFTERWORD

Children are abused every day across the world. Most professionals estimate that the rate of sexual abuse may be anywhere from 8% to 20%, but in truth, the real numbers will never become known due to a low record of reporting.

As you may have already guessed, our hero Victor suffered greatly during his childhood while in the care of a relative. We neither wanted to glorify abuse, nor portray a weak hero, but we did want to create a story about a man's transition from victim to survivor.

For some reason in our culture, male sexual abuse receives less coverage and sympathy, and it was this very idea that inspired us to write Victor's story. While we never outright say it or have him admit it in the novel, Zoe was obviously sharp enough to grasp that it happened. Thankfully, he's also had the friendship of Doctor Oshiro and Ethan to help him along.

Everyone isn't as fortunate as Victor. If you or anyone that you know has been sexually abused, consider visiting this RAINN.ORG

https://www.rainn.org/get-help/national-sexual-assault-hotline

ART

We have an entire backstory that we made up about Victor and Ylona. She saved him at a time in his life when he felt alienated from everyone. He had an unsupportive fiancée in favor with the rest of the crew and few friends of his own on the Glenn.

Why did he choose to deploy again? In our hearts, we feel that Victor deployed to exchange places with someone else. With a member of the crew waiting for the birth of his firstborn and no one else willing to take his place on the ship. We figure it had to be something worthwhile that Ylona supported.

While deployed those years during their marriage, she often visited him at ports, giving her a chance to see the world beyond her home planet. Nowadays in our present time, it isn't uncommon for sailors to let their spouses know about planned liberty stops.

At the time of our story, marriages between aliens and humans are viewed similarly to how interracial marriage was treated in past decades. Will it change during the course of these stories? Possibly.

COMING SOON

We intend for each book to read as a standalone, however readers of the series will appreciate learning more about the characters you already know and like. Here's your sneak peek at the upcoming stories by title.

Across Our Stars: Hamish
Across Our Stars: Evangeline
Across Our Stars: Ethan